The Streets Bleed Murder 3

Jerry Jackson

Lock Down Publications
Presents
The Streets Bleed Murder 3
A Novel by *Jerry Jackson*

Lock Down Publications
P.O. Box 870494
Mesquite, Tx 75187

Visit our website at www.lockdownpublications.com

Lock Down Publications
Facebook: Author Jerry Jackson
Like our page on Facebook: Lock Down Publications @
www.facebook.com/lockdownpublications.ldp
Cover design and layout by: **Dynasty's Cover Me**
Book interior design by: **Shawn Walker**
Edited by: **Mia Rucker**

Jerry Jackson

Intro

The first shot hit Kash in the back of his thigh as he backed up, shooting at any cop he saw. He winced in pain and turned around to aim but got struck again, two times in the stomach. Chavez snatched Kash, pulling him to cover and shooting his gun towards the Feds. The cartel of Mexicans had the first load of Federal agents at bay, hiding behind things not to get hit by the spray of bullets. Kash was losing breath as he reloaded his clip.

Jerry Jackson

Chapter 1
Gangsta

I was finally at peace in life, accepting the circumstances that surrounded me and learning lessons as I grew mentally stronger than my current situation. Prepared were my actions but not my notion. I was not ready to walk that journey of confinement for however long the courts saw fit.

I wouldn't lie, that was the choice I made. My life was not my life anymore. I gave it to my son. The easy decision to make that sacrifice stemmed from being a true father to my son, doing everything in my will to care for him in the correct manner.

I failed once, I knew that, but I would not fail twice. My sacrifice was the reason I was humble in my approach and at peace with God. I walked with my head up. I spoke with sureness. I respected the disrespectful, though I was not a saint. Matter of fact, I was nowhere near being a saint, but what I had going on was between me and God.

It was not up for judgment. My desires nor my family wants were to be up for discussion. My decision had been made long before I knew I would make it. Everything that had happened in my life had been written, stamped, and sealed in the book. God knew that one day I'd be standing in the courtroom awaiting my fate for all the wrong He knew I would do since birth.

I guess I couldn't be mad, or could I? I sometimes wondered if God wrote in two books because one moment we'd say that it was already written how our life would play out, but then it also states that the only power we possess is choice.

We have the ability to choose either wrong or right. So does God write in two books? I could have been a successful football player, a movie star, hell even a rapper. I could have been your normal everyday nine to five worker. I could have been a doctor, a preacher, a lawyer, or anything I wanted to be because God gave me that choice right? But life. It's also wrote in his book right? So do we really have choice? I guess I will never understand the understood. Though I honestly felt everything that happened was reasons behind actions and that karma was due, either good or bad. What you put into something, you will get the same out of it.

I stood before the judge. I stood before my family and friends. I stood firm and not worried of what would happen in this life time or the next.

All that ever mattered to me was my family being okay, my team being on top, and my kids being taken care of and safe. I made that sacrifice and now my team was on the way up, my family was safe, and my son was doing better.

Junior was still unresponsive but his vitals were great and he was no longer supported by a machine. My mom said, "All he do is just sleep, looking just like his daddy." My mother knew those were the words I worked so hard to hear. I waited so many nights to see this day and all praises go to God.

"Mr. Jackson, I understand your counsel has submitted a plea of guilty on all charges brought up against you," the judge spoke, looking directly at me over the rim of his glasses

"Yes, sir, your honor," my lawyer answer for me because it was what he was paid to do.

"And you are well aware that you are going under a blind plea?" the judge asked.

I nodded my head, confirming his question as Mr. Swinn spoke up again.

"Yes sir."

The judge looked down to the paperwork and read from it. It took him a brief moment. Then he looked over to the district attorney.

"Have all these cases been processed and closed?" the judge asked.

"Yes, sir, all witnesses, families, and statements are on file," the district attorney replied.

"Mr. Jackson, you are charged with twenty-two counts of first degree murder, fourteen counts of armed robbery, fourteen counts of kidnapping, twenty-eight counts of aggravated assault, and you're willing to enter a guilty plea on all charges as a blind plea?" the judge asked me.

"Your honor…"

"Counsel, I spoke to the defendant. Please allow me to hear from him. I've heard and seen enough of you already," the judge cut my lawyer off, and then fixed his gaze on me.

"Sir, yes, sir." I finally opened my mouth to speak. Looking around I saw Monkey sitting behind me next to my mother and NeNe.

"Okay, and you don't want a trial?" the judge strangely asked.

"Sir, no, sir," I replied and truly meant it. I heard a few mumbles from those that loved me, wishing my mindset had changed since the last time we'd spoken. They just did not understand the true meaning behind me being so willing to just give up and give in. but I knew and God knew, and that's all that mattered.

"So how do you wish to plea, Jackson?"

"Guilty, sir," I quickly shot back, which got a reaction from my mother that I cared not to hear. She had broken down Again, but this time standing to her feet. Monkey had to grab her as she cried her heart out.

My mother, she was a strong woman who did all the correct things a mother should do as a mother to her kids. When she lost Cool, he took a piece of her with him to heaven and it took years for her to even think of getting over the loss of her first born. Now there I was, standing at the mercy of the judge, about to lose my life to the system, also taking with me a piece of my mother and making her life a bit harder to deal with.

Today, no matter what, I had to stay firm in what I believed, leaving all emotions to the side because not only was it hard on my family and friends, it was extremely hard on me to go through with this ordeal. The judge finally looked up from typing. He fixed his eyes on me before he spoke.

"I never met a man like you before, a man who committed crimes and got away with them, just to turn himself in, a man that confessed that he was the one that we had been looking for all this time. You are a brave young man I must say." the judge paused, and then stared at me before asking, "Son, did you truly kill all these people?"

I looked back at the judge and smiled a slight smile, not a proud smile, but an honest smile, when I said, "sir, yes, sir, I did."

"Damn, son." The judge shook his head, and then began to type on his computer. "I must follow this protocol. It's more murders than I've ever seen in my thirty-six years of being a judge, son." He paused again, and then said, "The court has to impose the death penalty to this case. It's only fair."

As soon as I heard those words, the court room erupted in cries and yells. My mother could be heard over everyone. The police had to detain her and take her out while everyone else broke down, except me. It seemed I was the only one holding my head up and facing this situation head on. I was okay with my sentence. I wasn't mad at all because I made a deal with God and I intended to stick to it.

"Gary Jackson, the state of Georgia sentences you to death by lethal injection."

I heard the judge but his voice was no match for my mother's screams. She had to be removed from the courtroom. I looked over my shoulder and saw my nigga, Veed,o and my cousin, Eric, showing their support.

It made me smile to know my niggas were out. Poonie Man would soon hit the streets because I also took his charges. Zay and

Patman were also out, which was a good thing. I knew Kash was gon' take over the streets. It was gon' be turnt up in a major way and my faith was that my nigga was gon' hold it down like I hoped and planned.

Once my mother was removed from the court room and the judge finished with the proceedings, I was walked out, escorted by six deputies who were ready to take me down if I started to trip. It was no pressure, like I said beforehand, what I had going on was between me and God.

Jerry Jackson

Chapter 2
A New Beginning
2003

Kash and Monkey pulled up to the Blue Flame strip club where Asia met them in the parking lot. Monkey parked the Porsche truck and killed the lights.

In the next car over sat Asia. She was driving a two-door Benz with pink and white jolly rancher candy paint on 23-inch chrome flats. Asia had the stripper game on lock. She was stamped as the baddest stripper in Atlanta, which gave her the extra popularity and helped her gain clientele to push work. She was serving most niggas that came through the club, and bitches too.

Asia stepped out of her Benz. She leaned into the Porsche on the passenger side where Kash was. He had the phone to his ear when she reached in to give him dap, and then reached over to dap Monkey.

"What's up, y'all?" she was the first to speak.

"Wassup, peeps?" Monkey spoke.

"Is the nigga inside the club still?" asked Kash about Lucky, a New York dude.

Monkey had already filled him in on all that he knew about Lucky. For the past two months, Lucky had been frequently spending time in Atlanta and almost always pushed up on Asia and other dancers with questions about Kash.

Little did Lucky know, none of the dancers could speak on Kash. Hell, even Asia was oblivious to most shit about her boss. All Asia knew was that he was Gangsta's brother who'd just got out and he was the plug.

"Yup, he in VIP," she stated.

"Cool, we on our way in," Kash replied while hanging up his phone call. He knew Lucky didn't want any problems when asking of him. All the nigga could want was to link up.

"Alright, I will be inside," Asia said and walked off. Kash watched her in lust as her outfit hugged her body like paint.

"I'ma fuck that lil' hoe," Kash mumbled to Monkey who was looking at her fat ass also. They both got out of the Porsche truck and approached the club.

"I done hit it like twice. She can fuck, too," Monkey boasted with a smile, dapping Kash as they walked.

Since the day they met, they had become cooler than either one of them thought they would. Kash had come to like the type of dude Monkey was.

They both entered the club after paying the bouncer a grand a piece to get their straps inside just in case this meeting didn't go as planned and something stupid happened.

Asia met them at the door and led both guys to the VIP section where Lucky sat with at least six bad bitches, all dancing to the loud music. Monkey noticed that Lucky sat in the same exact spot the last time.

"Come on, shawty," Kash said, and walked straight over to where Lucky was posted.

Lucky didn't really notice the guys approaching until he saw his own men moving in towards the two men who were closing in on him. With a one-hand motion he made the dancers stop dancing and leave. Then he spoke.

"Yo, introduce y'all self now that you up in my private space."

At least ten of Lucky's men surrounded the two. Kash looked over his shoulder, and then looked back at Lucky. He shook his head with a slick smile.

"I should be asking you the same shit. See, what I wanna know is why are you around my city asking who I am and shit." Kash never took his eyes off Lucky.

"Who are you, son? You riddled me with them questions," Lucky said because he was confused about what Kash was talking about. He sat up.

"I'm Kash, nigga, the motherfucker you been asking 'bout. See the thing with me is that you don't even reside in my city and keep inquiring 'bout me. So you tell me what's so important," Kash got straight to the point. He was more aggressive than Gangsta. Kash would act first and put thought into it later. His words must have spooked Lucky because he sat up even straighter and then waved his men to fall back off the two. Then he told them to take seats.

"Yo, no lie, son, I was expecting you to show up. That's word," Lucky said as Monkey and Kash took their seats and got comfortable

"So what's hap?" Kash asked, no beating around the bush.

"Listen, B, I don't have no type of beef with you or your man's here. I'm just admiring you from afar. Any man that get out the slammer and take off as you have is amazing to me. And I'm no hater, son, and I don't mind following greatness. So I was thinking maybe me and you can link up and talk some numbers," Lucky quickly explained while pouring up them all some drinks from one of the many bottles on the table. Lucky spoke with so much respect that Kash couldn't do nothing but nod his head and take the drink given.

"Okay, I hear you. But what's up though? Talk numbers," Kash shot back.

"Well every strong leader needs an army in this lifetime. I see your movement and pattern. It's correct. So let me be that nigga to surround you with more opportunity. I hear you already got good coke prices, but I don't hear nothing on you with weed. And that's where I come in at. I can supply you with whatever you can handle," Lucky boasted and took a swallow of his drink. But what Lucky didn't know was that Kash had the connect on any drugs he wanted from Loco. Kash already had his mind made up but wouldn't tell Lucky shit just yet.

"Maybe we can get something going, figure something out," Kash replied. And for the remainder of the night, they sat around and kicked it, calling all the dancers back to entertain them and ordering up more bottles. Lucky's crew of at least thirty New York niggas filled the VIP also, which gave Kash the chance to process all the faces he could while at the same time peeping Lucky's every move. He had to admit Lucky was alright. He was cool and you could easily tell he was a made nigga by how he kicked it.

Kash had Asia sitting across his lap after a dance she'd just recently gave him. He wanted to fuck this exotic looking beauty and she knew it. Her loyalty to Gangsta was what caught Kash's attention when he first met her. Plus her hustle game was official and money was never short. Kash had plans for her though, but first things first, he had to bust her just to get it out of his system.

"What time you get off?" Kash asked. His lips brushed her ear.

"Bout an hour or two, I'm tired," Asia stated, feeling a slight chill run up her spine from his voice.

"You fucking with me tonight?"

When he asked, Asia looked down at him from his lap. He was leaned slightly back.

"I can if you want."

"Fuckin' right. I done had enough of just looking, I'm tryna see what it hit like."

"And I wanna see the same," Asia shot back quickly. Kash was already nearly hard and knew she felt him pressed into her back side.

"Cool, just pull up to the condo." Kash had a condo downtown Atlanta because his house was being built from the ground up and the condo was the place he kicked it at, being that he was single. Since being free, many different females tried to get with Kash but his focus wasn't on being in a relationship. All Kash did was freak 'em and go about his business.

Ebony, his baby's mother, was the only female that wouldn't fuck him when he tried to bust her. *When you ready, then you will make me yours again. But until then, you'll run these streets,* Ebony had told him. He was smashing so many new females in passing and tonight he would add Asia to the collection.

***

Kash was in the condo when Asia knocked on the door. He opened it to find her in some tight jeans and a fly shirt to match, showing off her belly ring. She was still shorter than him, even in her heels. Kash allowed her in. Music played softly from the speakers overhead. The lights were dim. Kash already had a bottle on ice and blunts rolled up. Asia put her bag down by the sofa and sat down to take off her heels.

"Honey, I hope you don't want no more dances 'cause I'm all out of those," Asia said and laid back on the softness of the sofa.

"Nawl, shawty, you straight. It ain't like that. All business is out the door right now. It's just some kicking it going on," Kash replied and joined her at the sofa. He lit up one of the blunts.

"And no drama, wifey, or baby ma?"

"Nawl, shawty, you good," Kash laughed. It had only been two months and he meant to enjoy every day of his time spent on the streets. Three years was a long time, but being locked up, it was the longest he'd ever done and he vowed not to go back by any means. He made promises to himself to get rich and some kind of way get his brother off death row.

This time on the streets, he would mimic Gangsta's movements and calm demeanor rather than his own fiery personality. He promised to trust no man and to make sure everyone was good around him because everyone the Feds snatched up was out and the streets were live. Every day was a party in Atlanta.

Veedo was on the team. Poonie was a nigga Kash didn't like when they first met back in the days. He'd wondered why Gangsta had him stamped as a stand-up guy but Kash let Poonie pick up money from three major spots. Zay and Eric hit the streets like they never left, but neither was selling dope. That was strange to Kash because them two niggas were balling, buying houses, cars, and running a few businesses together.

Kash kept it to himself, but he surely was gonna look into it. Kash had bricks going for the low so everybody was eating and everyone was being low key doing so because the Feds were so mad that niggas beat them that they was lurking, asking questions about Loco and Mr. Play, but nobody could or would break and give up the information. Loco only dealt with Gangsta and Kash. They were the only two that could give up the info, but everyone knew they were solid.

Kash and Gangsta were considered legends in the hood, pulling off acts no one else had. And now that Kash had resurfaced on the scene, he had taken the city by surprise. He was surprised himself when he got to the warehouse and found a thousand kilos waiting on him. He instantly called to confirm with Loco, who wanted nine grand a brick. Kash fronted the bricks to everyone for twenty-two grand a pop, but if they straight up purchased one, they could get it for eighteen.

Asia was one of the top people who moved drugs fast. All her plays were niggas trying to fuck and shop the weight that she sold at good price. She would go through a brick or two per day, slanging quarter bricks, halves, and even fourths. Asia handled good business but Kash had something else in mind because he'd already fronted two new niggas and a dyke hoe named Juice from Old National Highway. Kash was slowly but surely putting his stamp down on the city. He had his movement going strong and his crew on point.

Kash and Asia smoked two loud blunts and killed half the bottle

"I'm going to shower, you can come or not, or meet me at the bed." Kash stood to his feet. He was a little drunk so his words were a bit slurred and slow.

"I did all that already," Asia shot back.

Kash made his shower quick, only washing twice and rinsing off. Since being in prison, Kash had beefed up, now weighing two hundred ten pounds, all muscle. He walked naked into his room with his dick semi hard and swinging side to side. Asia laughed at him as he approached the bed naked, dick swinging. He joined her in bed. She was also naked. Asia pushed Kash to lay flat on his back.

She leaned over and kissed his chest, running her hand up his stomach, across his ripped six-pack, and down to his big dick, which was hard and thick. Asia knew this was about to hurt but she still kissed his stomach. Positioning herself on her hands and knees, she kissed the head of his dick. Asia gripped it at the base. Then she moved it side to side, looking at how big he was. She licked around his head three times with her tongue ring. Then she took him into her mouth.

She started jacking and sucking at the same time. Her mouth was so warm and wet that Kash started gyrating his hips. With one free hand, he held her head, and with the other, he gripped the sheets. Asia lightened up on the pressure with his dick slipping in and out of her mouth. She pushed his dick up till it laid flat on his stomach. She suckled one of his balls while still jacking his hardness.

Asia took the other ball into her mouth, then licked around them both a couple times before sticking the dick back between her lips and going to work on him good.

"Damn girl," Kash moaned more so than said as Asia gave him some amazing oral sex until he was about to cum. Kash pulled his dick from her month.

Asia got up and straddled him. Standing on her feet in a squatted position, she eased down on him, painting only his dick head with her juices as she bounced lightly three times. Then she slid down him a few inches, holding her balance with one hand on his stomach. The other was on her knee and her eyes were closed. Kash held one of her ankles and the side of her thighs as he pushed up into the tightness of her.

"Oh, umm, shit, baby, yo dick big as fuck," Asia cried out in pleasure and pain.

"I got you. I'm not gone hurt that pussy. Just do your thang baby," Kash shot back and let her get her ride on. Asia got down to her knees, stomach to stomach, and Kash grabbed her booty as she rocked back and forth on him.

Kash raised his knees a little and caught the movement she had created. His hands slid from her booty to her back. When he had her locked in, he began grinding into her.

"Shit, take some out, baby."

"I got you, just…"

"No." Asia was trying to slide up but Kash held her in place as he pushed up into her a little deeper. "Oh shit, oh, baby, it hurts."

"Com'ere," Kash flipped her over onto her back with his dick still inside her.

"It hurt, Kash," Asia cried.

"Okay, I got you."

"You keep saying…" Her words came to an end when Kash started fucking her again. Asia thought it was about to be more pain but was quickly surprised when pleasure came. Her pussy was so warm and tight that Kash could no longer hold it in. He pulled out and shot a big load of sperm over her pussy and stomach. Asia stroked and squeezed it for every last drop.

"Damn, that pussy good." Kash laid on his back, tired and out of wind.

Asia got up to clean herself. She stopped at the door, turned around, and said, "Your dick is big as fuck, boy." she rolled her eyes and disappeared into the bathroom.

The duffle bag with straps was large and heavy. When Kash pulled it out, the first thing he noticed was a letter taped to its side with Kash wrote on the front. He opened it, read it, and then he quickly folded the note and looked at his baby's mother, Ebony.

"Where is the key?"

She reached into her nightstand and retrieved a tiny gold key.

"Charles, I know that being free was a surprise blessing and that you don't have a plan on your steps. All I can say is take your time out here. You have another shot to do it correct. I'm here if you need me. Believe me or not, I got your back. You are my kid's father. I can't help but to give you that. If you need anything, I got you."

Ebony felt the need to say as she closed up the laptop that sat across her lap. She climbed out of her bed. She wore boy shorts up under her t-shirt. Ebony was a sexy black female. She was thick and had a big booty to go with her small waist. Her hair was long like she wore a sew-in, but it was her natural hair.

That was something Kash liked about her, she was natural with her shit. Ebony disappeared into her bathroom and came right back out.

"I need to be dropped off on the west side," Kash spoke.

"Your mother wanted me to bring you to her house when we all woke up. She has plans for you and the kids."

"My mother don't want nothing but to sit round. I got a lot of stuff to do today. We'll go over there around noon. She don't know what time we waking up, but I need to be getting out of here like right now though, for real," Kash shot back. He wanted to jump on top of things early. He reopened the note and read a phone number from it, speaking the numbers out loud.

21

"Okay, well let me get the kids up and dressed," Ebony replied, leaving the room after putting on some jeans.

Thirty minutes later, Ebony pulled into Gangsta's mother's yard. When Kash laid eyes on the money green 442 Cutlass, he instantly fell in love with it. Gangsta never ceased to amaze him.

He had everything already laid out. all Kash had to do was follow up on the way Gangsta had shit set up, meet the people he wanted him to meet, and fuck with the ones that were written in "the will" as Gangsta called it. Kash kissed both his kids and hugged Ebony before he got out of her car, prepared to journey a brand-new road. Fresh out the grips of hell, and he was crowned king by his brother.

Now it was all up to him what he would do with the blessing, how he would put things in order to make shit work. Kash knew Gangsta's mom was at the hospital with Junior, everybody was, so he jumped right into the 442. It had butter yellow leather guts with soft butter yellow carpet running through the two door monster. It had the digital dash and oak wood everywhere. It smelled brand-new when he climbed in. then he heard a car horn blow behind him. He looked back to find Ebony still parked.

Kash smoothly cranked up the 442. It roared to life as he got back out of it and approached Ebony's door.

"What's up?"

"Charles, where is your license? I know you not about to jump in and just get to going, are you?" Ebony wanted to know.

"Girl, I got this."

"No, you don't, you're already going about this the wrong way. I'm just being honest. I can take you to get your license in the morning. All you need is a little patience. That's it. I just don't want you to get into no trouble, fresh home off a life sentence," Ebony stressed.

Kash gave her the shake of his head. "I got this, Ebony, damn. I thought you said you won't police a Nigga."

"Oh, low blow, Charles, real low."

"I'll see you at twelve." Kash wasn't trying to deal with her emotions right now, he had bigger fish to fry. Plus, he was a grown man and he did what he wanted to do.

Kash knew that she held his best interest at heart, and he understood that, but at the same time he didn't need a mother watching his every move, especially not the real police.

"Bye, Charles. I see you tripping again." Ebony placed her car into reverse. Kash took a step back. As she pulled out of the driveway, he let her be and jumped into the 442. He pulled out also and hit Bankhead.

Nothing was on his mind but the note from Gangsta, yet he knew to drive safely and be careful. Kash found the phone Gangsta said would be in the glove compartment. He powered it on. Traffic was nice. The sun was beginning to show itself. The 442 pushed up Bankhead on 26-inch rims with its money green paint and crystal clear windows. He wore his seat belt just in case the police did decide to be around and saw him riding through.

Kash looked at the phone and scrolled through the contacts. They read Loco, Monkey, Asia, and Poonie info. Gangsta's mother's number was also programmed, and a few more people. Kash continued to look through the phone. In Gangsta's letter, he wanted Kash to see that all the folks in his contact list were cared for, saying each of them played a loyal role in helping him find Bam and taking him out.

The next day, Kash woke up with money on his mind and pussy next to him. Asia was sound asleep, looking good as ever, Kash noticed as he climbed out of bed. He picked up his phone to see a couple missed calls from Poonie and one from Loco. He redialed Loco's number and walked into the bathroom. He brushed his grill and listened to the phone ring.

"My friend," Loco answered.

"What's up, amigo, my main man?"

"I need you to pull up tonight, my friend, for important discussion," Loco replied.

"Just gimme a time and date, and I'm there," Kash shot back, and then rinsed his mouth and began to wash his face.

"How is Gangsta holding up?"

"Bruh good. My nigga slick, too slick to go out like dat. Plus, I'm working day and night to figure something out that's gonna move that sentence off shawty," Kash admitted.

"Well I'm with you on that, so let me know. Anything I can do, it's done on behalf of my loyalty and family. I'm with you and Gangsta."

"Say no mo, amigo," Kash laughed, and then asked, "So what time?"

"Ten thirty sharp," replied Loco. Kash hung up the phone, walking back into the room.

"Say, get up, baby girl," Kash spoke to Asia while redialing Poonie. Asia moved a little but stayed nestled under the silk sheets. Kash continued to the kitchen.

"Hello?" Poonie picked up.

"What's up, Homie?"

"Man, I went to Dill Ave to pick up from Rat and the check short."

"How much?" asked Kash.

"Like a ninety," replied Poonie. Kash could tell he was still sleep in bed.

"Okay, what about the other spots?"

"Everything else Gucci."

"Cool, I'ma pull up on Dill later. But hold tight with that paper, I'm coming to grab it," Kash informed Poonie and then they ended the call.

Asia was sitting up in the bed when he entered the room. Kash went to his closet to find something to wear. Asia also climbed out the bed. She was still naked so she found her panties and bra.

"Good morning," she spoke, putting on her clothes.

"What's hap, baby girl?" Kash turned and looked at her.

"Bout to leave, I got a play at eleven, and plus I gotta meet up with Poonie to drop that money off," Asia said.

"Have you ever been locked up?" Kash wanted to know, asking out of nowhere

"Never," replied Asia.

"Do you smoke? Do any drugs?" he asked again.

"Hell no." Asia balled her face up, shaking her head side to side. It was evident that she was offended.

"How far you went in school?" Kash didn't pay any attention to her being in her feelings.

"College, why?" Asia wanted to know.

"I got some plans for you, a better position," Kash replied while pulling an outfit out and tossing it on the bed. "How much work you got left?"

"Half a brick probably, that's what I was gonna talk to you about when I paid off today. I wanted a double up," Asia shot back.

"Nawl, just take that half to Poonie and keep that check for yourself. Put it up. I told you I got a plan I'm putting in motion that I need you to play a major role in that's gonna benefit the whole team, even Gangsta." When Kash said Gangsta's name, Asia's face lit up.

"Okay, cool, so what you're saying is you want me out the game?" she questioned.

"Exactly."

"If that's what you want, then you know I'm with y'all on it, especially if it helps Gangsta," Asia admitted.

They both got dressed. Kash took her to eat breakfast, where he explained that he wanted to get her in the prison system as a secretary or counselor so she could be in the front office and have access to paperwork.

"So answer me this, how long will this take?" Asia wanted to know as she was stuffing her mouth with food.

"Ion know, shid, a couple years I guess. That's why we start ASAP, feel me?" Kash shot back, also eating his food. They both were hungry. She nodded her head with a mouthful of food.

"As long as I don't want for nothing and it's gonna help Gangsta, I'm down." Asia meant every word that came out of her mouth and Kash could see in her eyes that she was dead ass serious. He liked that a lot. He like the choice made by Gangsta to even fuck with her.

"Say no mo, baby girl, I like yo gangsta. I'ma take care of you on everything, just go 'head and fill out the application. That's the first step," Kash said, taking a drink from his juice and looking at her.

"To what prison?" Asia wanted to know.

"In the GDC, baby girl, Jackson State."

"Oh, okay, say no mo," Asia replied with a smile.

Chapter 3

It was an early morning. The sun was bright in the blue skies. The wind was calm and the air was clean. Veedo sat in the driver's seat of his S550 Benz coupe, talking on the phone to his lawyer. He was at a red light when this white Lexus pulled up next to him.

Veedo looked at the driver and instantly was captivated by the driver's beauty. Veedo honked his horn to get her attention. She looked over. He waved. She waved. Then Veedo began to roll his window down. But the light turned green and traffic was thick, so she pulled off. Veedo he got behind her and trailed her until she pulled over in a gas station. He jumped out of the coupe fresh in polo gear. He approached the driver's side window and noticed there was another girl in the car.

"How you doing, Queen? And you, how are you?" he asked both girls.

"We good, what's your name?"

"My name Veedo and you?" he smiled as the girl he was talking to gave him an approval nod of her head.

"Trish," the beautiful woman spoke back. She was taking in full view of Veedo's six-foot three-inch height and dark chocolate skin. She could tell he was physically fit and saw that he was amazingly handsome as well.

"Nice to meet you, Trish. So check this out, I know y'all must be busy and I'm grateful you stopped to grant me your time. I would like to get to know you though. But I don't wanna hold you up from business. Can I give you my number?" Veedo said.

"Sure, that's fine," the woman said.

He quickly wrote his info down, and then let her leave as he climbed in his own car. Thirty minutes later, he pulled up at one of Kash's female friends' house. Veedo pulled up behind the green 442. Kash was in the yard with no shirt on, a cup in one hand, and a blunt in the other. There was a girl standing next to him who Veedo instantly recognized but couldn't place the face.

He got out of the whip and him and Kash gave each other dap. Since being in Rice Street and Gangsta linked them, they'd created a nice solid bond that neither planned to break.

"What's good, homie?" Veedo asked, and then kinda tossed some respect to the woman in the yard with a wave of his iced out hand.

"Coolin' this way, look though, come walk with me right quick." He and Kash walked out to the street, out of ear shot, then Kash spoke again, "Tell me what you think about this. The niggas Eric and Zay just bought another night club, this shit over here by Vine City. I think it's a strip spot, ion know."

"What's that, two clubs and two restaurants?"

"Hell yeah," Kash replied.

"I think them niggas both some hoes first off. Them niggas left Gangsta to die 'cause both them pussy ass niggas had the money to give bruh and these suckas knew that this nigga Bam was up to some fuck shit but neither said shit," Veedo stressed. Kash knew he was only being real. He also told him of the beat down he gave Zay and why.

"Then I tried to plug in wit both of them fools. Neither jumped on team and these niggas hit the ground running."

"I know, right?" Veedo stated.

"I got something for them niggas. So what's good on the spots? Is everything moving as planned?" Kash was asking about the three trap houses they had on Hollywood Road that Veedo controlled.

"So far everything Gucci, had one situation with a lil' GF nigga, but it got straight," replied Veedo.

"How many niggas we got in each spot?"

"It's four in all, two servers and two gunnas," Veedo was happy to say.

28

Kash nodded his head in approval before asking, "How often do we get the money out of there?"

"I just wait till Poonie pull up and that usually be one time in the wee hour of the night mostly. Should I change that up?" Veedo answered and asked.

"Yeah, move the money three times per day and get a shooter to play them routes with Poonie. I'm surprised these niggas ain't tried his ass yet. Back in my hay days, I was lurking on niggas like Poonie. He wouldn't've make it out fucking with my team," Kash admitted.

"Consider it done. Let me ask you something though. That female in the yard, where she from? She look like I've seen her or that I know her," Veedo had to know.

"She from Albany, bruh, a nurse I met when I was locked up. Let me ask you this, have you ever been to Augusta medical when you did your bid?"

"Hell nawl, but I had Albany fucked up before I got knocked off. She might know me or I know of her folks or something. She still working there?" Veedo asked as they walked back into the yard.

"Yup, we got big plans to get my motherfucking brother out, at least off that death sentence," Kash boasted, throwing one of his arms over the woman's shoulders, which made Veedo smile because it sounded good when Gangsta's name was involved.

Veedo left shortly after and sent the girl Trish a text. He ended up at one of the trap spots on Hollywood Road. When she called him as he'd asked her to in his text message, Veedo posted up in the yard, seated inside his car.

"Hello?"

"Is this Veedo?" the sexy voice asked. Her voice made him remember that amazing face of hers.

"Yeah, what's going on beautiful?"

"Nothing much, you said to call, so I did. I'm only following orders"

"I can dig that. so look, I know we just met two hours ago but ever since I met you, I cannot get my mind off the fact that you're very beautiful and, believe it or not, I have never had the opportunity to befriend a woman as beautiful as you are," Veedo spoke while looking around in the car for a blunt wrap to roll up some loud.

"Oh really?" asked Trish with a smile.

"Yes, I'm being honest. So I take it you single, but why are you when beauty prevents you from being left alone by the thirsties," Veedo said.

"Well, I am single and my job and school has never been supported by my so called boyfriend. All men want to do is fuck me til I'm pregnant and stop my mojo. Most men these days are lost on what's important," Trish replied.

"True, it's like us men are timid when it comes to being real. We don't hold dear to morals anymore, nor do we show respect that's due. So you still in school? Where do you work?" Veedo wanted to know what kind of nigga would not support a bad bitch like her, no matter what she did.

"I'm out of school, finally."

"And your job?"

"You wouldn't believe me if I told you, and if you did, then you will still judge me for choosing this lifestyle."

"You hell, Ms. Lady. I'm not in no place to judge nobody but I am trying to know who you are. I'm not trying to let you get away without putting up a fight," Veedo joked.

"Well I'm not comfortable talking about my job right now, but if you make it past go then yes, I will tell you everything about me," she shot back.

Veedo had found the wrap and began to roll it up with some loud.

"I'm cool with that, so what's your age?"

"I'm twenty-nine, and you?"

"I'm thirty. I got two kids, one baby mother," Veedo quickly slid in.

"No kids," replied Trish

"You want any?" he asked.

"If it happens, then cool. But let me ask you what is it you do to make money? School or work?" she questioned because it was something she wondered of him.

"To be honest, I'm not doing nothing at all, I'm living off old luck and patience now-a-days. I'm an ex street champ who once had my hand in the game, but I just recently got out from a federal case that could've left me fucked up." Veedo was being honest on top of a lie.

"Oh lord," was the only thing Trish said.

"I'm just being honest."

"Yeah, I know, and I appreciate it. But you know the saying goes, once a street nigga, always a street nigga. Like when your money run out, then what? What do you have to fall back on?"

"I got a plan. I'm working on a business as we speak. I just left my lawyer's office looking at my options of what I can and can't do," replied Veedo. By now he was getting out of the truck, being met by one of his workers. Veedo put his finger to his mouth, telling the dude to not say anything, and the dude got the picture.

"Well that's good, and how long have you been out?" she asked

"Two months almost, I guess. Nothing major, I wasn't in long 'cause the charges got dropped and that's how I got out."

"Oh, I see. Well listen, I'm pulling up to my mother's house. Can I call you back?" Trish asked.

"Yeah, I hope I ain't running you off by being honest." Veedo felt her voice and mood change. It made him wish he would've lied in the process.

"No, you didn't. I like an honest man and I will surely give you a ring back. I promise."

"Okay, cool, I'm waiting," Veedo shot back and they hung up. He looked at his worker. "What's hap?"

"We got an issue," the worker said.

***

She was in her yard with Roxanne and Nikki when Kash pulled up and jumped out fresh from head to toe. Terry smiled as Roxanne look in lust. Everyone else knew that since Kash got out months ago, she'd been crazy about him. He walked up on the girls, hugged Terry, and then waved to Nikki and Roxanne.

"What's up, Terry? Where is Zay? I been calling and he ain't been picking up."

"You too?" a pregnant Terry said. That got a laugh from her friends, but Kash didn't crack one smile at all. Instead he nodded his head and then looked to Nikki.

"I heard you was pregnant, girl. Is that true?" as soon as the words left his mouth, Terry looked at her best friend like she had lost her mind. Nikki was the mother of three already and could hardly take care of them. If it wasn't for Kash putting Poonie Man on his feet, then it would be worse than it was.

"Bitch," Terry said, and then went to lift up Nikki's shirt. "You pregnant?"

"Ion know yet, Poonie ass just want me to be. But I will know Monday for sure," Nikki replied, moving Terry's hand away from her stomach.

"And you?" Kash turned toward Roxanne.

"Could be," she laughed. Terry hit her and Nikki laughed too. "But it got to be with a boss."

"Well look, Terry, when Zay get home, tell him to get at me ASAP. And what's up with your daughter and unborn?" Kash pointed to her stomach. She was pregnant by a fuck nigga.

"Keshana good, and I will be having this baby in a couple months. I'm so ready, too," Terry rubbed her stomach with a smile.

"That's what's up. Don't forget to tell bruh I'm looking for him," Kash said then nodded towards Nikki and Roxanne before walking off.

As soon as he did, Roxanne exhaled and said, "Lord God, that man is one fine something. His ass can sho' get it day and night, no lie."

"Bitch, don't tell us, tell him," Nikki cut in, rolling her eyes as Terry laughed. She was at a point in her life that she was happy with how it was going. She was happy for both her friends and her family. She was especially happy that Zay was out the dope game now, so they could live a happy life away from the cops and violence in the world. She just wanted to raise her kids and enjoy the remainder of her life.

And if Zay did choose the streets again, then she was leaving at a drop off a hat. With him having the restaurants and clubs, that put them good at life. She adored his business mindset. Zay was always a money man, a go-getter in all he did, and for that, Terry was lucky.

She was also thankful for Gangsta and all he'd done for her and the sacrifice he made to set Zay free. Even though she did not want Gangsta to go to jail again, she was still happy he had it in his heart to help so many people when he was truly the one who needed the help. She was proud to be his baby's mother, his friend, his family. Terry vowed to hold him down while he was in prison, no matter what, and Zay would have to respect it.

She knew that Zay always despised Gangsta and always would, but he had to let that childhood hate rest in the past. Terry and her two best friends walked back into the house. She was cooking dinner tonight and hoped Zay didn't miss another meal at home by coming in at the wee hours of the night. She was dealing with it as it came, but at the same time, she was getting tired of it and she was starting to complain more than usual.

"Bitch, I'm about to go. I'm not doing no cooking. I'm sorry," Nikki said once Terry stopped in the kitchen.

"Girl, you said you would help me. Hoe, you know I can't be on my feet too long," Terry said with a mean expression on her face.

"First of all, I didn't say no such thing, and second, yo ass ain't cooking no Thanksgiving dinner. You better make some quick shit, honey. Anyways, Zay ass might don't even show up," Nikki said.

Terry knew she was right but that still wasn't about to hold her up from cooking for her family. Hell, she and Keshana would eat all the food if they must. Terry excused herself from her friends. She went into her bedroom and sat on the edge of the bed. She called Zay's number and, to her surprise, he picked up.

"What's up, baby?"

"Hey, Zarack, you coming home tonight to have dinner with us?" She was glad he was at least on the phone because, since being out, he was always busy.

"I mean, the club will be getting live soon and Eric is out at the restaurant tonight, so I'm holding it down solo. What time will dinner be ready? I can swing through. Then I'ma have to leave right back out," Zay said, which made her feel a little better about the situation at hand.

"Well, if you come now, then dinner will be ready. I'm in the midst of cooking right now as we speak," Terry replied.

"Okay, I'm leaving in thirty minutes."

"Okay, love you, I'll see you then," Terry shot back and they got off the phone. When she walked back into the kitchen with her friends, they saw a glow on her face, meaning her mood was bright. Nikki instantly rolled her eyes and Roxanne burst into laughter.

"Y'all hoes help me real quick. My baby on the way home."

***

He had two trap houses booming on Glenwood Road with loud and crack. His name was spread all over Zone Six and the surrounding areas. Monkey couldn't complain at his life right now. He was just glad that he chose the right way to go. Messing with Bam was the worst mistake he'd ever made, and helping Gangsta was the best thing he could've pulled off.

Monkey didn't know Gangsta at first, but still was willing to go out there with him. The more he was around Gangsta, he saw how real and solid the man was. He was surprised at what Gangsta did, turning himself in. But at the end of the day, he had freed so many people in the process, and for that, Monkey saluted him.

He pulled his Benz up behind one of his partners' whips and jumped out. There were a few cats out posted. Every one of them knew who Monkey was because he was who paid them. So with respect, all the niggas spoke and showed some form of love. Monkey walked up the steps leading to the door as Black Boy walked out with the phone to his ear.

"What's up, bro?" he asked Monkey as they gave each other dap.

"Coming to holla at you real quick, step back in and get off the line," Monkey said and led the way inside. They were inside the trap house that sold all the weed you could buy. It pumped anything from grams to pounds of all types of flavors, pulling in at least fifteen grand each day. The only problem was Black Boy liked to keep too many niggas hanging around who weren't contributing to the cost.

It made the trap hot, first off. Then in the long run, the niggas who were just sitting around would peep a slick way to come up with cut throat intentions, and Monkey just wasn't going for that right now.

"What's up, bro?" Black boy asked. He was a childhood friend to Monkey.

"You gotta clear these niggas out that don't serve no purpose here, bruh, like yo baby ma lil' brother and his lame ass home boy, Steve, and that dat nigga with them dreads, he most definitely in the way," Monkey pointed to one of the many dudes he saw inside the crib.

"Okay, okay cool, I'll handle it, bro, say less," Black Boy replied.

"Yeah, we bout to switch our offense up anyway. I'm sending two shooters and another nigga to help you push the work. Money will be picked up three times a day instead of one. We just getting our security beefed up so money can flow. Plus, I'm dropping a double up from now on," Monkey explained the entire plan to Black Boy, and he was with it, hands down. Monkey left the trap spot.

Chapter 4

Zay and Eric had a club called Zero Below that was pumped up every weekend in Atlanta. It was one of the main spots everyone went to after the Hip Hop closed at 3am. Zero below had a laid back environment that mostly grownups attended, but after 3am, you could find all types of ages there turning up. Kash parked the 442 in a spot reserved for Eric. *Fuck that nigga,* he thought as he slid the gun under his seat and replaced it with a kitchen knife.

He slid the knife into his sock, jumping out of the whip, smoking a New Port. He tossed it to the ground while looking at the half filled parking lot. It was only midnight so the club wasn't as live as it would soon be. Kash made his way to the front entrance and was met by the club bouncers. He paid twenty bucks to get in and was amazed at how well put together the club was. It was laced from what Kash's eyes noticed as he strolled to the bar for a drink. The speakers were pumping *Monsta Swole.*

"What can I get you?" a bartender asked him.

"Lemme get a bottle of hen and a cup, no ice."

Kash got comfortable on his stool and looked around to the many faces of the club. He didn't see anybody important, though he did recognize a few. The waiter returned with the drink he requested with a smile.

"Anything else?" he asked Kash, watching him rip the bottle open.

"Yeah." Kash started pouring him up a drink. "How long you been working here?"

"I'm not sure, a couple years, I guess."

"Where is your bosses? Eric or Zay?" he downed his entire drink and fixed another one.

"The new owners? Yeah, Eric isn't here tonight, but Zay is in the main office. He had an important call, but he's been out on the floor most of the night."

"Cool, say no mo." Kash removed himself from the bar. He walked around the entire club looking for the main office. Once he found it, he did not waste time walking right into the room that was more plush than the club. It was a sound-proof room. Wall to wall carpet, flat screen TVs mounted on the walls, a red oak desk, and soft big chairs decorated the space. Zay held a shocked look on his face when he and Kash locked eyes. He couldn't believe somebody let this nigga just walk into his office. He was still on the phone as Kash closed the door.

"What's up, nigga? You look like you just saw a ghost." Kash smiled and took a seat in one of the leather chairs. He sat the Hen bottle on Zay's desk.

"Nawl, bruh, just surprised that you just walked in so easy. Could've been anybody, feel me?" Zay tried to act normal, like he wasn't feeling the pressure, but Kash peeped his hoe card instantly.

"Yeah, I feel that," Kash said while looking around. "Damn, this spot here is nice. You and that boy Eric did y'all thang with this one. Matter of fact, where is shawty anyways? I ain't really seen him." Kash decided to play mind games with Zay because he knew exactly where Eric's bitch ass was hiding from the world.

"Ion know where that fool at, might be on his way here or to the other spot, ain't no telling," Zay replied while hanging up from his phone call.

"Y'all niggas got four spots, huh? Ain't sold not one ounce of dope to get the money, y'all niggas got old paper, huh?" Kash asked and got a hesitant answer from Zay. At first, it was a look that Zay gave him. Then he shook his head slowly before speaking.

"It's not old paper, bruh, it's loans we've taken out and common sense. With the right lawyers, you can make all type of things shake," Zay replied.

"Oh yeah?" Kash asked skeptically as he poured another drink into his cup.

"Yeah, I let my mother and Eric mother do all the paper work" Zay said. Kash had stood to his feet. He started walking around the office, not saying anything. He walked over to Eric's desk.

"Y'all niggas been sending Gangsta something on the books?" He took a seat in Eric's chair, throwing his feet up on the desk and knocking over pictures and pens. They shattered to the floor. Neither Kash nor Zay flinched.

"Yeah, we bout to start. We got something going to him every..."

"You know shawty is the true reason all of us is out, don't you? Bruh been locked up almost three months and y'all just now about to break bread. What's up with y'all two niggas, you and bitch ass Eric?" This time when Kash stood to his feet, Zay saw something different in his eyes. Kash walked towards him.

"It's not like that at all, my nigga. We fucks with Gary..." Zay's words came to an abrupt end when he noticed the knife in Kash's hand. Zay wanted to hit the panic button but he didn't have one in the office. He vowed to get one if he made it out of this ordeal alive.

"What is it like then, pimp? See y'all niggas don't fuck with bruh so don't act like it. I'm the wrong nigga to try and play, see, 'cause I'll hurt one of you pussy niggas," Kash stated.

"Come on, bruh. It's not like dat at all, my nigga," Zay pleaded.

"Nigga, fuck you. I tell you what, though, where is that paperwork? I wanna see how much this pussy ass club bring in 'cause y'all niggas finna pay to play. Gangsta get twenty-five percent of everything y'all do, nigga, and I get ten, that's thirty-five percent of everything you do, pussy nigga."

Kash came around the desk to get face to face with Zay. He punched him in the mouth, sending him crashing into the wall, still in the chair. Then Kash stuck the knife deep into his thigh.

"Ughh ahh," Zay yelled out in pain.

"Think it's a game?" Kash snatched the knife out. He grabbed Zay's shirt and wiped it clean. Zay fell to the ground holding his leg as Kash walked out of the office.

***

Right now, nothing in life mattered to her but her son and Gangsta. All NeNe wanted was her family back. She wanted her son to make it and his daddy to come home.

She wanted her life normal like it once was before all these things took place. NeNe and her sister were sitting inside the room with Jr, hoping and praying that he pulled through as the doctors had said he would. He was no longer on life support, which was the best thing of all out of the situation. His entire face was wrapped with two tubes running from his mouth and nose.

It was a sight she cared not to see but NeNe dealt with the reality. She was overly grateful that God spared her only child, giving him the chance at life. Her wish now was that he made a successful recovery so that he could grow up like every other kid, big and strong. NeNe looked up when the room door opened and in walked Kash, holding some flowers. He smiled down at NeNe before speaking.

"What's going on, sis? Erica, what's up, how y'all?" Kash placed the flowers on the counter along with other gifts people had brought when they visited.

"Hey, Charles, we good. What's up with you?" NeNe asked as she got up to hug him. She was proud of Kash for holding everybody down straight out of jail. He was a true friend turned brother in her eyes.

"I'm just coolin', had to come see my nephew and make sure he good. Do y'all need anything? Have y'all ate?" Kash asked concerned.

"No, we hungry, too," Erica cut in. "You buying?"

"Whatever y'all need," Kash quickly shot back. NeNe noticed for the first time a scar on Kash's face.

"What happened?" she asked and pointed.

"Got stabbed twice there."

"Oh my goodness, stop lying." Nene reached to touch it. The scar was from his ear to his jaw. It didn't look too bad, but it most definitely looked painful.

"No flexing, so what y'all tryna eat? And when is my lil' nigga coming home?" Kash wanted to know.

"He got to wake up first, Kash," Erica stated.

"Well get 'em up."

"I wish," NeNe replied and touched Jr's tiny hand. "The doctors said that he can awake at any moment, so that's what we're waiting on. Plus, once the wraps come off his face, the doctor said he should be coming back, said we also gotta do plastic surgery if his ear do not heal correctly," NeNe told him.

"You found the doctors that can do the surgery?" Kash asked.

"Well a few have come down and left their cards. See, we may don't need them, at least that's what I hope."

"Cool, give me the cards. Let me get some info on what's going on."

"For what, Kash? You must finna change your appearance," Erica asked in a joking manner.

"Some like dat," replied Kash, not paying attention to her jokes right now.

"Boy, hush, but where we going 'cause I'm hungry?" Erica stood to her feet and her and Kash eyed one another. NeNe noticed and she would have loved to see them back together.

"Where y'all wanna eat? It's up to y'all," Kash said.

"Just bring me something back. I'm not going. I wanna be here when my baby open his eyes," NeNe said.

"Oh, you going?" Kash turned to Erica. She reached down and grabbed her pocketbook. She looked at Kash with that *what you think* look. Then she led the way to the door and opened it.

"Boy, you better come on," Erica said as Kash hugged NeNe once more. Then he followed her out the door. When the both of them left, NeNe found her seat and sat down. She grabbed the letter Gangsta had sent to her through his mother. NeNe had yet to open it because she wanted to read it alone, without any interruptions. She opened it with a fearful heart. Her hands began to sweat as her eyes embraced the first line.

Nya,
Beautiful woman you are, oh how happy I am to be a part of your life and that we share a son together. First, before anything, I hope that this letter embraces your hands blessed with a peaceful mindset and a day's joy...

Nene, baby girl, I know life right now is extreme and it's difficult, if not impossible, to hold on. But please do because behind every frown, there's a smile. Our son will be okay, baby. God told me so. It's what I asked for and God said he'll give it. I love you, okay, baby girl? Always know that, alright? Nya, I want you to also know that I never meant for this to happen to us. It was never my intent to lead us down this road. And actually, I was walking the right path to get us where we needed to be.

I was doing what was right as a man and a husband, and especially a father. Baby, I don't know why this nigga chose to fuck with me, but he did. And for that, I am sorry. All I want, Nya, is for our son and you to make it, and for you to be proud of me at being your child's father because I am proud just at the thought of you being my son's mother, my friend, and with hopes that one day you will become my wife and that we may have more kids.

Nene, I know you may try to figure out why I chose to turn myself in like I did and admit to all my wrongs. Well, to be totally

honest with you, I made a deal with God to spare our son in ex-
change for my freedom and clean slate. I was tired of the many
wrongs I've done, so I decided to kill two birds with one stone. I
did not know what else to do, baby girl. I ran out of option's and
God was our only route, so please don't hate me but respect and
love my reason for being here on death row awaiting my fate.

I love you, Nya. I respect you fully and I look up to you for
being a strong woman walking this even stronger life. Trust God
that Jr will soon open his eyes and smile again. I have both y'all
names on my visiting list so I'll see y'all sooner than we both ex-
pect. Kash got anything you'll ever need so when that time comes,
just ask. Kiss my son for me and send me some pictures and you.
Be safe, okay, baby girl?

Always,

Gary

Nene didn't even realize that tears were rolling down her face until she was finished with the letter. Her heart was heavy. She was wishing that all of this was a dream and that she'd wake up in Gangsta's arms next to their son. Reality told her that it wasn't a dream, that what was playing before her eyes was real life.

She put the letter in her bag and got up. She walked over to Jr's bed. For a brief moment, all she did was look as tears fell rapidly down her face. She bent down and kissed his wrapped face. "That's from your father." as soon as she came up, she noticed Jr's arm move. Nene was stuck at the moment, not knowing what was going on. She started to reach out to touch him again, but this time Jr's legs started to kick out. His hands moved. His head moved side to side. He started moaning.

Nene jumped back then yelled, "Help. Help. Doctors." Nene quickly ran out of the room as the machine started making all types of noises. Nene saw nurses and doctors running in her direction. They told her to go stand in the waiting room and closed her outside of the room. Nene wanted to faint. She wanted to put up a fight and stay in the room to see what was going on with her son. But she decided to let God handle it because he was the reason behind it all anyways.

***

"What's going on?" Veedo asked his worker as they both were walking into the trap spot.

"Two lil' blood niggas pulled a stunt last night and robbed June for a half of kilo coming into the spot. They took thirty grand, too," the worker said.

"Whea June at now?" Veedo asked.

"Home, I guess," the worker stated.

"Who is these two lil' niggas? Do you got a read on them? Where they hang at?" Veedo didn't like what he was hearing. He saw two niggas in the kitchen sacking up dope. Veedo took a seat at the table and pulled his phone out.

"Ah, they from Etheridge, Lil' Quin and Blade lil' bad ass wanna be thug," the worker said, shaking his head side to side.

"And they bloods?" Veedo asked, his mind formulating a plan already to straighten the situation before word got to Kash, It was one thing Veedo nor Kash allowed and that was taking out of their mouths. It was no pussy in their crew and any nigga should know that they don't play those types of games. It was a new boss in town. This wasn't a New York crew, it was niggas born and raised in Atlanta, GA who was eating off this plate, niggas who weren't snitching or bitching, just a group of hungry hood niggas chasing a bankroll.

"Yup, they big homie name is Block. I'd holla at him first if I was you 'cause bloods run the apartments," the worker let him know.

"Block?" Veedo asked.

"Yup, that's him."

44

Veedo sent a sweet text message to the beautiful girl he had just met, then got up and put the phone away. He walked over to the counter where the leftover dope was being sacked up. He only saw a few ounces and nothing else.

"Come here," Veedo walked away and back into the living room. "Where is Fred?"

Fred was the accountant of the house. He kept all paperwork straight and had inventory on all drugs pushed in and out of the trap spot.

"He upstairs sleep, last I checked," the worker replied.

"Okay, go get 'em."

The worker quickly disappeared upstairs and was gone a moment. When he returned, he had Fred behind him. Fred was an older cat that lived off loyalty. He was a big dude with grey side burns and green eyes. He was a guy Veedo had known all his life and since knowing Fred, he'd never heard bad things about him at all. All business was A1 when it came down to it.

"What's going on, V?" Fred rubbed cold out of his eyes as he joined Veedo at the sofa.

"Have any of the money been picked up?"

"Yeah, Poonie picked up last night but I got a sixty upstairs. you need it?" Fred asked.

"Nawl, Poonie can get it. I'm just trying to figure out what's what around here, that's all. So where was you when June got robbed?" Veedo wanted to know.

"Inside. Hell, I ain't hear or see shit. All I know is June came in saying he was jacked in the yard by two teenagers," Fred replied with a look Veedo couldn't read. But he did notice when Fred looked at the worker, he kind of rolled his eyes his way.

"Okay, cool, y'all niggas continue to hold the spot down. I'll have a load pull up in a few hours and I'ma get the situation with June handled. Y'all just watch yo self. Things are about to change, anyways, for the safety of us all. I'll let you know what's what with that as soon as I hear anything official," Veedo explained to his crew. He was disappointed with them because he knew it was some slick shit going on. He couldn't put his finger on it, but he wouldn't stop until he did.

Forty-five minutes later, Veedo pulled up to June's crib in Summer Hill. He watched niggas watch him as he parked the Benz. He jumped out and headed to the door. It was cracked when he walked up on the crowded porch with its old sofas, old chairs, and two floor model TVs.

Veedo pushed the door open a bit, careful not to rush into the house, but at the same time looking hard. He saw that the living room was empty. The house was quiet but reeked of a smell, a fishy sex smell that obviously started in the living room with clothes and shoes tossed everywhere. Veedo noticed two small bankrolls of cash, two ounces of cocaine, and a .45 on the coffee table. What mostly caught his attention was a book bag and a store sack of candy. He also saw a lil' lip gloss and a bottle of lotion that smells good.

Veedo made his way toward the back to the bedrooms, slowly watching everything he saw until he made it to the threshold of a door and saw June with his pants dropped to his ankles and his shirt off, sweating like a slave at work in the sun. Veedo couldn't see the girl because her head was down as she gripped the sheets.

"Say, June?" At the sound of his name, he almost jumped out of his skin. He quickly turned to see who had just walked into his house. June stopped and snatched his clothes up when he saw that it was his boss-man in his room. This movement gave Veedo a chance to see the girl who raised up embarrassed for being caught in the act.

"Wha-what's going on, Veedo?" June said. He looked high. He looked nervous. Veedo, on the other hand, didn't say anything to June. Instead, he stared at the girl. He saw that she was only a baby, a mere teenager, probably in the 10th grade. June had to be in his late thirties.

"Put yo clothes on, homie, we need to talk." Veedo finally looked at June with pity in his eyes. He couldn't believe the nerves of this nigga to be fuckin' a little girl. She was too young for Veedo as it was, and June had him by at least ten years, so she was definitely off limits to June. June pulled his shirt on and followed Veedo into the living room.

"What's good, family?" June asked, picking up a New Port and taking a seat on the sofa. He still had beads of sweat on his forehead.

"What happened last night?" Veedo asked.

"Man ion know how these two niggas got up on me so fast. All I know is as soon as I get out the car, they pop up out the blue skies, scaring the life out of me, no lie. I had just picked up a half and had the lil' money for Poonie on me, just in case we get together in traffic. I let them niggas have it cause at the end of the day, I know both of these lil' niggas and they families. I'm just glad them pussy niggas didn't whack me," June stressed.

"What's up with you bustin' a child, though? That lil' girl in school, my Nigga. You know that's some sucka shit," Veedo changed the subject.

"She eighteen, bruh," June quickly defended himself.

"Eighteen?" Veedo questioned. Then he said, "Get the fuck outta here." He walked away back into the bedroom and locked the door because June was sure to follow. Inside the room, the little girl had gotten dressed. Prepared to leave, she held a fearful look.

"What's your age and don't lie," Veedo nicely demanded, looking directly at the child who was scared out of her mind. He gave her that *don't fucking lie to me* look.

"Sixteen. Can I please go now?" the girl asked.

Veedo walked to the door, unlocked it, and June walked in. "Yeah you can go," he said and watched the girl pass June, who wanted to say something but didn't. He just let the girl leave, feeling as stupid as he looked. June knew he had fucked up big time, fucked up for crossing that line with a kid, and even more fucked up that he left his gun on the coffee table because Veedo had pulled out a Gloc. He held it down by his leg and glared at June with hate in his eyes.

"Wh-what's up Veedo?" June nervously asked, hoping that he didn't get shot or, better yet, die.

"Ain't shit up, nigga. Where is yo money stash at?" Veedo push the gun in June face.

"My who?" June balled up like a hoe nigga, eyes closed and hands up with his palms out like a bitch.

"Take me to yo stash, nigga, or get whacked. Fuck wrong wit y'all fuck niggas playing with a gangsta?" Veedo had become heated because niggas were taking his kindness for weakness.

June took him into another room where he had a stash of money. That's when he saw the bail of weed with one of Lucky's stamps on it. Veedo knew that Lucky was a New York nigga that flooded the streets with bullshit weed for stupid low prices. He figured June was trying to play both sides of the fence by getting work from both connects, but Veedo had another thing coming for his ass.

"Man, V, don't take me out, my nigga. You know I'm the most loyal…"

"Nigga, shut the fuck up talking to me. So you getting work from Lucky and me, huh? You tryna be slick, my dude, huh? We don't fuck with New York niggas. We rob and kill them niggas, you hear me?" Veedo aimed the gun at June's face.

"No, no, no, my nigga…"

Boom. Boom. Two quick shots left June slumped and brain mattered spread all over the wall.

"Pussy nigga." Veedo looked around. All of a sudden he was mad at himself for doing what he'd just done but at the same time, that was the game you played when in the streets. Veedo was just one of the types of guys that played by the rules, so if it caused for death, then death was what you'd get. Veedo made sure to wipe everything down he thought and knew he'd touched. He got the stash of money, leaving the bail of weed for the police findings. He quickly got up out of the house and jumped into his ride. Veedo saw the young lil' girl standing at the bus stop down the street. He stopped, pulled up next to her, and rolled his window down.

"Get in. I'll take you home," he spoke. He noticed the girl was hesitant to move. Veedo looked to the road ahead, then back to her before saying, "I'm not gone hurt you, just come on 'cause I'm holding up traffic. But I need to talk to you 'bout something." At that, the girl inched forward, but stopped again. Veedo leaned over the console and opened the door. "Come on. You straight."

The girl heard a few horns blow. She saw a host of cars behind the Benz, waiting on her to decide. She finally climbed in and Veedo pulled off. Her book bag sat between her feet on the floor.

"Just take me to a train station," the girl asked.

"OK do you know the nigga June you was fuckin'?" Veedo wanted to know what was on her mind.

"Yes, June used to stay by us last year."

"You know how old he is?" Veedo questioned.

"Ah twenty something," she answered.

"Wrong. He's in his late thirties, and twenty something is far too old for you. You sixteen, baby, you not ready for a grown man, especially a street nigga, drug dealer. June don't care two bits for you. He got kids yo age. He have no business with you. He is tripping. So what's up with your parents?"

"They're at work."

"Well here." he reached in his pocket and pulled out some money. "Forget you ever met me. This is a couple grand. You will not see June anymore, so don't go to looking for him either. Go find a boyfriend yo age, alright?" Veedo handed over the money.

"Okay."

"I'm serious. And if the police step to you, no matter what they say, you have not been over here and you have not seen him, got it?" Veedo asked for her understanding.

"Okay, I heard you loud and clear," the young girl pushed the money into her book bag. Moments later, he dropped her off at the train station. Veedo's mind was in limbo. He knew word would soon spread about what happened to June and that his name may surface. He had to figure out some kind of way to throw it off him if there was an issue.

Niggas doing something about the murders was the last thing he was worried about. It was police and police ass niggas that had him afraid. He knew that it was time to retire out of the game because his guilt trip was invading his thoughts and prison scared the life out of him.

Veedo pulled up to his baby's mother's nail shop, a spot he'd funded for her, just in case something happened to him and he couldn't do for his kids. April didn't do anybody's nails. All she did was charge a percentage off each customer. Veedo parked and sat inside his Benz for a moment. He had to add some shit up right quick, figure his next move out, and question himself about rather he should tell Kash what went down and about the weed from Lucky. Veedo knew he would not hold that type of information from his partner, so he dialed Kash's number.

Chapter 5

Kash was standing behind Erica on the phone with Veedo. They were in line to get their Red Lobster take out. Erica wore some blue jeans that hugged her hips and some low cut boots with the open toe front. It'd been years since he'd busted her up and all the thoughts in the world wouldn't change his mind of wanting to fuck her right then and there. He watched her move. With each step she took, her ass bounced in the jeans.

Erica was still as beautiful as ever, nobody could deny that. It was just how she treated him when he was locked up that made Kash look at her different. Erica turned her head to ask him something and noticed his eyes glued to her booty. With a quick blush, she turned fully around to face him, making him look up from her bottom to her eyes.

"So how do it feels to be free?" She didn't know what else to ask.

"All this shit feels the same," Kash laughed. "Nawl, I'm just glad my nigga bailed me out."

"I know that's right. Now all you gotta do is make something happen for him to get out," Erica replied.

"That's the mojo. What's up with you, though? You married yet? I'm surprised you don't have no lil' ones running around the place," Kash shot back.

"Honey, no, I'm good on babies. I'm just waiting on Jr to pull through, me and Nene is leaving GA once he wake up."

"Oh really? Why?" Kash wanted to know.

"GA is just our bad luck, I guess. Shit, so much has happened to us for the bad that we just want a change, at least for a moment anyways," Erica replied.

Finally, they made it to the counter where she paid for the food. Kash was the one who grabbed it as she took the drinks. Kash cranked up the whip once they were both inside comfortably. Erica went into one of the bags. She was hungry and couldn't wait another minute.

"So what's up with you, though?" Erica decided to ask. Kash pulled into traffic, his music beating *Velt*.

"I'ma get this money."

"Better slow down," she added.

"And I'ma get rich and murder trying," Kash laughed at his own joke.

"You got jokes, huh? I'm so serious, Charles. You realize you had life in prison?"

"I'm just chilling. My main focus is my kids and my brother," Kash admitted. He jumped on the highway.

Erica turned fully in her seat, her back against the door. For a moment she only looked at Kash and, ever so often, he'd steal a brief look her way.

"Charles, could it ever be us again?" Erica wanted to know. She needed to know.

Kash cracked a smile at her question. He smiled because when he was in prison, stuck with life, he had hoped and wished for a day like this, the moment and time when Erica would ask for another chance. Kash had no idea that he would be on top this much, but he still knew he'd be doing good enough to make her jock.

"Being in a relationship is the very last thing on my mind," Kash replied, knowing she wouldn't accept the answer.

"Boy, I said ever, not now, but it's gonna come a time when you need that rider."

"Rider?" he questioned with a smirk on his face.

"You know what I'm saying, Kash." Erica turned back in her seat and slapped her hand down on her thigh. She grabbed her food again and started back eating.

"I know you thought a nigga wouldn't get out, shawty. That's why you stopped riding and I know that. Ain't no pressure, I ain't mad at cha. But ion see myself in no relationship no time, real shit.

I'ma still take you out and kick da shit wit cha, but I'm cool on anything else." Kash didn't want to hurt her little feelings, so he kept the door open to fair grounds. He didn't want any drama with her and he most definitely wanted the pussy again, just for the fuck of it.

"Well, you right, but I had realized that back then. I wanted to come back, but you shut me out, Kash. You wouldn't write and you know for a fact that I sent you at least eight letters that you never responded to. You know I'm not lying 'bout that, now don't front," Erica defended herself and Kash agreed. She had a point, but the fact remained the same. She made the wrong choice no matter how she wanted to put it. He already had his mind made up about her since seeing her the first day he got out.

True indeed he wanted to fuck her again, but it would never be the same with them. It was a dead issue.

"I fuck with you though," Kash stated.

"No, you don't," Erica rolled her eyes. She wasn't feeling how he was acting and it showed in her mood. It showed on her face. She did not ask another question or speak another word. She just stared out the window as the car eased down the highway headed back to the hospital to give Nene her food.

When they made it back upstairs, the floor was more crowded than Kash had ever seen. So many people came with gifts. So many news crews and big time people of importance were there.

The area where Junior's room was had too many folks there. Police were telling people they had to leave. But the growing crowd was acting as if they did not hear any commands given by the cops. Kash and Erica looked at each other while making their way to the front. Neither one knew what to expect but both hoped for the best. What made the situation good was the fact that they found not one person crying and many people walking around happy, when just about an hour ago, the hospital floor was empty, calm, and chill.

Kash made it to the room door and they walked in. the sight he saw made his heart drop to the pit of his stomach. Chills ran all over his body as he stared at Nene holding her son, a son who had his eyes open. He still wore a breathing mask and his face had a bandage on it from the gunshot wound. Erica quickly rushed in when she saw what was going on. She couldn't believe it.

Mrs. Jackson wore a big smile on her face as well. More folks Kash did not know were also inside the room, everybody laughing and smiling through conversation. Kash was amazed and happy. He knew that was all Gangsta prayed for, so he knew his partner was about to be one happy man, no matter the situation at hand. He sat the food down and got a hug from Mrs. Jackson before going to hug Nene again and Junior

"Y'all call me," Kash said to Nene, and then looked to Mrs. Jackson because his phone vibrated a text message from Loco. He had a meeting today. Kash hugged a happy Nene once more. This was a good day, a very good day. He and Erica locked eyes briefly, then Kash left them to go handle business.

***

"Whoa, what's mobbin'?" Meco answered the phone. Kash hadn't heard from him since he got out of prison. He considered Meco to be a true partner. He was loyal to the core.

"What they do, fooly, you good?" Kash was joyous to hear Meco's voice again.

"Fuckin' right, bruh, I'm holding it on the road. What's up with you, though? What do you got going on out there?" Meco wanted to know.

"Man, a lil' of it all, bruh, no lie. I'm eating on these fuck niggas out here. What you need though?"

"I'm straight right now. I won my appeal, bruh, I'm just waiting on Rice Street to come get me," Meco was happy to say.

"Damn, that's the mojo. Boy, I need a nigga like you out here with me to hold these streets down. It's a lot of lames out here in your way, my nigga. I mean these niggas ain't got no swag," Kash said while driving a little over the speed limit.

"I'm ready, bruh. You know I'm mobbin', right?" Meco boasted.

"Well, I got you locked in. Call me if you need anything, my nigga. It's no pressure, I got cha." He and Kash ended the call. It was good hearing from Meco and Kash hoped like hell that Meco gave the courts back the life sentence they'd given him ten years ago.

Kash knew he could use Meco for muscle with the numbers he had with the mob. Meco was capo over most good fellas' members and could make shit shake in no time. Kash just prayed Meco got out, and if need be, he was willing to skin down for a lawyer for his partner. Kash finally pulled up to a Mexican restaurant in Gwinnett County, where his GPS directed him.

Once he parked the car and entered the establishment, he was escorted to a table, a large table with a group of Mexicans. Loco was the only person he knew out of the five of them. Loco held up his glass of wine and nodded his head.

"Welcome, my friend." Loco stood up to shake hands with Kash, like they always did. "Let me introduce you, my two sisters, Melody and Mya." Loco waved to his sisters, two very beautiful Mexicans girls. "And my two best mens, Longo and Jeter," Loco said.

"What's up, ladies? What's up, fellas? Nice to meet the family, I'm Kash," Kash spoke and took the seat open to him. It was next to one of the girls.

"We have yet to order, so have your choice," Mya spoke and Kash took up the menu.

"So I hear you just got out recently," Melody bumped shoulders with her questions.

"Yeah, I did," replied Kash, while looking at the menu.

"So, my friend," Loco cut in. He wanted to get right to the matter at hand. "I see you doing very good on pushing the product. I appreciate all gestures made, and our family's trust with you is extreme. My father wanted to make you sole distributor over Georgia, Florida, Texas, and New Orleans, but I do not want to put too much on you," Loco said.

Kash sat the menu down, and then sat up straight in his seat. He wanted to be sure he heard correctly, that his ears weren't playing tricks on him. He looked to Loco and asked, "So you want me to take over four states?"

"Yes, but not only will I provide you with security, but also a trustful team." Loco waved to the other four Mexicans. "Plus, a place to stay in each state. Reasons are federal government is aimed at my father, and I so we would hide for a while."

"So will I have access to all I need? I mean all everything? Will I be in contact with you?" Kash wanted to know.

"Yes, you will have all that you need and contact will be made only through Melody. Nobody but her will know how to reach us. I wanna send you up to meet the main source in each state, learn every route, every move. This training will take sixty days, my friend. No contact with nobody. You will be with Longo and Jeter to show you everything. Do you have trust in your people to hold Atlanta down for sixty days, or should we pull the plug until you get situated?" asked Loco.

"I got Atlanta, but when you talking 'bout leaving?"

"I'm speaking as soon as possible, my friend. I'll be out of the U.S. by sunrise, but I'll give you two weeks to mend things to your liking. Then be prepared to grab a sixty-day leave," Loco said.

"I'm good with that. So, question, the feds do I have to worry about them or am I in the clear?"

"You clear, trust me?"

Kash stayed around and ate dinner with them, getting to know the other four Mexicans. He and Melody seemed to click more than any one of them. Kash knew she was on him because she acted a certain way when he would speak to her sister, and one time during conversation, he caught her rolling her eyes at him interacting with Mya. It was funny and cute.

Kash knew before long he would get the pussy, but right now his focus was what Loco had going on. Was this too much? Should he just chill? What would Gangsta do? These were all questions Kash asked himself over and over again as he drove home.

***

When she got the call that Zay had been stabbed, Terry almost lost her mind not knowing what to think. All she knew was as soon as the call was made, she shot out the door and was driving at top speed headed to the hospital. Her daughter was with Nikki and Poonie, so she was alone. Her phone began to ring as she cut in and out of traffic. Terry picked it up in a panic.

"Hello?"

"What happened? I just heard." It was Roxanne.

"Girl, I don't know. All Zay mom said that Zay had been stabbed in the club said he's in surgery. I'm headed dat way now," Terry replied.

"Which hospital?"

"South Fulton."

"Okay, I'll be down there, girl, I'm leaving now. I'll text you when I get there," Roxanne said and they ended the call. Terry wondered what had happened in the club. What type of mess was Zay into that would make someone stab him? She didn't understand and prayed that it had nothing to do with the drug game because it would disappoint her if it did.

"If it ain't one thing it's another," Terry said out loud as the car exited the highway. She punched the gas up Cleveland Avenue, rushing through traffic. All her mind could think about was her man and his well-being. Tears threatened to fall out her eyes, but she aimed herself to be strong, strong for her unborn child and strong for Zay because all he had was his mother and her. She did not want to lose him like this, so suddenly, out of the blue skies.

Terry pulled into the hospital parking lot. She quickly parked and ran into the hospital. At the front desk was a woman around her same age. Terry cracked a smile through teary eyes and asked the lady where was Zay. After giving his personal information, the woman looked it up on the computer, then told Terry where to go. She didn't spare another second.

She made a dash to the elevators. The ride up seemed like it would take forever to get there. When the doors opened, Terry shot up out of there fast, and rushed down the hall to be met by Zay's mother and other family members. She hugged Zay's mother and then questioned, "Is he okay?"

Terry let the tears flood down her face, scared for the life of her man. Not knowing what to expect, she could only hope and pray that everything would be good for Zay.

"Yes, he's out of surgery right now. He just got stabbed in the thigh. Knife went seven inches into him and was snatched out, tearing veins and meat and tissue with the ridges on the blade. Doctors said he will be okay. He will have to go through physical therapy to gain his full motion of walking again. We'll be able to go see him in a second. Police is in there now," Zay's mother told Terry, which made her feel a whole lot better.

"Okay, that's good, thank God. Thank You Jesus," Terry said full of joy and hugged Zay's mother one more time.

Chapter 6

After another hour, Terry and the family were allowed to visit Zay. He was sitting up in bed eating the hospital food. As soon as his eyes laid on Terry, a bright smile painted his face. He also saw his mother and other family. He and Terry shared a kiss and a much needed hug.

"Baby, I was scared," she whispered.

"You know I'm hard to kill," Zay boasted, but he was fronting, he rubbed her stomach, feeling the baby move.

"I know, baby. So what happened?" Terry along with everyone else wanted to know what went down.

Zay took her small hand. He kissed one of her finger tips and looked her in the eyes. "Baby, I couldn't even tell you even if I tried. It was too much going on, too many people, too much noise," was what Zay said, but Terry didn't believe him for one second. She sensed something else, but she wasn't sure, so she agreed with a nod of her head. A knock came at the door. Then Eric walked in, followed by Roxanne.

"What's up, bro?" his concerned voice asked Zay, walking over to his bedside. He also acknowledged the family and friends. But his main focus was Zay, his childhood friend and business partner.

"I'm taking it day by day, my G. What's up with you?" Zay shot back as he sat up in bed correctly.

"Sounds true, so I need to know da business," Eric stated because word was already out that it was a hit on him and Zay's heads. Eric just wanted to know if it was any truth to it. He turned to the entire family when he saw that Zay was hesitant about telling him what was going on. "Excuse us for a brief moment, five minutes in private please."

"I guess," Terry was the first to agree. Then everyone else followed because they all figured Eric could get down to the bottom of what was going on. Everyone filed out of the room. Eric closed the door behind the last person and instantly turned towards his partner.

"What's up?" was all Eric said.

"It was Kash," Zay replied, which made Eric's heart skip a beat. He was shocked to even hear Kash's name of all people.

"What?"

"Man he talking about we haven't been fucking with Gangsta and all types of other shit. Nigga said we got to pay thirty-five percent of everything we own. Then the nigga stabbed me in my fuckin' leg."

"No way."

"That's what I'm saying," Zay replied.

"Thirty-five percent of what? What da hell wrong with Kash?" Eric was overall confused.

"Thirty-five of everything we worth. Nigga said we owe Gangsta."

"Man, fuck Kash. He must don't know who he fucking with. I will not give him one red penny of my money. Fuck what he stressing 'bout. Gangsta is my first cousin. He musta forgot or sum."

"I don't know what's wrong with that nigga. He need to be worried about a job instead of fucking with niggas who gonna have him knocked off," Zay said. The situation had Eric heated at knowing what went down. He really didn't like the act Kash pulled, no matter what anybody said or would say. Yeah, it was true that Kash and Gangsta were partners, but at the same time, he was blood to Gangsta and nothing to Kash. So the odds were different.

"So what we gone do?" Zay asked.

"We gone get that Nigga took out. Fuck Kash. He ain't no God," Eric stated. but did he truly mean it? They were words from anger and heated emotions, so did he really want to go at Kash? Did he truly want a war and to cross out his cousin because his respect was on the line? Everyone who knew Eric knew he wasn't a killer, but he did have murders on his hands, being the buyer of hit men. He wasn't scary, he just wasn't built for the action as Kash was. So was he truly ready?

**

Kash met Veedo and Monkey at the condo later that night to discuss what was going on. He planned on telling them about the meeting with Loco over blunts and drinks. Even though he was with Loco on the movement, Kash also had other plans. He parked the Benz in his designated spot as his phone started vibrating in his pocket. He opened the door, had one foot in and one foot out, and answered.

"Yo?"

"What you doing?" It was Erica, sounding as sexy as ever. He smiled then looked up just in time to see a car creeping by with tinted windows. The tint didn't hide two pair of eyes that were on him. That's when Kash reached for his gun. The car sped away through the condo's parking lot as Kash came up out of the car. The phone was on the seat. He was in the middle of the parking lot with the gun out, held down by his side. "Pussy niggas," Kash said, already knowing it had to be Zay or Eric's scary ass that sent a fake ass hit.

Erica's phone call just might've saved him some bullet wounds. Now that he had escaped death, he decided to always wear the vest Gangsta left for him. Kash walked back to the Benz and retrieved his phone. Erica was still on it.

"What's up, pretty?" he asked, walking to the building. He watched the parking lot just in case them niggas came back. He really wanted them to try their luck anyways. Kash slid into the condo and made his way upstairs

"What you doing?" Erica asked again, because he'd had her on hold.

"Just got to the spot."

"Oh, so you busy then?" she asked.

"Some like dat. what's up though, baby? You still at Grady?" Kash made it to his door. He used his key to walk inside. Monkey and Veedo were posted, playing the video game.

"Yes, Nene is feeding Junior now as we speak."

"So he's doing good? " Kash asked excited.

"Yes, he's doing very, very good. It's a miracle, he got to be here for two weeks though," Erica replied and smiled.

"That's amazing. That's real good then. Yeah, so what's up? You must tryna link up with me or something?" Kash wanted to know. He walked over and dapped each one of them up.

"Yes, if you want," replied Erica. Just that comment alone made him envision them fucking in some hotel room somewhere.

"Hell yeah, we can do something. I'ma hit you up when I leave the spot. Give me 'bout an hour," Kash told her as he sat down.

"Okay."

They disconnected the call and Kash placed his phone on the table. He caught the rotation of the blunt when it passed his face. The game was being played on Kash's 70-inch TV, showing as real as ever.

"Roll up another one, shawty," Monkey said to Kash, his face not leaving the big screen TV as the game went on.

"Nigga, I'm next," Kash told the both of them and grabbed a wrap. He didn't even care to tell either of them about the attempt made before he came in. He didn't bother to tell them because it was no big deal to him, or at least that's what he thought. Right now wasn't the time to have them worried about simple shit when it was major movement going on right under their noses. Kash rolled the blunt and began.

"So y'all niggas check the move," Kash said when he lit the blunt.

"It's bout to go down, bigger and better than we expected it to go. This Mexican is really fucking with us all around the plate. He's now trying to put the whole menu on our table. He want me to have three more states, being the sole distributor, and y'all niggas know I took him up on the deal," Kash smiled.

"Huh? Is I'm hearing correct?" Veedo paused the game. Now his and Monkey's focus was on Kash.

"Yeah, thing is the plug is slick hot and they wanna hide until the heat blow over. That's where we come in at," Kash explained.

"So it's gone be us the feds gone focus on instead of them?" Veedo asked. The feds were the last people he wanted to deal with.

"Fuck nawl. We ducking the cops in all we do. We just got to out slick the slicker, be on point, be on every move, and keep these suckas names out our mouths. See, as long as we play ghost, then how can we get popped? What I'm saying is all of us will be able to play the background, you know, coach from the sidelines."

"So who will supply us?" Monkey wanted to know.

"Same people. The main line still available to us, plus more. We get whips, houses, security, and artillery. We get a state to ourselves."

"Ion know, bruh. Don't this shit seem too good to be true though?" Veedo asked. By now, they had cut the game off and another blunt was in rotation. "I mean, best believe if the feds on them and we fucking with the same line, then that's gonna eventually lead to us."

"Could be true. But my plan is to get the position they giving, and then respectfully pull away from fucking with them. Give them everything and everyone back, but already be established. And within the sixty days I'm with them, getting the ins and outs, we link up with Lucky, rock him to sleep, and see if we can peep a weak spot 'cause we gone take him out for being too slick," Kash added.

Veedo had told him about the weed he found at June's house so instantly Kash made a mental note to get Lucky some kind of way because that was strike two. He wouldn't give him another chance to get over because the next time may just be his best time.

"I'm with it, my nigga," Monkey said.

"Hell, I'm in, too, bruh. I'm just not tryna play around with them feds just yet," Veedo replied with a shake of his head.

"Nigga, me either," shot back Kash.

All three of them rode over to the warehouse to do a count up on the product. It took over an hour for them to total up six hundred kilos, kilos Kash ordered to be moved the next day. They also did a pull up on the money spot to make sure everything was everything. It was almost 11pm when they all split up and went their separate ways. Kash called Erica like he said he would. He had beauty on his mind.

Chapter 7

Later that night after leaving the warehouse, Kash picked Erica up in front of Grady. He drove another whip this time. It was a honey white four-door truck that Erica didn't recognize. When it pulled up directly in front of her, Kash let the tinted window down. They both locked eyes, and then she opened the door and jumped inside, looking and smelling good.

"Hey," she spoke while putting on her seat belt. When she looked, she saw on the console a handgun and a bowl of weed. The bowl made her remember the times he did things like that at her house. It made Erica smile on the inside.

"What's up, sweetie?" Kash pulled off. It was around midnight. The sky was cool and dark with stars everywhere. He had made plans to take her out to dinner and then take her to a room and get his smash on. He was just hoping she was down for the action because he could've scooped up a begging Roxanne who wouldn't stop calling or texting his phone.

"Nothing, tired of sitting in that damn hospital. I'm just glad it's over with and my nephew can finally come home now. I know his daddy gonna be happy once he finds out that baby woke up and he's doing better than expected," Erica said.

"So have y'all heard from him yet?"

"Him and Nene been writing, but he's yet to call. You know how stubborn he can get at times," Erica said.

"I need his GDC number ASAP," Kash shot back. He needed all the correct info on Gangsta because once it came down to helping him out, he didn't want anybody acting as if they didn't know who Gangsta was.

"Okay, NeNe got it, I'm sure."

"Bet that."

"Boy you and Gangsta are twins," Erica said out of the blue skies, which made Kash look at her.

"What makes you say that?" Kash questioned. Now she had his full attention.

"You oughtta to seen him out here without you, man. I mean, he was holding shit down and all, but it wasn't a day I seen him smile. It wasn't a day that went by that Gangsta wasn't putting something together to help us out here and when I see you, I see him. 'Cause you have yet to smile and I see with my own eyes you handling stuff. So yeah, y'all are twins," Erica responded, and then started messing with the radio.

"That's my nigga, my G, my nigga for life," Kash admitted with a nod of his head.

"I know," she agreed.

Erica was still bad, three years later, Kash saw. He had so many nights of hate for her and she still had it going on. Her smooth skin tone and her pretty face matched her small waist and phat ass. She was thicker than a slim NeNe but also was small with it.

What Kash liked most about her was her smile and that she had some super cute toes. He was a feet man so it was a plus, a must, that his female had pretty feet. Erica was wifey type to the niggas who were not in the streets, because she most definitely wasn't the rider type for a nigga doing a prison bid. Kash could never put his true trust in her as he'd done before.

Kash pulled up to Taste, an upscale restaurant in Buckhead that was owned by Zay and Eric. Kash parked his own whip versus using the valet. He gave his name at the door and was escorted to a beautifully put together table. The seating was cream soft leather with golden trim. Music played softly overhead. The entire atmosphere of the restaurant was amazing. He and Erica took seats. She held a big smile on her face.

"God knows I haven't been anywhere since them boys kicked in our door. I'm somehow nervous just being anywhere. I guess I just feel brand new," Erica said while looking at the menu on the iPads at the table that were used to order from.

"Well, just sit back and relax, baby girl, you wit a real nigga. Nobody gone harm you while I'm on these streets, so order you a meal for champs and enjoy your safety," Kash assured her and began looking at the menu also. He was hungry and more ready to get her naked than anything. After the food arrived, he took the time to survey the room, watching everyone who worked there and noting every door they walked in and out of. He had plans to pay Eric a visit, just to let him see his face because he knew Zay had told him what was going on by now. Kash knew that the so-called hit sent was right up Eric's alley, with his scary ass.

He and Erica ate in silence just every so often they'd look at each other. Erica would slightly blush and Kash just looked. It was hard for her to read him, even though she still tried. But it was nearly impossible to know what was truly on his mind.

"Baby girl, I'll be right back," Kash excused himself from the table. He had already peeped the way he would get back into the office, so he went straight inside the cooking room. The cooks and waiters strangely looked at him as he walked through, but nobody dared say anything, even if they wanted to. Kash saw the door that belonged to Eric and Zay because it was marked private. He walked right in on Eric and two niggas Kash had never seen. Eric was seated behind a desk with his hand hidden under it.

The two guys were each posted in the corner of the office. Kash noticed the video monitor and instantly saw Erica seated at their table, meaning Eric was watching him the entire time. Kash smiled that wicked smile.

"Shawty, you that shook?" he asked Eric. Then he looked to both the dudes. "You know what's up with me, bruh, I'm an animal. Two or three ain't enough," he was talking about them being deep and looked to have straps on them.

"Come on, Kash, why you wanna bring drama into this shit, my nigga?" Eric asked.

"Nigga, why yo hand under the table?" Kash asked and pointed. Eric looked down to his own hands then back up to Kash face before saying.

"We don't want no problem, my nigga, but…"

"But what, Eric? What, nigga? You know what's up. Boy, stop playing. Y'all niggas gotta pay dues." Kash was ready for whatever. He knew that all three of the dudes were strapped, but at the same time, he knew that Eric wouldn't allow gun shots to go off inside the restaurant.

"What dues, my nigga? You tripping, bro," Eric said, his hand still under the table. Both the dudes started clutching their weapons also, but Kash was bar none, especially at the moment.

"Dues for being fuck niggas, niggas who owe Gangsta their lives," Kash said fast as his face hardened.

"That's my first cousin, bro. Gangsta know I got him on whatever. So what is you talking about?" Eric said.

"Bitch, ion give ah fuck if he yo son, you know you fake kicking it, he know you faking it, and I know. Like I said, my nigga, you got the message I sent Zay. Oh, and I got that message earlier today." Kash paused, and then looked over the two dudes again and asked, "Is these them lil' niggas who was scared to bust something when they saw me?" Kash laughed at his own question.

"Man, Kash, you on some mo shit. I don't know why, but you are…"

"Nigga, name one time you sent shawty some money to his books."

Kash knew that neither Zay nor Eric had sent Gangsta one penny. And the more Eric was playing stupid, the madder Kash became. "You know what?" Kash shook his pointer finger at Eric. "It's thirty-five percent every week, boy, no flexin'. You don't have enough niggas in this world that can protect you from me, so play with it, nigga."

And just like that he walked out of the office, slamming the door and walking back into the front where Erica awaited him at the table. Instead of sitting, he stood there with his hand held out for her. She took it.

"Everything okay?" Erica wanted to be sure everything was good because his facial expression had change instantly.

Kash just winked his eye. "Everything's perfect, baby girl," he responded and led the way out of there with plans on returning however he saw fit. Outside he jumped in the truck, then reached for the fresh rolled blunt. He needed to smoke one badly. Kash was a weed head and had always been that way since he first started smoking. Erica cracked her window but said nothing about him smoking because she felt something was wrong and she was not trying to add fuel to flame.

They rode listening to music. Erica text Nene back and forth while Kash smoked. His mind was on something else now, like Lucky, the New York nigga. Kash felt in his heart that Lucky was indeed a killer but he was old school and Kash was on go-go like a 90s baby, so he knew that the pressure could be applied. it would just have to be finessed the right way. He tossed the blunt roach out the window then checked his phone as he punched down the highway going to the Marriott downtown Atlanta. He stole a look at Erica, looking like heaven in the passenger seat, and couldn't wait to get her in the room to do her something bad.

***

Veedo opened the picture message from Trish and was captivated once again by her beauty. She looked so young and adorable too be the age she was with long jet black hair, the kind of hair that had her baby hair cute. She was your typical redbone, but you could confuse her for being a mix breed. It was just this certain look about the woman Veedo noticed.

"What's good, baby girl," he sent a text back. Inside his grandma's house, he was posted at her dinner table counting money and thinking.

"Nothing much, just got off work," the text came back.

"You so beautiful. Wish I could hang with you but I know you just got off so rest up, baby girl, and get at me later," Veedo text again. His grandmother was in her room somewhere as Veedo continued his count of the stacks of block of money in wraps. He had well over half a million dollars on the table in his face. Veedo was ready to cash out the game, let it go, let everyone else play because he now had the money to invest into something legitimate.

While he was fresh out, he could start over. But the streets were calling his name. His loyalty to Gangsta was what had him, and murder was what came with selling bricks of cocaine. His phone vibrated again. It was Trish.

"You can come chill if you like. I'm not sleep or nothing, nor tired."

Surprised was Veedo to get the message. He didn't look at it like she was a freak or something, but he was still surprised that she even considered him to come over so fast.

"Text me the address." He sent his reply as his grandmother walked into the dining room. She took a seat at the table and slid him a note. He looked at it and nodded his head.

"That spot back there is getting full," his grandma spoke. She opened her bible like always and began to read her word.

"I know, ma, that's why I'm moving some of it to another spot. Just hold what you got so I'll always have me something in life, and I'll make sure nothing else come here," Veedo told his favorite woman in the world. All he had ever become stemmed from his grandmother. He could never deny her that.

"That's fine, baby," was her reply while still looking at her Bible. She was always there for him and that was his security.

After Veedo loaded the money into the Benz trunk, he left Dill Ave and followed directions from his GPS to Trish's house. On the way over, Veedo had thoughts of his partner Gangsta. He wanted to visit him and have a face to face talk with the man he looked up to in some form, being that Veedo was older.

He just wanted to make sure Gangsta was okay, make sure he was still level headed. He needed a real nigga like Gangsta on the streets. He didn't deserve the amount of time they'd given him. Veedo didn't care what Gangsta did. His cell phone rang showing the caller was an unknown number. Veedo looked at it and decided not to answer it.

He made a mental note to get his number switched while he was safe. Veedo was plotting to act as the ghost Kash said they all should be. To Veedo, that was a great idea. Veedo planned to stick with it, at least until he was able to escape the game fully. The phone rang again with the same number, which was private.

He paid it no mind as he followed the GPS to Trish's house in Riverdale, GA, deep on the south side. It took him longer than what he thought. When the Benz turned on her street, Veedo was surprised to see how nice the homes were and the nice cars parked in driveways. Trish's house was fairly big with three brand new whips in the yard. Veedo pulled into the driveway and killed the lights to his Benz. He sent her a text message, telling her he was outside.

"I'm here."

He sent it and then sat there waiting on her reply, but didn't get it. Instead, he saw her door open up and out she came, looking as amazing as the first time he saw her. Veedo got out of the Benz. He walked over, meeting her at the steps leading to her door. She wore regular jeans and flats with a nice shirt. Her picture perfect face was the main attraction, and her body was banging, too.

Veedo didn't know whether to shake her hand or hug her, so he just opened his arms, looking down at her sexy frame. Trish smiled and then walked into his arms for a quick embrace. She smelled good, Veedo thought to himself as he released her. Then he followed her lead into her house. Trish's living room was nice. It had a warm feeling to it. Plus, it was well put together.

"Make yourself at home, I'll be right back."

Chapter 8

Erica pushed at Kash's shoulders. Her legs were locked straight out but Kash held her from underneath with his hand coming around holding her in place while he drove his tongue in and out of her pussy. She gyrated her hips. She moved up and down and still couldn't escape his mouth as she came hard. She was nearly in tears because she wasn't strong enough to get out of his grip and he wouldn't stop sucking her clit, circling her clit, and fucking her wet tunnel with his long tongue.

It felt like heaven but at the same time she was sensitive after she came and this was her third time. Kash finally came up from between her legs. She slapped his chest with the palm of her hand. Kash smiled and then sucked one of her breasts into his mouth. Erica cupped his head with one hand and rubbed his back with the other one. He slid up to her neck. He sucked her enough for her to feel the pleasure but not enough to leave a mark. With an arch of her back and a push from him, he was sliding into her warmth, her tightness, the wetness. It felt so good as Kash started grinding, making sure to go deep into her.

Erica pushed at his hips like she always did. But this time, like most times, she didn't run. She rolled her hips but pushed his hips to keep him at bay. Kash had a pretty big dick and he was a freak to make matters worse. Sweat started forming on his forehead as he raised up from her neck, looking down at how sexy she was, how adorable the sight of her was. It made Kash want to melt inside her. He went deep again and then started stroking her with two or three inches of his shaft and his dick head.

Erica moaned while wrapping her arms around his neck, grinding her hips, and squeezing her pussy on the tip of his head each time he almost slipped out of her.

"Damn, daddy, I miss this dick," Erica moaned.

"You miss this dick, huh?" Kash asked and took his Dick out of her at the same time. "Come taste yo pussy, it tastes good."

Erica wasn't surprised at his outburst because Kash had always been that way. She sat up and then got comfortable on her knees. Kash laid flat on his back, dick sticking straight up, hard as a brick.

Erica took him into her mouth with no hands, at first, then she gripped him with one hand, stroking him at the same time. Her free hand ran up and down his ripped stomach. Erica looked at his face as she worked him with her mouth.

"Shit, bae," Kash silently moaned. He started gyrating his hips, pushing his dick a bit deeper into her than she wanted him to go. Kash moved the fallen hair out of her face. He tucked it behind her ear and placed the same hand at the back of her neck. She sucked him good for at least ten minutes. Kash fought to hold his in, and did. He turned her over on her hands and knees and entered her from behind.

She could hardly take the dick in that position, so she was running from him every chance she got. But Kash held on to her, keeping her in place as he worked his magic on her, making her cum again.

"Oh my God, oh my God," Erica cried out in pleasure, also trembling from head to toe. She was still running so now Kash had her pent down with his hand in the small of her back. She was on her stomach. Kash didn't wear a rubber, so when he felt his nut about to pour out, he pulled out of her. He slapped her bubble booty.

"Turn around and suck this nut out," he said, and she did as she was told.

Erica turned around and placed the dick in her mouth. She sucked and pulled. She stroked and locked until she felt him swell up in her mouth and warm sperm, with its salty taste, spilled onto her tongue. Erica quickly sucked him dry but didn't swallow. Instead, she got up from the plush bed with a mouthful of cum and ran to the bathroom to spit. That was something she'd always done so it didn't shock Kash at all. He held a wicked smile on his face while picking up the phone that started ringing.

"Yo?" It was 2:30am and it was an unknown caller.

"Kash, hey it's Asia." She was talking low.

"What's up, baby girl, everything good?"

"Yes, I was just calling 'cause it's the only chance I got. We're not allowed phones here at training, but I called to ask did you handle that for my mom?"

"Yeah, that's handled, baby girl. So when this training shit over?"

"It's four weeks. Okay, I gotta go." Asia quickly hung up the phone as Erica was getting back in bed.

"I see you still a freak," she said.

"I see you still can fuck," Kash shot back laughing. She laid back to get comfortable and started playing on her phone. She had nine missed calls all from Nene. Erica sat up. Instantly, her heart dropped to the pit of her stomach. She dialed her sister's number, knowing something bad had happened and she wasn't there.

***

When Veedo opened his eyes, he felt Trish still cuddled in his arms from last night. The both of them dozed off in conversation after she had fixed them some fish and fries. Trish was beat from work and Veedo was tired of the streets. The last thing he remembered was telling her about his first time on a real date. He remembered them both laughing and that was about it.

Trish felt so good in his arms, he could've stayed like that forever and a day. Last night he learned that she was from Augusta, Georgia, the south side, which was the hood. He was surprised by this fact because she seemed like the nice home, great background type kid. But she wasn't, and that made Veedo like her more.

She shared with him about her drug dealing boyfriend that got killed by another drug dealer. Trish said that she was attracted to thugs with a hustle about themselves. Veedo told her all good girls like bad boys, it's a given.

"Beautiful," Veedo softly spoke, which made her stir. "Beautiful."

"Hmm."

"Get up, ma."

When he spoke those words, Trish instantly opened her eyes to find her living room sunlit. She sat up and looked back at Veedo, her eyes red from sleep. She braced up on his legs and stood up.

"Good morning. Oh my God, what happened?" Trish asked.

"I guess we passed out," Veedo responded, also standing up. It was 7am his phone read with only a few miss calls. He had one message from Nene, saying that the baby was out of his coma. That was some of the best news he could ever get, Veedo thought and silently thanked God for the blessing of having brought a miracle to that baby because he didn't deserve to die at such a young age.

"Goodness," replied Trish as she walked into her bedroom. Veedo found his keys and pocketed his phone. He'd enjoyed last night with her. Trish was most definitely a female he could wake up to every day. She was wifey type, no doubt about it. But he wouldn't focus on that just yet with her. He would take his time and make things work right with her.

"Hey, I'm 'bout to leave, baby girl, for business this morning. You work today?" asked Veedo from the living room to her bedroom. Trish reappeared.

"Yes, I do."

"Wanted to bring you lunch, if possible."

"Aww, how sweet, but it's Wednesday. My boss always have his wife prepare us lunch at my job. How about I buy us both dinner tonight at some nice restaurant?" Trish shot back.

"Sound good, just text me a time and place, I'll be there," said Veedo, and he left.

Outside, he activated the Benz by phone and noticed she also had a Benz in her yard, along with a dodge viper and a BMW truck. He wondered what kind of job she had what she did for a living. She looked like a nurse type, or lawyer, if anything. Hell, maybe even an assistant to some big corporation somewhere downtown.

She never discussed where she worked or what she did, and now that he liked her, he wanted to know everything about her that could be known. He was trying to lock that woman in.

Inside his Benz, Veedo called the number back that last called him. It was Monkey, but he got no answer. So Veedo left a text. He was hungry, so he made a stop at the Waffle House by the highway. He parked the Benz and jumped out.

Two drunks sat outside the store drinking on one bottle of something. Veedo walked inside and his nose was embraced with the smell of some good cooking. He found an opening at the counter with an empty stool. A white woman was waiting to take his order.

"Good morning, sir, you ready to order?" she asked nicely.

"Yeah, let me get two patty melts with cheese and extra onion, two waffles, extra butter, three pancakes, no syrup, with cheesy eggs and a hash brown," Veedo placed his order.

"Anything to drink?"

"Yeah, water"

"Ok," the woman replied and turned around. She yelled out his order to one of the cooks. Veedo sent Trish a quick text telling her how much he enjoyed her company and that he couldn't wait to see her again. When he finally pulled his face from the phone screen, he notice someone watching him from afar, a person he didn't recognize off top. She had cut her hair low real low and had gained weight. When the woman finally smiled and stood to approach him, Veedo knew who she was. It was Lisa Pay, the old school smoker from Albany.

"What's up, V? How you?" Lisa Pay asked with that same country slang.

"What's going on, Lisa? What you got going on in the A?" Veedo got up to hug her. She was his road dog when he was grinding. Lisa Pay was loyal like no other smoker he'd met.

"Rehab, man, I quit that shit. When you left, yo homie came down and stuck a gun in my face for your money. I had to change my life honey," Lisa playfully said.

"So you still in the program?"

"Yes, in with one of my mentors now just getting something to eat. We headed back to the center now. But what's up? How have you been? And when did you get out?" she wanted to know.

"I been home a few months now, Lisa, and I'm holding it down how it go. You know me, forever chasing a check," Veedo replied while his food was being placed on the counter in front of him.

"Well, that's good. I miss you, man," Lisa said as another female, a bit older than her, joined them. Lisa hugged Veedo once again. He gave her some cash and his cell number. It was good seeing her, he thought and smashed his food, leaving a ten dollar tip. He wanted to see his kids today so he made a call to April, telling her to have them up and that he was on his way over. Outside, Veedo stopped at both the junkies outside. He reached in his pocket and pulled out a bankroll, peeling off six hundred dollars. He gave them three each.

"Before anything, y'all go buy something to eat."

He jumped back into his whip and mashed out. He didn't mind giving blessing out as he did because he was blessed by Gangsta years ago and hadn't fallen off yet. So every chance he got, he made sure to share.

Dear Gary,

God is good, I must say. God is amazing and so are you, the father you are, the man you are. Your respect and morals are correct, Gary you are a king forever and always and I am thankful to have you in our lives. Baby our son is woke! Your prayers was answered, your promise was handed down by the grace of God, so thank you.

Thank you and thank God!!! So yes, Jr woke up two days ago out of the blue skies. You told me to kiss him for you and I did. And when I did, I promise to God he woke up. Baby, could you believe three radio shows wanna talk to me and two TV shows have asked me to come on. It's a miracle is on TV every day about our baby. The doctors have become famous. Hell, everyone is practically famous. Yes, God is good. He's amazing.

Gary, thank you once again for all you've ever done for us, for me, for our son. I want you to know that I'm sorry for how I shut down when our son got shot. I'm sorry, but I was so scared. I was so confused and heartbroken, but not once did I give up or stop believing in you. You are a great man, a great leader, so don't think you're not. Gary, I want you to come home so bad. I want us to be together like the old us. I want us to be together right now. I don't care because you're where you're at, I'm willing to ride every day with you if you allow me to.

Me and Jr will be to see you as soon as the doctors clear him. I miss you, baby, I want you to continue to pray and continue to stay strong for us, for you, for the sake of love. Your mom is always around us. She is an amazing woman who has not left our side for one moment. She's like the mother I never had and I love me some her.

Terry and Keshana are doing good. Kash is doing good, as far as I can see. All of your friends have showed their support. Everyone is looking nice. we just need you home. I need you home. Your son really, really needs you home. Do you need any money on your books? Need me to do anything? Gary, I love you, honey. I love you so much. You're all I need, all I want. Hey, maybe I'm just rambling off with words, but I mean them and God knows this. Please write back soon we love you.

Always, Nya and Jr

Nene folded the letter and stuck it in the envelope. She sealed it up and sat it up next to one of Jr's bears. He was off with the doctors having tests run on him so she used the time to bathe and write Gary. It always felt good to put her thoughts on paper, especially to him anyways. Nene's hope was for another miracle. She prayed that God blessed her with Gangsta's presence one more time. She prayed faithfully for him not to die in prison. It was hard dealing with the fact that it was very possible that he would one day get the lethal injection. It scared and worried her.

Nene was so ready to close this chapter in her life and get her things together. She had already made plans to leave GA. She was moving to Texas with her grandparents until her home was finished being built out there. Erica was leaving as well so that the both of them could get their fresh start. Nene had two jobs lined up once she got settled in, and Erica could work for her grandparents, who owned a funeral home in Texas that was popular in the state.

Nene wanted a change of pace in life. She wanted a slow humble life and being in Atlanta wasn't slow at all. Then she had Kash, and Kash was already doing the most in the two months he'd been out on the streets. That lifestyle was the one she was trying to escape. True indeed, she loved all her friends and family and they loved her, but it was time to get away from everyone, everyone but Gary and his mother. Nene was more than ready to go, more than willing. God waking Jr from his coma was also a wakeup call for her.

It was a miracle that had the entire world shocked. Nene finally was able to see God's grace, and even though she was raised in a God fearing home, this was the first time she'd actually saw his power. Grateful, she was and forever in debt. Last night, Erica left and did not return and Nene wondered what her sister had going on because Erica hadn't left her side the whole time since the kidnappings. Now, all of a sudden, she didn't show up last night and only sent a text saying she was going out to eat with a friend. Nene sent a text.

"Where is you?"

Then she put her phone down on its charger. Doctors said that if all Jr's tests came back good, then she could take him home. She could only pray everything was good with her son because it had been three months since she'd laid in a real bed. A bed was so much needed at the moment. Her body longed for the softness. She needed to feel that cozy feeling, the warmth and comfort of home.

She no longer had that house they got kidnapped from. She would stay at a home Gary's mother rented for her and the baby in Cobb County. It was just something for the time being until Jr came home, and it was a place Nene could call her own. Erica text back.

"Omw. I'm with Kash."

"Ok," replied Nene.

"You hungry? Have you ate?" Erica text.

"I haven't ate."

"Ok."

Nene took her phone with her, leaving the room. She decided she would stand outside for a minute. She couldn't remember the last time she walked outside. She rode the elevator with two other people down to the bottom floor and got off to a crowded downstairs. She made her way out the door. The sun was out and beautiful in the sky. The air was warm and the sky was blue and pretty. Nene inhaled a lung full of fresh air.

"Thank you, Jesus," she said while looking up to snow white clouds in the sky. It was only by God's will that her son was living.

"Excuse me, aren't you Nya Robertson?" asked a white woman who was standing outside smoking a cigarette. She was an older woman with grey and black hair, smooth skin, and bright eyes. Nene studied the woman first before she spoke.

"Yes, I am. And you are?"

"My name is Gwen. I'm just a woman with some ideas. Come, let's talk," the woman replied at the same time pulling Nene to walk with her. They both walked into the hospital where Nene found out the woman was a major movie director. She offered Nene two million dollars up front and royalties off sells.

Nene had a lot of offers on the table, but nothing like this. Authors wanted to write books. Talk show hosts wanted to take their shots. The whole world had their own questions. It was too much at the moment and Nya had too many other things to think about other than money. She told the lady she needed time to think on it and they parted ways. When she made it back upstairs, Erica and Kash were standing outside of Jr's room, talking.

"Hey y'all," Nene spoke.

"What's up, Nya? Where is Jr? We looked in and he's gone," Kash spoke back.

"With the doctors." Nene looked at Erica one time and knew by the way she was standing that she'd been fucking with Kash. She was too clingy and gave it away instantly. Though Nene said nothing about it, she knew what was going on.

"Everything good?" questioned Kash.

"Yes, they're just running tests to see if they will discharge him today or not," Nene was happy to say as she took the food Erica gave her. It smelled good, making her realize she hadn't eaten anything at all today.

"Okay, that's the move. I need Gangsta's info, too, so I can send him a letter," Kash added.

"I will text it to you," Nene replied while sitting down with her food to eat because she was for sure hungry. Kash he left both sisters alone. Erica went into the bathroom and Nene kept eating.

Jerry Jackson

Chapter 9

Trish sat beside her desk looking at the screen to her computer as Veedo's face stared back at her. She was shocked at knowing he was one of the guys linked to the case they'd lost two months ago. This news devastated her. He was one of the ones she didn't get to interview.

Trish read his entire file. He had been to prison twice, both times for trafficking drugs. He had never had a job in his life. He was the father of two. Trish just stared at the screen stuck, not knowing what to do. She was heartbroken. Veedo was petty compared to Bam, which was their main man at the time. But he went down in the sweep the feds pulled off over GA.

She had to admit Veedo was a nice man. He was sweet and chill. There was something she liked about him. There was an instant attraction when she'd first met him, not knowing he was a criminal. Even though she liked guys with a lil' street in them, she didn't want a drug dealer, and drug dealer he was. She just couldn't do it.

Veedo did tell her he was an ex street champ, and that he'd just gotten out recently. He was being honest. He had given her that much, right? He did tell her that he was no longer in the streets, at least he was honest and didn't lie, right? Trish found herself confused because one part of her said no, but the other half said yes.

It said no because she wasn't into criminals and nothing dealing with crime. Yes, she adored the mere thought of a hard man, true enough, but she didn't want a thug in her life. It said yes because Veedo was so her type. Everything about him she liked. He was physically perfect in her eyes, and full of charm and grace.

How he spoke to her always gave her chills, and being around him was so amazing. Trish was stuck between a rock and a hard place. All she wanted to do was enjoy her life, but it seem what she liked wasn't good for her. Finally, she closed the page and loaded her to-do list on screen. Trish was recently handed down leads in the Mr. Play and Chavez connect, a case that the government had been working on for the past six years, trying to penetrate the organization, and still couldn't.

Commissioner of the FBI gave Trish a shot at going at Mr. Play, a Mexican cartel that ran an underworld in GA, and a host of other states. Trish started at the bottom and eased her way up to the middle of things, and so far so good. Veedo crossed her mind again. She wondered what he was doing at the moment. She looked at her phone to find it just there, no texts, no calls from him. But it was still early so he was busy, had to be.

Trish went through some notes on Mr. Play and Chavez. She scrolled down to Jeter and Loco and Longo. She decided to put her focus there first. She'd look into what they had going on, since the last word was that Mr. Play and Chavez were gone out of the U.S. After she copied some numbers and addresses down, Trish prepared to leave her desk. She grabbed her Glock and badge and she was off on a mission, a head start to something good was all that she hoped. But first things first, she wanted and needed to get Veedo off her mind.

"Ms. Williams, you have a call on line three," her secretary announced as she peeked her head into the office. Trish smiled at her coworker and reached for the phone. Her mind was so gone over Veedo that she picked up unprofessionally.

"Lo."

"So you couldn't return not one of my calls nor text? And last I heard is that you was letting ol' boy come over," her friend Brit said into the phone, catching Trish by surprise. She didn't know what to expect. She smiled an embarrassed smile.

"Believe it or not, girl, we both fell asleep in the middle of conversation. I woke up in his arms."

"Yeah, yea…"

"I'm so serious," Trish shot back cutting off her friend who didn't believe her.

"I hear ya."

"Whatever, anyways, I'm busy at work, unlike somebody I know." Trish's friend Brit was a successful business owner that never went to work but always wanted to be paid. She wasn't lazy, she was just one of them type of females that tried to get around things to work in her favor. Some say she was slick, some say she had good grace. She said she just had common sense.

"Well, honey, get to work and make sure you ring me when you get a moment," Brit said. Then they ended the call with air kisses.

Trish got up from her desk. She slipped on the pumps she had kicked off and grabbed her cell phone, walking past her secretary into the hallway. She ran into her boss, who had the phone glued to his ear. Mr. Donald looked at Trish and with one hand motion told her to follow him.

Perfect timing, she thought while rolling her eyes at the back of his head, but she followed her given orders. She wondered what he wanted. What had come up? She hoped it was good news instead of something she would not like.

Jerry Jackson

Chapter 10

Nothing in life is free. Nothing is promised. And most times, nothing is real. And at all times, all things are what you make them out to be. Those were the thoughts that ran through Kash's mind as he sat and watched his kids and Gangsta's lil' girl run around Footlocker school shopping for shoes. He also had Roxanne following them while he played on his phone.

It'd been almost two weeks since he and Loco had dinner, and the time was now, if it was a time. He knew that today would be his last play day, so he wanted to give his kids some time, plus put the dick in Roxanne's hot ass. Kash's phone began to ring. He saw that it was an out-of-town number, so he picked up.

"Hello?"

"Yes, a Mr. McCants please," the very proper voice stated through the line, clearly sounding like a white guy.

"Yes, this him." Kash replied.

"Okay, I'm doctor Swizits. You arranged a phone call?"

"Oh okay, yeah, I did." Kash now knew whom the dude was. "I would like some work done, but I got to sit down with you,"

"Well, yes, that can be arranged, but business is business. So my question to you is what's your occupation?" the doctor wanted to know what he was dealing with. Who was he talking with? Was it real? Was it some prank?

"I'm a movie director, if you must know," Kash quickly said because he knew the doctor was fishing for something solid to go off.

"Okay, well I'll have my assistant book you in say two weeks?" the doctor asked.

"Let's say after sixty days. I'll give you a call back, just don't forget me," Kash shot back.

"That's fine by me," replied the doctor.

"Daddy, can I get some Pradas?" Kash's son asked as he skipped and jumped towards his father. Kash hung up his cell phone.

"How many pair of shoes you get?"

"I got me eight, and Unique got twelve pair of Jordan's. She crazy, daddy," Charles Jr. said.

"What Keshana bought?" asked Kash.

"The same as Unique." when Charles Jr. said that, Kash started laughing. That was when Roxanne and the girls appeared.

"It's pay up time," Unique said. She ran between her father's legs and hugged his neck. Kash scooped her up and kissed her candy lips.

"How much I owe, pretty lady?"

"Ten thousand, daddy," Unique joyfully said. Kash stood up with her still in his arms.

"Say it's nothing, daddy," Kash told his daughter.

"It's nothing, daddy." Charles Jr. said crunk before his sister could get it out.

"And you how many pair you grabbed?" he asked Roxanne, who was looking real good to the eye. Roxanne was your typical cute, brown skinned girl from the hood. She was one of them females everybody wanted to fuck because she always had a booty. Kash never really paid her any attention growing up, when he used to visit Johnson Road, chilling with Gangsta. But now he was.

"I didn't get anything. I'm cool."

"Say no mo," Kash put his daughter down and tossed an arm over Roxanne's shoulder. They all walked up to the counter, where it was loaded with kids' shoes.

"Unique, how much I owe, baby?" Kash looked down at his beautiful little girl.

"It's nothing, daddy." She jumped when she said it.

"That's right." Kash pulled out a wad of money and paid the amount given. He also paid to have the shoes loaded into his whip.

The day had just got started for them. The girls were going to get their nails done while Charles Jr. and Kash went to get haircuts. After he dropped the girls off, he drove ten minutes down the streets to Trill Cuts, owned by Juice, the dyke he fronted the work to.

When Kash entered the place, he found Monkey getting groomed up. He didn't notice Kash because his eyes were closed. Kash saw Juice talking to one of her stripper friends. The place was crowded with people trying to get fly before the weekend started. He spotted a couple guys he knew, though most of the niggas he didn't know were young. Kash and his barber locked eyes as he took his seat in the waiting area.

"Baby boy, what's up, homie?" Juice said once she turned and saw her connect in her spot. It was always a pleasure when Kash walked through the door. Juice stuck her hand out for some dap.

"What's up, Juice? You know I'm pulling up with the support team," Kash gave her dap.

"Glad you here," she spoke and then touched his son's head. "Hey, lil' man."

"What's up, brother?" Monkey opened his eyes and saw his partner.

"Shit, cooling, my guy."

Kash never noticed the black Crown Vic pull up to the shop with four niggas inside.

"What's word, Lil' Charles?" Monkey spoke to the baby. He was almost finished with his haircut and shave.

"Nothing much," Charles Jr. spoke back. He had his game boy in both hands. When the door opened, Kash noticed four guys walk in. All of them held serious looks on their faces, which instantly made Kash get on alert. The leader of the four dudes was a tall slim dude with short dreads. He was the first one to look around until he spotted Kash, He wore all black and Kash could tell he was strapped by the bulge in his shirt, and so were the other three dudes with him.

"Say, fooly," he pointed toward Kash. The entire salon had gone still, nobody said anything, and nobody moved. "Let that be yo last time rolling up on my fam, Zay and Eric," the dude said. He had a mean expression on his face, tattoos on his face, and looked geeked up on some type of drug.

Kash stood to his feet, not an ounce of fear in his heart. The only thing he worried about was his son's wellbeing.

"Fuck is you nigga, and yo partners, too? Fuck going on?" Kash asked. "Sit down," he told his son and walked into the middle of the salon to meet the dude. But by now, the barbers, Juice, and Monkey were stepping in to make sure things didn't get crazy.

"Nigga, I'm Don Kill Sum, and like I said, that was your last time pulling up on my fam. it's over with. Don't nobody owe you shit, bruh," Don Kill Sum said, not backing down.

"Pussy nigga…" Kash was about to step closer so he could slap the spit out the nigga's mouth, but Juice stepped in. she pushed Kash's chest and Don Kill Sum's chest too.

"Hold up. Hold up. Rico get out of here with that shit."

"Lil' homie, what's going on? What's this about?" Monkey added into the play of things.

"What's up, Don?" another dude spoke, one who was with the tall slim dude.

"Fuck you mean, lil' nigga?" Kash aimed his finger at the dude. He pulled out his strap. Everyone else did, too.

"No. Uh-uh, hell nawl. I'm calling the police," Juice said, which made everyone calm down.

"Y'all niggas tripping," Monkey said.

"Man, this mob shit this way, my word been spoke out. It's over with," Don Kill Sum said.

"Fuck you, nigga. Zay pussy ass and Eric can't pay for no motherfuckin' protection from me. Them niggas owe a real Don. Y'all niggas just some peons, pimp," Kash said.

Juice was pushing them out the door while one of the barbers held Kash. Kash was the only one who wasn't holding a gun. It was in his car and he vowed to not slip like that again. He was lucky today that Zay and Eric were pussy niggas who hired another pussy nigga to do their dirty work.

Kash had calmed down when they left. He looked over to his son, who sat there playing his game without a care in the world. Kash liked that.

"Kash, sit down, baby boy," Juice said while looking at the Crown Vic pull off.

"Man, what was that about?" Monkey wanted to know. He still held his gun out, confused about what was going on.

"Juice, whea that nigga from? You called him Rico," Kash ignored Monkey's questions, asking his own.

"That's Rico. He one of them GF boys. They from Etheridge, honey. Rico, he just wild and shit, that's all," Juice told him.

"So he so-called mob?" asked Kash.

"Yup, him and a million other niggas around here," added one of the barbers.

"Okay, check."

"Man, what's up, bruh?" again Monkey spoke. He tucked his gun and stood face to face with Kash, They had just come close to death and that wasn't a good idea.

"I'ma put you up on it, bruh. Right now, let me get my shit cut. We gone rap, my nigga," Kash replied. One thing about Kash was that he hardly showed his emotions. Rather he was mad or not, you'd never know because Kash kept such things tucked away, making it hard to read him. He would make the lil' GF nigga pay for even thinking he could confront him like he was pussy or something, especially for a sucka nigga.

Kash also knew he had bigger fish to fry right now, so the lil' pussy nigga would get what was due to him once Kash got done with the big business. After the next hour had passed, he and his son were back in the ride going to pick up the girls so that they could finish their day of fun. Kash wouldn't let what happened in the salon dictate the remainder of his day. Roxanne, Unique, and Keshana all were dolled up when they got into the ride with their nails and feet done.

"Daddy, look, daddy," Unique showed off her nails when she got in the truck.

Kash smiled and said over his shoulder, "It's pretty, baby, but not as pretty as you are."

Later that night, before Kash boarded the plane, he, Monkey, and Veedo had dinner. They discussed everything that was going on, and neither Veedo nor Monkey agreed with Kash putting the pressure down on Zay and Eric.

"We gonna miss our blessing fucking with them lames," Monkey stated.

"Boy, them niggas gone pay my brother," was all Kash said, and that talk was over with.

"So everything else in order, right?" Veedo changed the subject.

"Yeah, everything is a go. Y'all niggas just hold it down and when I get back, it's on and popping," Kash replied.

"Okay, we got shit under control," Monkey told Kash. They stood shoulder to shoulder hugged once Kash made it to the Airport. Veedo did the same.

"Say no mo," was Kash's final reply. He soon after boarded the plane and sat back comfortably in his seat, his mind consumed with how life would be after he took on so much responsibility. Kash never imagined being this far in position. Even when it was him, Dank, and Gangsta pulling off petty licks, Kash's mind never thought that one day he'd be the brick man, let alone run a drug empire in four different states.

He'd never had the type of money he was seeing now, and all thanks went to Gangsta for putting everything to work the way it was working. Kash felt no remorse for Eric nor Zay and planned to deal with them accordingly, and fast. Plus, he already had his shooter that was scheduled to pick up the money from all four spots or give problems when either Zay or Eric didn't comply.

He made sure all his business was handled correctly, all but the issue with the GF nigga. Kash decided before he took the lil' nigga out, he would hurt him first emotionally. He would rock that baby to sleep because he had no time to play with somebody else's kids. Kash was up in life, feeling himself. He had plans that were already in motion that would put him on top and all the people with him. He wouldn't leave one person out if they remained loyal as they were, and if not, then Kash would serve them a death sentence they deserved.

He remembered four years ago he and his squad had dreams of being top dogs in the game. Things were coming together back then until Dank couldn't take his fall when the time came. Dank fucked everything up, every plan they had. Everything they had situated, he fucked up by snitching his way to a man slaughter charge. He had fifteen years do ten while Kash was sentenced to life plus some, and Gangsta's death sentence stemmed from the acts of Dank because if he never folded on them, then Gangsta wouldn't have gone through half the shit he went through and Kash would've never done three years.

They would have, nine times out of ten, gotten Dank all the lawyers he needed to help him out. Dank knew this, but he decided he wanted to bring everyone else down on some sucka shit. Kash could never forgive him. Gangsta never would forgive him. And karma would prevail on him one day. Kash planned to be there to witness it with a smile. So many thoughts ran through his mental, his family, his love life, and especially his kids. Kash knew that things were about to get deep, so he had to calculate his every step so that he wouldn't get caught up in these streets.

He had people depending on him to handle business and he wouldn't let them down. As for his love life, he wasn't thinking about not one female. He only fucked bad bitches, not cuffed them. That was his motto. He didn't have the time. All he wanted was some good head and some clean pussy. They could keep that love shit. Kash's mind was in overdrive, his body was tired, his eyes got heavy, and sleep finally took over. He was out like a light.

***

Veedo met Trish at Huston's in Buckhead. It was a casual spot, very low key, and the food was great. Tonight with her it felt different. Tonight did not feel the same. True indeed, she was looking amazing in her skirt and nice shirt to match. Her hair was pinned up, she smelled great, and was even soft as a cloud when he hugged her. It was just a gut feeling he felt that made him watch her closely and pay attention to everything about this dinner date. Trish sipped her wine and blushed when she looked across the table finding Veedo staring at her.

"What?" she asked and couldn't help but smile.

"You're beautiful, baby girl. I'm blessed to even be near you," Veedo said, still not removing his eyes from her. She was bad and she knew it.

"Thank you."

"So how was work?" he asked.

"Work was good. Really a nothing too hard, nothing too much type of day."

"Where is work?" he smiled. The question made Trish pause. She locked eyes with Veedo and sipped her glass one again.

"I'm a lawyer. That's all I'm telling you right now," she nervously said and sipped some more wine. She took her eyes off him, but Veedo already felt something wasn't right and her reply confirmed his assumption, but he said nothing. Dinner had finally arrived and conversation was light. Trish did most of the questioning, while he gave almost honest answers.

The only time he lied was when she asked him something about the streets. Trish didn't believe him at all because she already knew a lot about him. Veedo didn't believe her because, even though she could go for being a lawyer, he didn't think she was one. He couldn't remember seeing one lawyer book around her crib when he went over. Veedo figured she had to be a dancer or something that she was shamed about. Little did she know, he wasn't the judgment kind of guy. Veedo knew how it was in life and respected all grinds.

"So how old are your kids?" Trish asked as she picked over her food.

"Six and nine, my daughter is the oldest."

"Same mom?"

"Yup, and why don't you have kids again?" Veedo questioned.

"Haven't met the correct man yet is the best answer I can give you," Trish she replied.

After dinner, Veedo took her over to a small bar for drinks and hopefully she would loosen up, open up more, maybe some truth would come out. *No kids*, Veedo thought about it. She had to be a dancer with the three whips she had. He smiled to himself because he thought he had it figured out, but little did he know, it was more to it than what the eye saw.

"Well, you have now met the right one so call yourself blessed. I feel with you I've met the right woman and even though all relationships start off exciting, I feel something true about this friendship," Veedo spoke. They were at the table awaiting more drinks.

"Is that so? How are you so sure?" Trish locked eyes with him again, playing with her glass.

"I'm just sure. It's a heart thing, I guess." Veedo reached across the table and took one of her hands. She jumped a little but allowed him to hold her. "I want you, Ms. Lady, plain and simple." when he spoke the words, Trish took her eyes from his. She softly pulled her fingers from his hand.

"I can't say I don't want the same thing, but I'm not sure if we compatible." Trish added, "But I swear this feels too good to be true."

"I agree with you on that. My only disagreement is that I'm sure we're compatible with each other, and you're not, but it's not a problem."

"How you know is what I'm asking," Trish stressed.

"Cause we wouldn't be here now. I would've never woke up with you in my arms, better yet, you would've never stopped the day we met."

"I'm saying, that's a physical attraction that made me stop," she shot back, playing harder than she actually was.

"Well, I already asked God for you, so at the end of the day, you will be mines," Veedo said and winked with a smile. Trish smiled also. They ate their ice cream cake and parted ways after a brief hug in the parking lot.

"Can I kiss you?" Veedo asked, holding her small frame. Trish looked up to his face. Veedo leaned down, going in for her lips. She turned her head and patted his chest.

"Next time," she said and left.

Veedo climbed into his Benz and pulled off into traffic. He had big business to handle. Now that Kash was gone, he was acting right hand man to Monkey. He had to put a lot of things in motion. But first things first, he needed to check one of his trap spots that got robbed last night by some Etheridge niggas. Veedo felt like he was constantly being tried by them niggas and he was about to put an end to it.

Jerry Jackson

Chapter 11

Blue Flame strip club was packed tonight because rapper Yo Gotti was in the building, and when someone famous showed up, the dancers showed out, and every successful street nigga was coming along to stunt as well. That's why Veedo and Monkey had one part of VIP locked down. It was Monkey's idea tonight to come out and kick it because Veedo wanted to plot a murder on the low. But Monkey was the boss right now.

They was deep tonight with his whole squad and some hoods. Poonie Man and his brother were there, along with Pat Man and his people. The club was popping this Friday night in Atlanta with all kinds of niggas and hoes. Bankhead Highway was the place to be tonight. Monkey was just laid back on a mission nobody in the club would expect, handed down by Kash.

He smoked blunts that were passed and drank Hennessey out of the bottle. Poonie was loaded on X pills and weed. He was messing with all the strippers that danced for him. Veedo laughed because it was funny and life was lovely, and niggas with money acted any kind of way and got accepted. Yo Gotti had a section of the VIP and the majority of the strippers were in his space. Veedo also spotted Lucky and a few niggas coming through the door. All them niggas were iced out in the fly gear and shoes to match.

The females flocked in behind Lucky, flooding the VIP section even more. It was bad bitches everywhere, all over, Veedo noticed. He was about to reach out and grab a bad lil' red bone when his phone vibrated a text message from Trish.

"Hey wyd?"

Veedo mistakenly dropped the phone in his lap. His drink had him feeling the effects. He sent her a text back, "At a gathering, wishing I could be around you. What's going on?"

"Real niggas in the building tonight," Poonie yelled standing up. Then he roughly gave one of the niggas with them dap. He was rolling up a blunt so most of the weed fell out into the carpet. He pulled out another sack and put more buds in the blunt.

"Order up some mo drinks," Veedo said loudly to anybody. Monkey saw who he was looking for standing across the room. They made eye contact and then the dude walked out. Moments later, Monkey got up from his spot. He excused himself and walked out of the VIP section. The bathroom was where he found the dude. Monkey walked in and saw the heavy set guy. He pulled out a Glock and passed it to buddy.

The dude took the Glock without any words being spoken. He just left out, leaving Monkey inside. Monkey washed his hands and exited the bathroom also. The club was packed so niggas and bitches were everywhere. Monkey left the club as planned and was picked up by his uncle and one of his uncle's trusted friends.

"Damn, boy, you stay up to some shit, don't cha?" his uncle asked while pulling off from the club.

"Gots to know dat," was all Monkey said.

***

Meanwhile, Veedo received another text message from Trish. It was a picture of her TV on Love and Hip Hop, showing him that was what she was doing.

"Whatever you doing, I wanna do."

He sent his reply and started back feeling on the dancer who was grinding on him. Veedo's dick was rock hard and the stripper felt him because she kept grinding on him. But it wasn't her that aroused him, it was thoughts of Trish that had his mind captivated. He wanted her badly. it was something about her that did something to him.

One minute the music was blaring through the speakers, the crowd was zoned out, the bartenders were doing their thing keeping everyone happy, and all the dancers were occupied with niggas.

Then, all of a sudden, things changed. The next given minute, the crowd went into panic when gunshots erupted.

Bloc. Bloc. Bloc. Bloc. Bloc.

Veedo pushed the stripper off of him as he witnessed the gunman standing over another dude, pumping him with bullets. The gunman tucked his gun and moved with the panicked crowd out the door to the crowded parking lot where he disappeared into the woods. Poonie and his people were all holding their guns out when they all made it to the car. Veedo wasn't that stupid. He knew to get off the scene so he jumped into his whip and smashed out, not knowing what the fuck was going on. He hit 285 and headed to the south side. He decided to pull up on Juice and her squad just to see if they had something going on. Plus, Juice kept a few bad bitches around. He still couldn't help but wonder what that shooting was about. He also was elated that it wasn't him or his folks that got caught down bad like that.

***

Monkey was at the condo with all the work and money there. He had the TV on the news channel where they showed the Blue Flame shooting scene on the outside. Dude got shot eight times, murdered in cold blood, and the killer got away as he was paid to. The dude who died was family to Don Kill Sum. Kash wanted to hit Don Kill Sum where it hurt, piss him off. He wanted it to be something perfect, and what better way than killing his peoples in cold blood.

Kash wanted him to get the picture and the frame, too. Plus, he had enough respect for Meco to not start nothing with the mob. This was personal, so that's how Kash brought it. He knew that once Don Kill Sum found out he was the reason behind his uncle's death, it would shatter him. and that was the plan from jump. Monkey's phone started blowing up back to back numbers. The first one he saw was Veedo.

"What's up, brother?" Monkey answered.

"What the fuck happened in the club? Where you run off to, my nigga? One minute everything is love, the next shit is wild. You straight?" Veedo asked.

"I'm at the condo chilling, 'bout to box up some of this money. Is the team good?"

"Yeah, everything Gucci. I'm over here on Old National with Juice nem, just chopping it up for a minute. I'll pull up in 'bout an hour or so to help you finish if you gone still be there."

"Most definitely gone be here," replied Monkey. He cut the TV off and walked into one of the rooms. Money was stacked from the floor to the roof. The room smelled strange, but that was because money had its own type of smell to it.

"Okay, cool, I'll be there," Veedo shot back and hung up the phone.

Fuck me, Monkey thought to himself as he looked at the bails of money. He didn't know where to start but knew he had to begin somewhere, so he took off his shirt, tossed it over a pile of money, walked into the living room, and began to make the boxes up. Was this the position Monkey dreamed to have? Why did Step just switch sides like he did? This could've been all them to themselves.

Gangsta probably never would've caught his time if Step would have flipped on Bam. But he let greed take him out of what was real. Monkey was happy about how things ended because now he was on top and all of his family was fed. This was everything he asked for and more. Now all he needed was a female to hold him down in ways no female had. He was childless, so the female that got him was the blessed one.

Three hours had somehow eased by and Monkey had four boxes packed with money that was scheduled to be picked up the next day. Kash wanted to go ahead and pay Mr. Play and Chavez the majority of the money owed. That way it would not be a problem. If anything crazy happened, he'd still have a clean face. Loyalty was all Monkey knew. That was how he got fed when he didn't have a pot to piss in or a window to throw it out of. He had his morals and loyalty, two qualities most people lacked. Soon, he would be a very rich man, and that was all he needed. fuck the rest.

Monkey retired to the living room. It was almost three o'clock when he started playing on Facebook with his phone. He heard the door and then saw it come open. Veedo walked in holding Zaxby's Wings and Things. It instantly lit up the room with its aroma.

"Brought cha something. I know you ain't ate shit, nigga." he gave Monkey the bag. "I already smashed mine." He walked into the room, which was still packed with money. He wanted to see what Monkey had done. Closing the door, he walked back where Monkey was, already digging into the bag.

"What the fuck happened?" Monkey played as if he wasn't the one behind everything. "I mean, one minute I'm coming from the bathroom, and the next minute shots popped off. Shid, my nigga, the door was so close so I got up outta there. I knew y'all niggas could handle that shit if it was us. I'm just glad it wasn't."

Veedo also took a seat, kicking off his shoes so he could relax before he got to work on fucking with the money he had to box up.

"I'm most definitely glad," Veedo shot back, and they both chilled out.

***

She had common sense. She had vision on what was best for her. She had expectations set high for herself. She was hard on herself, being her worst critic, but being her own best friend as well. Trish sat outside of Justin's waiting on Veedo to pull up. Right now she was going against her better judgment. She was again going on another date with Veedo. She couldn't get enough of him. He was so correct as a man.

His only downfall was his record, his past, his future. She had thought long and hard about dealing with him and decided that she would watch him for a couple weeks, and if he was clean, then she would go full throttle with him. She would go ahead and tell him she worked for the government. Trish knew that he would feel some type of way about her not telling him the truth.

With a deep breath and exhale, she opened her car door when his Benz pulled up next to her own. Veedo got out clean in black silk slacks with the shirt to match. He wore Mari gators slippers with just a plain watch on his wrist. When she hugged him, he smelled amazing, like he always had, and his strength felt so safe to her.

"What's up, beautiful?"

"Hey, you look handsome. Your body is nice," Trish said.

"Aw man, go head on." Veedo smiled it off, then said, "You're amazingly beautiful though, I must say." He took her small hand into his own and they walked into the restaurant to be seated. Trish was on cloud nine in his presence. Veedo was what men should be, so it was hard not to like the person he was.

Her every wish was for him to be clean from the streets so they could work towards being together. but if he was in the streets and had lied to her, then she would continue to mess with him until there was enough evidence on him to put him and whoever was with him behind bars.

Once they sat down at the table, a waiter approached with two roses that he placed on the table in front of Trish.

"For you because I feel you deserve it," Veedo said. He cut his phone off and also placed it on the table.

"Aww thank you. You're so sweet, I swear," she blushed and picked up one of the roses.

"I'm just me, baby girl," Veedo replied and started looking over the menu to eat something. He didn't notice Nikki until she walked past his table with her daughter. They both were headed toward the restroom. When she locked eyes with Veedo, Nikki stopped with a slight smile on her cute face.

"What's up, V?"

"Nikki, what's going on? Let me introduce you to my friend. This is Trish. Trish, this is Nikki, my home girl."

"Hey, how are you?" Trish she spoke with a smile. She and Nikki shook hands.

"Well it's nice to meet you and hope I see you often," Nikki told Trish, then added, "Let me get this girl to this bathroom." She walked away and left Veedo at the table.

"She's nice," Trish told him once they were gone. She was also reading from a menu, getting ready to order up something to eat.

Dinner was great, they laughed and joked and got to know each other a little bit better than they already had, and with each moment that passed and time was spent with this man, Trish found herself falling for his charm.

She honestly felt as if they could make the perfect couple, but this one issue stood in their way. One issue that she hope like hell wasn't anything serious because what they had going on felt so good that it scared her knowing that this all could end in a pretty bad way and that was something she didn't want right now.

Trish knew that she deserved to be happy because she wasn't a bad person. She wasn't a bullshit ass female that played games with men's emotions and led a man down the wrong lane. She was respectful. She was faithful. And most of all, she was loyal to the core if she was in a relationship, and loyal to her friends, too. Not everyone got her loyalty because, those that didn't show it towards her, got nothing in return.

Outside at their cars, while in an embrace with Veedo, Trish locked eyes with a man she thought she'd seen before but couldn't place his face. He was with the same female Veedo introduced her to. He quickly looked away and climbed into a car with Nikki and three kids. Trish never took her eyes off them.

"I enjoyed every second of your time, beautiful. I really mean that, and I so thank you. Okay?" Veedo said, looking down at her pretty face.

"I enjoyed us as well, sir, I must say." As soon as Trish spoke the words and looked up to his face, his lips met her own. She was in total shock but also captive in a lustful moment. She found herself holding his neck as she nicely kissed him back, feeling tingles run up and down her spine.

"Have a peaceful night, Veedo," she whispered, feeling lightheaded. She didn't want to let him go.

"Call me when you get home, lemme know you safe," Veedo said while walking backwards, still looking at her.

"I will, I promise," replied Trish, and they both climbed into their cars.

Chapter 12

Kash was inside the nice home Loco had arranged for the four of them to stay in. he stood at the window inside his bedroom, looking out to the beautiful yard deep in thought. It'd been three days since being in Texas and all he'd done was meet important people. He'd had lunch with the governor of Texas, who was a close friend to Chavez. He ate lunch with one of the judges and two lawyers. Kash was introduced to four different older cats who were major drug dealers, and he'd also met two dirty cops.

Today was the day he learned routes and places around Texas. It was Mya's day to show him what he had to do. She was in her own room getting dressed. Longo and Jeter had been gone most of the morning on a mission to handle some loose ends. Melody was downstairs cooking a quick breakfast for them all as she always did since being there. Kash could smell the aroma from where he stood in the window.

Melody liked him and he knew it. Mya wanted to fuck and he knew that also. But he acted like he didn't peep game. He wanted Melody to press more, and he knew before long, Mya would expose her hand to lust. He could tell by the way she looked at him. Sometimes he'd be doing shit around the house they stayed in and he'd look up to catch Mya just staring at him.

Mya let it be known because they always locked eyes and then she diverted her eyes down to his dick print. Just that thought made him smile and remove himself from the window. He found Melody in the kitchen putting the finishing touches on the breakfast, eggs, bacon, grits, and toast. It was an old fashion style breakfast. Melody was a Mexican, but she had a banging body like a black girl.

She was thick with it, just the right size ass to match her small waist. Then her face was pretty, minus the heavy makeup she wore. Her hair was longer than he thought because she kept it in a bun. But now when he walked in and saw her, it was down past her ass, which made him glare a moment. Then he grabbed a seat at the table.

"Morning," she spoke over her shoulder when she noticed him enter the kitchen.

"Good morning. It smells good in here," Kash replied.

"We got to eat," Melody smiled and winked. Mya walked in a few seconds later and took her seat.

"Hey y'all," Mya spoke. It seemed she was the one with the most swagger out of the two girls. Melody was older and Mya was younger, but both were bad.

"The two of you should eat up and hit the road. Mya, you know we're on a time frame," Melody said and tapped the watch on her wrist. She put a plate of food in front of him, then did Mya the same way. She fixed herself a plate and joined them at the table.

"Thank you for the third straight breakfast," Kash spoke, stuffing his mouth with food and looking to Melody, then to Mya.

"So what are you saying, sir?" Mya wanted to know. The entire table burst out into laughter. Kash and Mya quickly ate their food and soon were in the truck with a driver. They both rode in the back of one of Loco's custom made Tahoe trucks. Kash blew on loud and sipped Hen while he paid attention to everything Mya pointed out to him. They rode all through downtown Huston, Texas. Then Mya tapped the black window to get the driver's attention. The driver let it down and then looked back at Mya as she said something to him in Spanish.

"Go to Arbor Court." The driver nodded his head and the black glass eased back up.

"Now where we headed?" asked Kash, still pulling on his blunt. They'd been riding around three straight hours and he was getting restless.

"The apartments we invest into," replied Mya. She cracked the window because she didn't smoke and the car was getting fogged up.

"Say no mo."

Kash tried to pass the blunt, but she shook her head and then said, "How many times you gonna offer me your drugs?"

Kash laughed. He hit the blunt a couple hard times and tossed the rest out the window.

"I never know when you will change your mind, you know," he said back, looking over at her. She was a lot badder than her sister, with more youthfulness that Kash wouldn't mind test driving.

"Makes me think you trying to get me stoned to do something to me," Mya added into conversation that he took no offense to. Kash knew she was only talking, just joking around with him.

"Ion need drugs to get you, baby girl, all I gotta do is go." Kash decided to play games and spit game at the same time because he knew Mya wanted to fuck.

"Oh, is that so?"

"I think it is, but I can be wrong."

"Or you can be right," Mya shot back. She burst into laughter once they locked eyes and were quiet a brief moment. "Let me stop."

"Yeah, before yo young ass get hooked on a real nigga," Kash replied.

"Or the other way around," Mya wasn't going out without a fight. She always strived for the last word.

Kash only smiled and they continued conversation as the driver pulled up into Arbor Courts. A few turns and the Tahoe was parked by a couple high price whips. A few cats approached the Tahoe, which made Kash reach for his gun. But Mya placed her hand on top of his.

"No, these our people," Mya said and then rolled down the window to greet one of the dudes who walked up.

"Yoyo, what's up with it?"

"Mya, what's good? Who you got with you?" the dude Yoyo looked into the ride, making eye contact with Kash. Mya turned towards Kash, then back to Yoyo before she introduced them.

"This is the new plug, Kash. And Kash, this one of our main men in the state, most loyal cat I've met in a while," Mya said.

"What's hap, peoples?" Kash acknowledged the dude Yoyo then they all got out of the Tahoe and met a few more other cats that had the projects on lock down. And with Loco and Chavez being the plug, they supplied every drug. That night in the projects, Kash had to learn which nigga was which from the biggest to the smallest. He was street so it was easy to adapt to his environment. Blunts and drinks were being passed. It wasn't nothing but love being shown.

Kash did a lot of listening, not a lot of talking, because he wanted to come off as a serious nigga who don't kick it. He did hold convo with Yoyo, who gave him a quick rundown on what was what and who was who, what they made, and what they get fronted.

"Do you ever pay up front?" asked Kash, talking to Yoyo.

"Naw, I'm always fronted," Yoyo replied. He and Kash were walking through the projects talking and meeting the right niggas.

"Okay, well after every three fronts, you pay half the bill up front from now on. And instead of paying when you done, you pay as you go now. Find a method to move the money into one spot per week." Kash changed the main ways Yoyo dealt with Loco. He was showing that he was in charge.

"Okay, cool, I can work that Jones," Yoyo agreed and that was business in apartments.

Kash and Mya jumped back into the Tahoe. The driver pulled off after being told to head back to the house.

"You hungry?" Mya asked.

Kash looked at her and shook his head side to side. High as hell, he leaned back in his chair. "Nawl, I'm good."

"Well I'm starving," Mya shot back. She tapped the black window again and then asked the driver to make a stop at Wendy's.

"How old is you, Mya," Kash wanted to know.

She looked at him. "Old enough, why?"

"Shit, just wanted to know, dats it," Kash quickly shot back.

"Oh, I thought you was trying me like some young simple chick. I know I look young and all but, honey, I'm old enough for whatever," Mya said smiling and joking at the same time.

"Bet you can't take the D," Kash laughed his reply.

"What?" she didn't understand.

Kash smiled and shook his head. "Nothing."

"So you not man enough to say it loud and clear?" she joked.

"Oh, I'm superman, baby girl. I just decided that I'm not gone go there with you cause you won't know how to act with a nigga." Kash just stopped talking altogether.

"Honey, please," she rolled her eyes, "Yo ass can't handle what I got going on and that's a fact."

Her statement made Kash sit up. He looked at her with a smirk on his face. Then he leaned back in his seat.

"Girl, stop."

"I'm so serious." Mya was sure of herself.

Kash was sure of himself also but he said nothing else on that matter because he was slick ready to try her on some sexual shit.

Mya must've seen him hesitate because she slid over closer to him. She took one of his hands and placed it between her legs, making Kash feel the warmth of her phat pussy. She rolled a little. "Do that feel like I'm too young?" was her question.

"Most definitely feel grown," replied Kash, his dick now super hard. He was ready to smash her now more than ever. Kash removed his hand. he put it to his nose to smell her.

"Boy, I'm fresh." Mya slapped his hand, feeling offended by what he did.

Kash laughed. "I'm just playing, lil' crazy."

The truck pulled into Wendy's and went through the drive through, where Mya ordered her and Melody something to eat. She and Kash had been gone all day and she knew her sister hadn't eaten since this morning. She wasn't paying attention to Kash but jumped when he put his hand back between her legs. Mya was playing it off while talking to the woman at the window.

"Pussy too phat," she spoke low over her shoulder, then started back talking to the girl in the window. Mya got her food and moved Kash's hand so she could sit straight. She smiled at him before saying, "And now that you done touched phat ma, you can't keep yo hands to yourself."

Her statement made Kash pull all the way away from her. "Damn, my ba…"

"I was just playing, boy. Let me eat first," Mya said and started eating her food.

Kash wished he had his phone. He wanted to check on things in the city with his squad, but at the same time, he had to have trust in them. He had to show them he had faith in them to hold shit down. Plus, it was restricted for him to have his phone or any form of communication with anybody.

He only looked out the window as the city of Huston passed him by. The three days he'd been there he'd enjoyed the time spent and had plans to grab a spot down there somewhere, he thought. Ten minutes later, while he was looking out the window, Kash felt Mya's hand touch his lap. It instantly made him jump from feeling her near his wood like that. Out of nowhere, he just got hard. Kash placed his hand on top of her hand, making her grip his member.

"See you playing," he spoke.

"Am I?" Mya was a freak and Kash was about to find out. He let her unzip his pants and free his hardness. When Mya had him gripped at the base, she was amazed at his size. Kash smiled at how she was looking at him.

"Don't play wit it. There you go," Kash said and put one of his hands on top of her head to guide her mouth to him. Her mouth was so warm, so wet. Kash closed his eyes and leaned his head back to enjoy the pleasure of her oral sex. "Shit, girl," moaned Kash as he started grinding his hips up into her mouth, making his dick go deeper in her throat. Mya gagged and tried to come up for some air but he wouldn't let her.

"Umm ah mmm," she slurped him up and down.

"Yeah, get nasty wit that shit, baby. I like it nasty. Lemme see that spit," Kash said and Mya did as told. She let the juices from her mouth run down his dick then she stroked him. She looked up at his face to see his expression. She wanted to see if he enjoyed her oral pleasure and she got the answer she was looking for.

Mya she finally came up from sucking him. "Put this dick in me, papi," she said and pulled off her shoes, her pants, and shirt.

Kash was stripping also. He turned her over flat on her back and entered her raw. Her pussy was tight. It was warm and wet as ever. Mya put one of her hands on his stomach to keep him at bay. She couldn't take all of his dick, it was too big for her.

"Shit," she moaned as Kash slid in and out of her love. he was holding her hips, biting his bottom lip, and holding his nut in that felt like it was about to pour out of him.

"Don't run," Kash grinded into her deeper. He laid down stomach to stomach with her and started sucking her neck, her earlobe, and her chin. As he stroked her pussy with his dick, in and out, Kash he cuffed her legs in the buck.

"Papi, don't stop," she moaned and urged him to keep going. Mya ran her hand up and down his back as he fucked her. As good as he knew his dick was, he fucked her in that position until she came with loud cries.

Kash pulled his dick out of her and made her suck her pussy juice off him. Then he came in her mouth and she swallowed his load.

A couple minutes after they got dressed, the driver pulled up to the house. The driver opened the back door to let them out and he and Kash made eye contact. He gave Kash that *I know you smashed that* look.

When Mya walked into the house, Longo and Jeter were playing the video game and smoking weed. Kash went straight to his room after speaking to them. Mya went to find her sister. Inside the room, he pulled his gun from his hip and put it on the nightstand along with his bankroll and watch. He needed a shower and some rest time.

They would be leaving Texas in the morning going to another state to do it all over again. Kash was ready to get back to the city. He wondered what happened at Blue Flame. He wanted to know if Monkey handled his business as planned. Kash wanted Zay and Eric bad, too. He couldn't wait to make them pussy niggas pay for tryna send somebody at him. He would make life hard for their scary asses, point blank. He stripped down to his boxers and tank top. Then it was a knock at the door.

"Yo."

"Can I come in?" It was Melody.

"Yeah," replied Kash.

She walked in holding a note. She gave it to him and was about to walk off but he grabbed her hand.

"Tell me you fuckin' with the help," Kash said. Melody was lost for words at first because she was confused, but then she thought about what he was saying.

"From the looks of things you already got my sister-wife open," she said pulling her hand from his.

"You see the wrong shit, boo. Yo sister ain't for me, you are," Kash lied.

Melody thought about it a second. Then, without reply, she walked off leaving him alone in his room, which made Kash laugh and head to the shower. He knew Melody felt some type of way because she knew Mya was in her way.

***

"Let me make sure I'm hearing you correct, you said Veedo fuckin' with the Feds?" Monkey asked Poonie, confused as to what he said. They were outside parked in Poonie's driveway. He had called Monkey as soon as he made it home from dinner and told him that he saw Veedo with a federal agent.

"That's exactly what I'm saying," Poonie confirmed. Monkey sat there a minute to ponder his thoughts. Why would Veedo switch sides when shit was lovely for them? What would he gain by siding with the government?

"And you sure this the feds you seen him with?" Monkey wanted to be sure himself.

"I'm positive, bro. I was having dinner wit my family when my BM told me she saw Veedo with some pretty girl. They was seated around the corner so they didn't see us. I got up to peep the move, you know, about to go introduce myself. When I rounded the corner, I was shocked to see this FBI hoe and Veedo in deep conversation over dinner. Then, I saw them hugged up outside. Me and this bitch made eye contact, bro. I know it's her. It's the same hoe that came to visit me in Rice Street, trying to get me to flip. That's how I'm sure," Poonie said.

That was all Monkey needed to hear. He nodded his head with a thoughtful look painted on his face as he dialed up a number in his phone.

"Damn, Veedo, what he got going on?" Monkey asked out loud as he listened to the phone ring on the other side.

"Surprised the fuck out of me too, Bruh. I'm not gone even lie, when I saw them together I didn't know what to think," Poonie replied.

"Well we finna see bout this shit," Monkey shot back. He couldn't get nobody on the phone so he put it in his console.

"So what's the plan?" asked Poonie.

"Get you and your brothers, snatch that nigga up, take him to the warehouse on Fulton industrial, and call me when everything is a go." Monkey had made up his mind.

Poonie agreed and got out of the ride. Monkey pulled off, headed to the condo to move the money and drugs to another spot just in case Veedo was exposing everything they had going on.

He met up with his uncle an hour later at the condo, where they loaded up the two trucks full of kilos and another van pulled up to get four boxes of money. He wanted to be one step ahead of Veedo and whatever he had going on. Right now, the feds was not the folks he was trying to deal with.

Monkey still was lost on why Veedo would want to bring them down. What had the Fed's offered him that was better than their position right now? Monkey wanted to talk to Kash bad because he had to know what was going on, but he'd been gone only a week. Monkey knew he had to act now rather than later because later could be the end of them and everything they had going on.

The money and dope was taken to a storage place in College Park, GA, a place owned by Monkey's grandfather, so he knew it was safe there for the time being. He and his uncle rode around talking about Veedo because the situation had him fucked up. He didn't understand what was going on.

"Why don't you confront him, nephew? Maybe yo friend got shit mixed up, you never know," his uncle said, drinking a can of beer and smoking a cigarette.

"Ion know, uncle. Poonie said it was the same FBI hoe that tried to get him to rat. He said that he was sure," Monkey replied. He pulled the car over into some apartments and killed the lights.

"It's always two sides to a story, just know that."

"You right, Unc, but this just too much. If it ain't one thing, it's another. And I'm being honest when I say this, I'm not tryna go out bad fuckin' with no rat. I didn't fuck with Bam and he was a major plug, so I'm not about to allow my right hand to take me down, ya feel me?" Monkey began to roll up a blunt. He was stressing.

"Oh, I feel you on everything. All I'm saying is that you're going only off what Poonie saying. I mean, at least look into it yourself before you just go to acting 'cause you might just be doing the right thing but it's a chance that you could be wrong, too. You know I got yo back. I'm not just gone tell you anything."

Monkey pondered on what his uncle had just said. He had a point but his gut told him to act now and ask questions later, so that's what he intended to do.

Jerry Jackson

Chapter 13

Death row wasn't nothing like he expected it to be. Gangsta just knew that it was hell on earth, pitch black dark, hard walls, and cold iron. He thought that all niggas serving death row time were niggas who had given up hope, niggas who talked shit and kept up mess. But he was wrong because when he got there, death row was humble. Death row was clean and, to his surprise, the rooms were bigger than any cell he'd ever been in.

The few months he was there, Gangsta had met and befriended some cool old-heads that he talked with through the doors. One of his main partners was Flip, a legend who once ran the Atlanta streets. Growing up, Gangsta watched Flip paint the city red and also take care of his people. To Gangsta, he was a real stand-up guy, a real killer, and a very good hustler. When Gangsta first got to Jackson State Prison, Flip had everything running smoothly with the prison officials.

He kept weed and cigarettes to smoke, and occasionally he'd pull out a bottle of yack. Flip had this guard he was fucking named Ms. Pitt, a thick amazon female in her late twenties. She was tough for the chain gang, but just a simple something if a nigga was free. Gangsta also got cool with a white dude named Randy. He'd been locked up twenty-eight years and was looking to soon die. He was the first man in GA to receive a death penalty for drugs. Gangsta learned a lot from old Randy about mind control, and he painted out a solid way to launder money and move dope without being caught.

Gangsta always listened and paid attention to everything Randy said. He'd kept them up plenty nights, telling him and Flip stories. Gangsta didn't enjoy being locked up, but he enjoyed the time spent talking with real people. It was a couple more cats on death row with the death sentence, then you had other cats that couldn't be around other inmates who they housed on death row.

Officially, it was only ten niggas waiting to die in GA who were already sentenced.

Gangsta made the best out of his situation. He dealt with it how it came and went in every day like a champ. He was a man of honor so he stood up like a real nigga supposed to and did his given time, prepared to leave earth any day, any minute. He could be gone, missing, and Gangsta truly accepted that. It was shower call so Gangsta was doing his sit-ups and pushups before they made it to his cell. That was something he did every shower day, making sure to stay fit.

All Gangsta did was smoke weed, nothing else, and drink water. The only time he drank something else was when Flip and Randy talked him into it. He did a lot of writing music and business plans. Gangsta spent most of his mental time reading the bible, praying, and hoping God one day answered his prayers for the sake of his son.

Nene had been faithfully writing him once a week. It was something to keep him sane. It was what helped him get through each day that was hard to get past. He was glad to get positive feedback about Jr's surgery. Nene also kept him updated on Kash, and just knowing he was doing good on the streets holding it down was music to Gangsta's ears. He wanted the best for his family and friends. All he wished for was for them to be up in life, and so far so good.

"Jackson, you ready?" officer Johnson asked Gangsta. He tossed a letter on the cell floor and it slid across to Gangsta as he was doing the last of his pushups. The letter was from Nene. He picked it up and sat it on his bunk.

"Yeah, I'm ready," Gangsta replied to the question. He grabbed his towel, two face rags, his soap, shampoo, and extra pair of boxers. He pulled off his Jordan's and slid on his shower shoes. Mr. Johnson dropped the flap, Gangsta put his hands out through the flap, where Johnson placed cuffs on his wrists.

122

"I see you, Lil' G," Flip said. He was standing in his cell door just looking out. Well, to Mr. Johnson, he was just looking, but Gangsta knew Flip was really interacting with Ms. Pitts in the control booth.

Once Gangsta was placed in the shower, he was given ten minutes to bathe so he never wasted time spent in the water. He soaped his body a few times, washed his hair, and then his face. He was done, and minutes later, placed back in his cell.

"Johnson, let me get some hot water," Gangsta said when he was safely in his cell.

"Okay, give me a minute," Mr. Johnson said, then walked off.

Gangsta freshened up and got dressed. He got comfortable in his bunk after he fixed him a soup, waiting on his hot water. He got the letter from Nene and opened it up. It smelled just like he remembered her smelling, which was amazing. Gangsta began to read the letter and about halfway through the letter, Gangsta's heart dropped. He jumped out of the bed he went one way, the letter went the other way.

"Oh my God, yes," was all Gangsta could say as he took the letter and read again what Nene wrote, saying their son was woke and that he was doing good. Gangsta couldn't believe it. He was so happy with the news that his son was gonna be okay, that Junior was finally awake, he repeatedly thanked God for this blessing. So much weight was lifted off his shoulders. He felt brand new. He smiled as he paced back and forth in his room, still thanking God.

"What's going on out there, Lil' G?" Flip spoke through the cell walls, loud enough for Gangsta to hear him clearly.

He walked over to the door and looked out at Officer Johnson taking another inmate to the shower. Gangsta walked closer to the wall.

"My boy, he's out his coma," he yelled as the last tear he promised to ever drop fell from his eyes. This day was an amazing day he'd never forget.

***

He was sleep but still felt the bed move. His eyes quickly opened to find Melody crawling up on the bed with him. He released his hand from the gun under his pillow. Melody had her hair hung down. She had on a white blouse as she moved slowly towards him, being the aggressive one. Kash only had on his boxers and a tank top. He instantly got a hard on when her hand gripped his member. Melody pulled his boxers down enough to free his large dick.

"I see you came to your senses," Kash said.

She started slowly stroking him up and down his shaft. With her free hand, she ran it across his abs and to his chest. She straddled one of his legs. Her bare pussy sat on his shin as she continued to stroke him to a brick.

"Just be thankful I like you," Melody said. Then she took him into her mouth. She stroked and sucked him good, so good that Kash had to push her off the dick because she worked his sensitive part. She smiled through the darkness of the room, then slid her body up to his own. She grabbed his hardness and eased her pussy down on him.

She rode him slowly, up and down, taking most of his big dick. Kash gripped her booty as she placed both hands on his chest to balance herself as she worked her pussy up and down his shaft.

"Fuck me," Melody said. "Fuck me good," was her moan. She nearly dug her nails into his chest. Kash took her waist in both hands and started rolling his hips to meet her coming down. As soon as she eased down on him, he'd push up into her. With one flip, Kash was on top of her. Now her legs wrapped around his waist and he put both hands on either side of her head and leaned up, looking down at her while he went to work, thrusting inside of her.

Melody placed both her feet flat on the bed and began rolling her hips to meet him, thrust for thrust. It hurt but it felt great at the same time. She rubbed up and down his back and wrapped both hands around his neck. She encouraged him to keep going. Kash wanted to pull out when he felt his nut about to pour out, but for some reason, he couldn't help but to cum inside the pussy. His body locked up. He pushed into her deeper.

"Oh shit, papi, oh God, it's deep," Melody screamed out in pleasure and pain.

Kash rolled and rolled into her as he came. He bit down in her shoulder. She rubbed his head. They both were breathing hard. Melody kissed the side of his face when Kash kissed her neck and then eased his dick out.

"No, papi, don't pulled it out yet," she said and started squeezing her pussy muscles, draining him for the very last drop of semen.

"Damn, girl," Kash squeezed her thighs. They were soft as clouds.

Melody grabbed his face and started kissing him deeply. To his surprise, Kash started kissing her back. Their tongues danced with each other as their bodies moved together. She grinded, he grinded. Kash started sucking her neck as his dick grew inside her. Melody gyrated her pelvis when she felt him get back hard.

"Fuck me. Fuck this pussy good, papi," Melody urged him on as Kash started fucking her good. This was the first time since he'd been out that he'd taken his time with any female. He made sure to fuck her good for the next thirty minutes.

Melody fell asleep in his arms that night. Kash stayed up a minute or two, thinking, mind in wonderland. He was wishing Gangsta was around to reap the benefits of how things were moving for them as a team. If it wasn't for Gangsta, then nobody would have what they had, and maybe everybody would be locked up.

One way or the other, Kash would make something happen for his bother. He just didn't know what it would be yet. He continued to hold Melody as she slept, lightly playing with her long hair and thinking until his eyes finally got heavy and he gave in to sleep.

Chapter 14

Veedo was leaving Old National Highway but before making it to his car, he was ambushed by three niggas wearing masks. He didn't have the chance to make a move because he was caught off guard by the attackers. One dude hit Veedo upside his head with a gun, dropping him to one knee. When he looked up, he saw three barrels pointed at his face.

"What da fuck?" Veedo mumbled. He was dizzy from the blow to his head.

"Snatch that nigga up," one dude said. Veedo wanted to buck but knew it would end up bad, so he complied. Two guys took either side of him while the third one held him at gun point. They led him to a blue van and forced him inside where he was duct taped at his feet, hands, and mouth.

Scared wasn't the word, it was more like confused. Confused as to who these niggas were and what they wanted from him. He couldn't talk because his mouth was taped up also. The van pulled off fast into traffic. Veedo's mind was racing, trying to figure out what was going on. The last thing he remembered was seeing Juice's face as she also pulled out of the store parking lot they had met at.

It was a setup, it had to be. Juice set him up to be jacked. Did she really think she would get away with this? Greedy bitch. Why would Juice cross the team only for what he had? A couple hundred grand was nothing when loyalty would bring them wealth in all they did. So why? His head was hurting. He felt blood run down his neck and back from the gash in his head. He could hardly move as he tried to get a better position because his leg was falling asleep.

"Bitch ass nigga, stop moving fo I slump yo ass," somebody said.

Veedo couldn't catch the voice so he kept twisting and turning every so often to see if somebody else would say something.

"Just chill," a voice said. He thought he recognized it but wasn't sure. Veedo wondered where they were taking him as he felt the van make turn after turn. It seemed like forever and a day, but the van finally stopped and the door slid open moments later. Someone roughly grabbed Veedo and pulled him out of the van. His feet landed on the ground, but he couldn't walk so they drug him inside some cold place.

Veedo was totally shocked to find Poonie and his brother standing before him with another guy when someone snatched the black bag from his head. One, he didn't know at all, but it really didn't matter. When Veedo saw Poonie, he was more confused than anything now. He was shaking his head side to side.

"Surprise, surprise, pussy nigga," Poonie said and snatched the tape off his mouth, pulling away facial hairs and all.

"Nigga, y'all tripping. Kash gone kill y'all niggas, I promise…" Veedo couldn't finish his statement because Poonie's brother, Mario, walked over and punched him in the mouth.

"Shut da fuck up, rat ass nigga." The blow to his face made Veedo's head snap back.

"Fuck you," Veedo spit at Mario, wishing he wasn't tied up because he would definitely try every last one of them niggas. He knew neither one of them really wanted his problems, but right now they had the upper hand.

"Nigga, don't get sideways cause you'll get flipped before Monkey get here," Poonie said, and again Veedo was shocked.

What da hell Monkey got to do with it? Veedo thought when he heard that name. *Is everyone tryna cross Kash and I'm the only one in the dark? What the fuck is going on?* He wanted to know badly.

"Fuck you mean, Monkey? What da fuck y'all niggas got going on?" Veedo couldn't help but ask. His mouth was full of blood.

Poonie laughed, "I should be asking you that same question. You must didn't think I saw you that night at Houston's," Poonie spoke.

"Houston's, and so what?" Veedo stated, oblivious to what Poonie was saying.

"That was that same bitch that interviewed me in the county, nigga. The bitch tried to get me to roll and I see the hoe got you how you was hugging that bitch in the parking lot."

"Huh?" All Veedo could think about was Trish and him being at Houston's. So what was Poonie talking about? He was overly confused.

"If you can huh you can hear," Poonie replied.

"Ion know what da fuck you talking 'bout, nigga," stated Veedo, madder than ever.

"That police ass bitch you with, nigga. You working with the Feds nigga. Don't act stupid like we ain't peeped you."

"The Feds? Is you motherfucking crazy, nigga? Fuck I look like?"

"You look like a rat ass nigga to me, homes," the dude Veedo didn't know said.

"Man, real talk, I just met that bitch. Ion know nothing 'bout no police shit, nigga. She said she was a lawyer." Veedo now understood why she didn't tell him about her job. Now it all made sense to him why she was timid when it came to that discussion. So what was her plan? What was on her mind? Veedo knew he had not exposed his hand to her, so what was her agenda?

"Really? A lawyer? And you went for that?" Poonie sarcastically asked, looking at Veedo like a damn fool. He roughly placed fresh tape over Veedo's mouth again. He and the crew were waiting on Monkey, who said he was on his way over. He would be there in the next ten minutes.

***

Terry, Nikki, and Roxanne all met up with Nene and her sister at Nene's new home. It was beautiful and it fit her and her son. It had a large front and back yard with a circle driveway. Terry parked her ride. They got out and were met at the door by Gangsta's mother and his auntie.

"Hey y'all." Mrs. Jackson hugged Terry at the door. Then she hugged the other two and led them into the house.

"It's beautiful in here," Roxanne said, looking around at the well decorated home with its warm feeling and sense of comfort.

"Smells good, too," Terry added as they followed Mrs. Jackson and Eric's mom into the living room where Nene was sitting, holding a sleeping Junior The sight was something to see.

It seemed Nikki, Terry, and Roxanne all rushed over to Nene and the baby at the same time. Everyone hugged everyone and then sat down to talk. Nene explained exactly what was going on with Jr, saying he didn't need surgery but he was blind in one eye and that couldn't be fixed. But everything else was good and he could continue to stay home with frequent visits from doctors.

Erica and Nikki ended up in the kitchen cooking dinner with Mrs. Jackson and her sister. Terry and Nene talked about the future and the past. They laughed, they even cried, especially when Nene told Terry that she was leaving GA as soon as Junior was done with therapy. It saddened Terry to know this news, but she understood where Nene was coming from. She just wanted Keshana to have her brother around often, rather than every once in a while. Plus, with Gangsta being on death row, Terry knew Nene wasn't gonna make the brother and sister seeing each other an obligation.

"Girl, I'm going to miss y'all," Terry said. She wanted to cry.

"We gonna miss y'all too, trust and believe that, but it's for the best, you know, with all that's happened. And my sister needs to get away also, cause Atlanta is too fast for us," Nene said.

"Just know I'll be up four times a year at least cause the kids got to know each other, that's the least we can do for Gary," Terry shot back, and they continued in conversation. Terry told her about what happened to Zay at the club but couldn't tell her who did it. They talked about Kash and how real he was and all the good he's done so far.

"Them boys like twins." Nene thought of Gangsta. She missed him dearly.

"Sho is," Terry replied. They gave each other high five through smiles. Then they met up with everyone else for dinner, leaving Junior asleep in his play pen. Dinner was good. Everyone talked and ate. Nene enjoyed the company, she hadn't smiled that much in such a long time. She was really, truly happy, and she could never stop thanking God for seeing her son through and bringing him back to her.

She was thankful for Mrs. Jackson for standing by her side nonstop in prayer and pains. Those times when Nene just wanted to give up, Mrs. Jackson would say, "Let's pray."

She would pray for hours, her and Nene. They would cry, pray, and cry some more until they both became exhausted from tears. She was also proud of Erica for continuing to stand on her word and get herself together. So far so good was all Nene could say. Everyone went back into the living room. She woke Junior to feed him, then showed the girls around the house and went outside. Terry was holding Jr as he sucked his food through a straw. His jaw was wired shut so he was yet to eat his food correctly.

"Looking just like his daddy," Terry said, kissing the side of his face.

"Where is Keshana?" Mrs. Jackson asked.

"She's at daycare. So when will y'all visit Gary? I wonder is her name on the list?" Terry answer and asked.

"Yes, her name is on there. We haven't been yet though," replied Nene.

Terry stayed over a few more hours and at six o'clock she left to go get her daughter from daycare. After she got Keshana, she dropped her friends off, then made it home just in time to help Zay bathe. Terry she sat on the edge of the tub, carefully washing his leg. She was getting bigger by the day and Zay was loving it.

"Bae, are you gonna tell me what's really going on?" Terry couldn't help but to ask.

Word had travelled that it was a hit on his head, but she didn't believe it at all. She just wanted to know what was going on with her family. She wanted to better support him. Rather right or wrong, she wanted to be there.

"Real talk, baby, ain't no real pressure. Ion know who did what but when and if I find out, best believe you will know first before anybody else, I promise," Zay assured her.

"Okay, Zarack, I hear you." She gave him one of them looks. Then she went into the bathroom to shower before returning to the room to find no Zay. Terry ended up in Keshana's room, making sure she was good. Then she eased into the den where she heard Zay talking to someone low on the phone. Terry made sure she wasn't seen but she eased closer so she could hear what was being said.

"You think Kash had OG knocked off?" Terry heard Zay ask someone. "Man, that nigga tripping."

Terry crept off back into her room. She had heard enough to figure out something was going on, with Kash in the middle of it. Terry knew OG well, too. He was one of the west side favorites. Everyone loved OG. So to have him killed was a blow to his family. She wondered what any of this had to do with her man. Why was Zay being so secretive? Terry wanted answers and vowed to get them. As soon as Zay got in bed, she attacked him with question after question.

"What do you got going on?"

132

"What you mean?" Zay got comfortable in bed and looked at his girl who also was sitting up.

"You heard me, Zarack, don't continue to lie to me."

"Ain't nun going on, bae, real..."

"Okay." Terry she turned to get out of the bed, mad at the answer he gave. She knew he was lying. She knew Zay well. He grabbed her arm, pulling her back.

"Baby, where you going? Look, okay, listen, I just don't want you stressing, that's all. I got this shit handled," Zay said.

"What Kash and OG got to do with you being stabbed or a hit on your head?" she asked.

"Look, Kash just on some jealous shit 'cause me and Eric not trying to work for him. So he call himself wanna throw up Gangsta and demand we pay him and Gangsta for being on the streets."

"His ass need to pay Gangsta, if anything, for how that boy put him on. Kash ass needs to sit down somewhere."

"Exactly," Zay replied.

Zay went ahead and opened up to Terry about everything that had happened. She was happy they had that talk and, to her surprise, she wasn't worried. If anything, she felt like she could talk to Kash. So that night they fell asleep in each other arms, unworried about the wrath of Kash.

Chapter 15

When he pulled up to the warehouse, there were two shooters standing out front smoking a blunt in the cool of the night. Monkey and his uncle went inside and strolled further into the area until they found Poonie, his brother, and a tied up Veedo. When Veedo and Monkey made eye contact, Veedo started moving wildly, trying to speak, trying to say something.

"Take that tape off his mouth," Monkey ordered.

"What the fuck this about, my nigga?" Veedo said once the tape was off his mouth.

"You tell me, V. All I know is Poonie say he saw you having dinner with the Feds, and when you sitting with the police, that tells me you working with them, and that we don't tolerate at all, no ifs, ands, buts, or maybes," Monkey replied.

"Talking about Trish? Man, I just met the lady a couple days ago. She told me she was a lawyer, my nigga," Veedo said confused.

"She the Feds, nigga, how can you not know?" Poonie cut in. Veedo gave him a death look and then fixed his eyes on Monkey, who in return looked at him. Everybody was trying to read everybody.

"I guess this hoe lied, my nigga, but I ain't no rat, no sucka, no none of that. I'll never sell out, my nigga," Veedo pleaded.

"Veedo, my nigga, this some fishy shit," Monkey spoke back, pacing back and forth, trying to figure his best step. He stopped, turned, and pointed at Veedo. "So you didn't know the hoe was the cops?" he asked.

"I promise, I didn't," Veedo replied.

"And you," Monkey turned and pointed at Poonie, "know for sure she the cops?" he asked Poonie.

"I'm positive."

"Get his phone," Mario added.

"You got pics of the hoe?" Monkey wanted to know.

"Yeah, it's a few pictures of her in there," replied Veedo.

Poonie pulled the phone from Veedo's pocket and was given the code. He went straight to the photo gallery. He showed the pictures to Monkey, who grabbed the phone, looked, and then pushed the phone towards Veedo, asking, "Is this her?"

Veedo took one look. "Yeah, she said she was a lawyer and I fucked around and believed that hoe. No lie, my nigga, I don't fuck with the police," Veedo stressed.

"I sho hope not. So look, since you didn't know, and I can go for that 'cause that hoe is tough," Monkey said and looked at the picture. He looked back to Veedo and continued, "Since you don't fuck with the police, you gotta take her out the game," Monkey said.

"Shid, bet," Veedo replied fast.

"Call that bitch, get her to come to you," added Monkey.

"Nawl, call that bitch and tell her to come here. We bet not let that nigga out our sight," Mario cut in.

"You right," Poonie agreed.

Then Monkey spoke again. "Okay, call the hoe to meet you here, and kill the bitch. That's how I'll know you true to yo shit."

Veedo agreed to the terms and made the call to Trish. She was happy to hear from him, like always, and they could hear it in her voice. They talked about five minutes before he asked to see her and said that he had a surprise for her. Trish agreed and took down the address. They hung up with promises to see each other in the next couple hours. Monkey pocketed Veedo's phone when the call ended.

"I'm starting to believe you, boy, I ain't lying." Monkey shook his head, walking off. His uncle followed him. They walked down the range of the warehouse.

Poonie and his brother, Mario, stood guard over Veedo, along with another dude who still held his gun down by his side.

"So what you think nephew?" Monkey's uncle asked when they were far enough out of ear shot.

"Ion know, unc. For real, the nigga seem like he really don't know what's up with that bitch," Monkey said. His uncle nodded.

"Go read their text messages," his uncle advised.

Monkey felt that was a good idea so he went through the phone. He checked the date on the first message and saw that they indeed just started talking. He even saw one message where Veedo had asked her where it was she worked, but she never sent a reply.

"Yeah, you right, unc, look," Monkey showed him the message.

"See, I told you. So now what's the game plan? What you wanna do when this bitch will be here any minute now?"

As soon as his uncle said those words, something clicked in his head. Monkey headed back to Veedo.

"Untie him, he good," Monkey told Poonie, who had a disappointed look on his face.

"How you know?" Poonie asked.

"Untie him. Don't question me," Monkey shot back. He looked at Veedo and knew that the Fed bitch shouldn't see his face like this. It wouldn't be a good idea killing the bitch at the warehouse. She might've been wired or anything.

"Call that hoe and cancel tell her something came up."

Veedo couldn't remember a time when he was ever madder than he was right then. He wanted to kill every nigga in the room. He felt like he'd beat the shit out of every nigga there. At the same time, Veedo was shocked at the news of Trish being a federal agent. It totally took him for a spin. He couldn't believe it. But his lips and head had been busted by niggas he rocked with so it had to be some truth somewhere. He was just fucked up because he ran right into his own problem.

He was the one that stopped her and persuaded her. He was the one caught up in lust and near love with this woman. It was his own fault and he knew that, but he still wanted to choke Monkey the fuck out, and most definitely wanted to watch Poonie and his pussy ass brother Mario die by his hands. The other nigga could get spared. Veedo grabbed his phone.

He felt violated. He wanted blood for blood, but damn Trish was the Feds. The same type of people he was trying to not get caught up with, he was intertwined with and had feelings for. He dialed her number and let it ring a couple times before she picked up.

"Hey, I'm right around the corner," Trish answered.

"Ah I'm not even at that spot no more, baby girl. I had something that came up with my grandmother, a very important matter. Can we just do breakfast? I'll explain everything," Veedo said as calmly as possible in a deadly situation.

For a moment, Trish said nothing. Then she asked in a concerned tone, "Is everything alright?"

"Yeah, everything is good, I promise," Veedo replied.

"Okay, that's fine, just call me, I guess," Trish replied and then ended the call.

Chapter 16

When she first pulled into the warehouse, she felt strange. At first she was elated to follow her GPS, but when she got there, things changed. Something didn't feel right, and then the phone call. Veedo called her as soon as she turned the corner into the warehouse and saw two armed men standing guard at the door. She was confused and quickly agreed.

Something wasn't right. Something was going on and it made her a bit fearful being that she could've been shot when she rounded that corner at the warehouse. She was lucky the dudes didn't shoot. She was blessed they didn't. Trish drove and opened up her laptop. She wanted to pull up the location of the warehouse. She sent the information to personnel to pull up answers. All Trish wanted to see was what was going on.

Why was it two men standing outside at the address she was given to meet him at? It was a question she wanted answers to, point blank. She ended up at her office, mind in overdrive, when she got the phone call from personnel. The warehouse belonged to a white woman who probably had no idea what was going on at her work place. None of the information was helpful, nothing she could figure out. All Trish could do at this moment was wait on Veedo to make the first move. Shortly after she left her office, she got a call from Veedo. He sounded better than before, but those vibes were still there.

"Are you okay?" Trish decided to ask him.

"Yeah."

"I was just wondering," she replied.

"Oh yeah, shit had happened, but nothing to worry about. What's up with you?"

"Nothing much, just leaving the office. So what happened to you?" she pressed for an answer, and wanted it.

Veedo was hesitant to answer though. He didn't know what to say but he knew it had to be something said. How would he explain a busted lip and swollen head? He took a deep breath then spoke.

"I got robbed a few hours ago, beautiful. I didn't want to tell you because I didn't want you to panic in fear and I definitely didn't want you to think I'm into the wrong shit and stop fucking with me," Veedo replied with pure intention in his words.

"Oh my," was the only thing she could say at the moment. "I wasn't expecting you to say that. Did they hurt you? Are you okay? What did they take?" she kept asking question after question.

"Yeah, I'm good, just got roughed up a little bit. But overall, I'm blessed to come out alive. Some young fool judging me off my past and thought I was a come up, I guess," Veedo told her. And for some reason, she believed him and things started making sense to her why the guys were outside with guns. Now the big question was why did Veedo call her to the warehouse? What did she have to do with it?

"Okay, that's good. I'm happy you are safe," Trish said.

"So are we still on for breakfast?"

"How bout dinner tomorrow night?" she shot back. She started to say more but didn't.

They continued talking for the next twenty minutes, and then hung up the phone. When she made it home, Trish's mind was in limbo. She was confused. She didn't know what to do. So much was happening so fast, it was becoming harder and harder. She had to think her way slowly through this ordeal.

First things first, she jumped inside the shower. To wash off her actions of today, a shower was needed at that moment. Veedo wouldn't leave her mind. It was something going on and it worried her because Trish knew deep down she was falling for Veedo and his passion.

It was always the bad boys that caught her eyes, but what truly captivated her about him was his effort at staying out of the street.

Or was he a big lie? She was straight captivated, she couldn't lie. She was determined to get down to the bottom of this because now her feelings were involved.

Thirty minutes after the shower, she was propped up on her sofa, on her laptop, looking at still pictures of surveillance on Veedo the past week. Trish saw faces she'd never seen but also recognized one or two of the guys in the photos. Trish faxed the photos to face recognition and waited on the reply. She decided to call her best friend Brit and share the news of what was going on with Veedo just to hear her take on the situation. Brit always was the ear to Trish's voice and for that she loved her friend. Not even two rings, and her voice embraced he speakers.

"Hello?"

"Hey, girl, what you doing?" Trish asked, while getting more comfortable on the sofa. She had a quilt tossed over her legs.

"Nothing much. What's up? How was work flow? Or did you go?" Brit asked like she always did.

"No work today. So listen, you remember the dude Veedo right? Of course you do, he's the one I'm always talking about. Anyways, he called me tonight and asked me to meet him. I agreed and then when I made it to town, he calls and say he's not there anymore."

"Wow."

"Brit, but I'm at the given address, right?" Trish paused.

"Okay," Brit urged.

"And it's two motherfuckers standing outside holding semi-automatic shit. Later, Veedo admitted to bring robbed and what not. All I'm trying to do is figure out what's going on, girl. Should I believe him or not?"

"Where was the place?" Brit asked.

"The fucking warehouse," Trish told her best friend who laughed before responding.

"Yeah, that's a drug deal."

"You think? But why would he wanna bring me into what they had going on? Does that make sense to you at all? Not to me, I'm just saying."

"Yeah, you might be right. But didn't you say he didn't know you was the federal agent?"

"Yeah, he didn't know," Trish added.

"Well then, he probably thinks you're some street chick…"

"He thinks I'm a lawyer," she cut her friend off before she got started.

"Oh, okay, well yeah." Brit paused. "Girl, ion know."

Both girls were stuck trying to figure out what was really going on. Trish's fax machine roared to life and sent a copy to her. She got up with the phone glued to her ear and took the paper. She saw the name and spoke it out loud, "Charles McCants aka Kash." He was a face she'd never seen.

Records showed that he was a bad ass growing up. He was twenty-seven years old, standing five feet ten inches, and at least two hundred pounds. His record was full of assault and murder. He'd just recently gotten a reversal deal on a life sentence charge. Trish folded the paper, deciding to dig deeper into this matter later on.

"I'm confused, Brit," Trish said, taking her seat again on the sofa. She ran her free hand through her hair, shaking her head side to side.

"You want company? I'm not doing anything," Brit asked.

"I need some sleep. And when I wake up, I hope it's all a dream 'cause I can't deal with this. It's too much," replied Trish, They talked a couple more minutes and then got off the phone.

"We gotta come up with a plan, V. What's up with this federal bitch? You think she on to us?" Monkey asked. They all were still at the warehouse. Veedo was still heated by their actions and it showed on his face. He really didn't care to be around them niggas at the given moment. He cared not to speak one word. but he knew he needed to get right before he went to acting up and shit.

"Ion know. We'll figure something out. But right now I gotta go clean up and shit," Veedo said, looking Monkey square in the eyes. He couldn't hide how pissed he was at these niggas and Monkey saw that.

"Yeah, I know. I'm sorry 'bout the situation, but you gotta understand where I'm coming from. With so much fake shit around us, I just…"

"Bruh, you could've stepped to me, my nigga. You tripped out, bruh, real talk though. You let some suckas snatch me up and do me bad, my nigga. Nawl, ion feel that at all, shawty. But like I said, we'll deal with the fed bitch how it go. I've never been a rat, no flaw, my nigga, real Bankhead shit. So yeah, nawl, ion feel you, bruh," Veedo spoke and walked away from all of them niggas.

He was past just leaving out of the warehouse. He called his lawyer instantly to ask about him dealing with the feds. Then he called Trish just to butter her up. They spoke briefly, then ended the call while he waited on his baby's mother to pick him up. It took another fifteen minutes for April to pull up. Monkey took that time to apologize again and again, trying to explain why he made the call. Poonie and his brother didn't say one word to him as they left the warehouse, jumping into their ride.

Veedo saw two dead men walking, and one standing before him. He wanted to kill Monkey just because he pulled a hoe call on him. Veedo couldn't wait till Kash returned. He couldn't wait to see how he would play about this situation.

April pulled off when Veedo got in and closed the door of her small BMW. His daughters were both in the back asleep. She didn't say one word when she saw his face swollen. She already knew what type of Nigga her baby's daddy was, so she just drove to his grandmother's house like he asked.

Veedo had quickly made up his mind that something had to be done about him being snatched up. But first things first, he would wait and as far as Trish was concerned, he was not fucking with the cop's.

Really, he had caught feelings for this woman. He was in love with her and it was a big disappointment to him to know it was possible that what they were sharing was coming to its end so soon. For the next couple hours, Veedo chilled at his grandma's house. He got a bit of rest and all her wisdom. She hit him with some deep soul touching talk with the end statement, "Always be a man." His grandmother always told him that. He and every other guy in their family she'd told that to.

Chapter 17

Kash and Jeter did all the clubs and DJ's in Miami. It'd been a whole month down in the sunny state and even though it was lovely down there Kash was ready to get back home to the big business. Loco wanted Kash to learn everything it was to know about Miami because it was a money place that pulled in loads of profit.

The night life was good in Miami every night, which was what Kash liked most about the city, along with the many different flavors of females. The good weather and the money is what captivated him. But Atlanta was home, wasn't nothing like the city of Atlanta, Georgia. Kash knew that once he returned, shit would be different. He wouldn't be the same type of nigga he was before. His position had gotten greater. He was being followed as he led. It was a huge responsibility he had to take on, and yes, he was ready.

Jeter passed him the blunt they were smoking as they stood posted outside waiting on the dancers of Diamonds of Miami. They both had snatched a hoe to take back to the spot. Kash liked Jeter because he seemed more vocal than anything. Jeter had swag and was truly thugged out. He was a womanizer as well, all females flocked to him in every spot they rolled up to.

The bouncers of the club didn't say anything to them for smoking right out in front of the club because they knew Jeter and his family. They all knew that he was a part of the Mexican cartel. Everyone knew and respected Chavez. Both the dancers came out to link up with them, both were bad. The Tahoe and driver were waiting for them. They all piled in the back. Jeter fixed up drinks while Kash rolled up blunts to smoke.

"Go to the pent house," Jeter told the driver.

"This is the life," Kash spoke while the girl he was with seductively danced next to him to the music that played low. He was tipsy and feeling himself. The girl who was with was named Pinky, the other one was Star. Kash nor Jeter knew that both the dancers were new to Miami and really didn't know anybody down that way, and they most definitely didn't think the girls were trying to set them up to be jacked. The driver didn't notice the car that trailed with two guys and a girl inside.

"You haven't seen nothing yet, amigo," Jeter boasted while pouring up some more and passing them around.

"I done seen enough," replied Kash while looking at Pinky and her tatted up skin. She was a high yellow bone with good hair. She was a slim chick with a fat pussy, a pussy he couldn't wait to dive into. Kash put some fire to the blunt as the Tahoe flushed down the Miami streets.

He only had two more weeks and he'd be crowned king, taking over every state he'd visited with an iron fist. He couldn't wait to get back to his home. He was missing his kids the most, but just the power and position he missed. He was sure Monkey and Veedo had things under control. He knew his phone and inbox were full of different messages. He really couldn't wait to get back to see how Zay and Eric had been playing the game because he wouldn't hesitate to take either one of them out.

Kash saw that the Tahoe pulled up to a beach home right off the beach. The driver pulled into its driveway. Kash noticed but really didn't pay attention to Star. When she saw Jeter grab his gun, she flinched a lil', but caught herself and then acted normal. She was the first to get out of the ride, followed by Jeter and then Kash. As soon as his feet hit the pavement, they were rushed by two niggas, both holding up choppers.

"Get shot if you act up, Homie."

One of the guys was some Latin kid with tatts in his face. He was the one doing most the talking. The other guy was a black dude. He was the biggest kid of both with a mouth full of gold that he kept showing off. Kash didn't flinch as both girls started acting afraid, crying and all that fake shit. Jeter grilled both dudes.

"This the cartel you fuckin' with. I advise you to…"

"Shut the fuck up, bitch ass Mexican. Move everyone in the house now. Get the driver too," the Latin kid said with his gun aimed at Jeter's face.

"Fuck you, punta," Jeter spit, but still was forced inside the beach house.

"Tie them up."

As soon as the dude spoke, Jeter charged him, grabbing the barrel of the AK-47. The Latin and Kash moved simultaneously. Instantly, the Latin aimed his chopper and shot Jeter in the side and hip area three times.

Bloc. Bloc. Bloc.

Kash was pulling his Beretta out. Jeter winced in pain but wouldn't let the barrel go as he wrestled.

Kash aimed, at the same time ducking behind the girl Star. When the Latin kid turned the chopper on him, Kash hit him twice in the face.

Boom. Boom.

Shells hit the ground as the Latin kid's body dropped, killing him instantly as the other dude finally overpowered a weakened Jeter. By then, Kash shot him seven times, sending his body crashing into the glass table in the living room. Jeter was tore up but still breathing. Kash he aimed the Beretta at both the strippers about to kill them.

"No, aimgo, these the bitches got info," Jeter spoke through the pain. He was losing a lot of blood.

Kash wasn't about to call the police so he looked at the pain-stricken Jeter and asked, "What now?"

"Call Mya," Jeter weakly spoke, and then passed out. The pain was too unbearable. Kash did as Jeter told him. Then he started asking the girls his own questions

"Who was these niggas?"

"We don't know, I promise," Star said, tears still in her eyes, real tears this time instead of the fake ones.

"Bitch, stop flexing. I know y'all hoes had a nigga set up to get popped. Stop lying," Kash said, gun aimed at her face. He wanted to bust the bitch but he didn't because Jeter said so.

Ten minutes had passed, then six car loads of Mexicans armed with guns showed up. It was at least twenty Mexicans. They rushed in, took Jeter, and some of them took both girls. Kash was led outside to a cream Rolls Royce with tinted windows. He was let inside to find Chavez and Loco.

"My friend, what happen?" Chavez asked. He shook Kash's hand.

The Rolls Royce pulled off the scene and Kash explained exactly what happened, giving Chavez full detail from the time they hit the club until they left, not leaving out how they met the girls.

"Jeter always like to freak. Thinking with your manhood isn't correct, my friend," Chavez said with a thoughtful look on his face.

"Yeah, I know," replied Kash.

"No, you don't, my friend," Chavez's statement surprised even Loco, but really Kash. "And let the time you bedded my daughters be your last time. We will keep business as business, not personal. Okay, amigo?"

The big man had spoken. Kash couldn't do anything but agree with a nod off his head and a shake off his hand. Money was most important right now, so he could deal without fucking either girl, and his loyalty would remain the same.

Kash was taken to the house to get all his things packed up. Chavez had left, sending him back a ride to the airport. Mya was out with Longo, going down to the hospital, leaving Melody as the only other person in the house. She watched him pack, not saying anything for the few minutes she stood in the door frame.

She held a sad smile as she adored just the sight of him. She wanted to speak, but couldn't, wanted to tell him, but could not fix her mouth to open, and Kash spoke no words either. He just packed his stuff. He looked over at the beautiful Melody a few times, but said nothing at all. Kash was ready to get back and be boss status.

Eric and Zay had to pay, and that GF nigga had to pay also for trying him, along with anybody else who wanted some action. He was stronger than ever with Don powers to make shit move. He was the shit around town now. He had all Loco's plays and connections to four states and major cities, and an unlimited supply of different kinds of drugs. Kash's job was to keep order in those four states and make sure the money was right at all times, and he was prepared to do it. His ride finally had pulled up. Melody saw him to the door. Kash turned around and looked at her.

"Be safe, beautiful. You amaze me," he said and hugged her.

"Ah, Kash," Melody began, and then paused. She looked up into his eyes. She tried to read him but couldn't. She smiled and then hugged him before saying, "You be safe also. Okay?"

***

Veedo was in his Bentley, black on black, riding shotgun while one of his shooters drove. After promising himself to never slip again or be caught slipping, that was how he rode everywhere. It'd been a whole month since he got banged up. He was well healed but the hate was still fresh. It couldn't be priority that he got Monkey and Poonie back, he had to put that on a later plan.

Things had gotten serious in Atlanta. Ever since OG got killed, the GF members raided the streets, killing everything that moved that they thought had anything to do with it. Veedo had his traps jumping more than not, and at the same time, he was fucking with Etheridge heavy. He somehow linked up with Block and they talked numbers. He was one of the only niggas out of GF that wanted some money rather than blood.

As far as Trish went, Veedo continued to act as if he was oblivious to her being the cops. They still dated and talked almost every night. He still had not had sex with her yet, though that was his mission. That was the main mission with him because his lawyer said it was a good idea to have intercourse with her. It could help him out on any case the government presented.

Veedo knew that he couldn't let Trish see him playing in the streets. So when he rode, he watched who watched him, or at least that's what he thought. He knew the feds were lurking, building a case on them. He made sure not to touch no work or keep large amounts of money on him. He kept it straight at all times. He was gonna beat them at their own game.

He would also beat Monkey at his own game, but that could come later. The Bentley pulled into Etheridge Apartments. The shooter was allowed through by two blood members at the top of the apartments. The Bentley parked next to Block's '64 impala. Block was posted on the hood. He jumped down and got into the Bentley with Veedo.

"What's up, my nigga?" They dapped each other up.

"Shit, cooling, just making my rounds early, ya dig?" Veedo shot back. Then he handed Block a bag that contained four kilos inside it. Block took the bag with a nod off his head. Then they dapped each other up again. Block and Veedo linked up because Block owed him the favor for not killing his two homies. All Veedo asked to be paid was loyalty.

"The rest will follow," Veedo told him one day when they met at Bankhead Sea Food. Since then, everything had been straight. The trap houses had been moving good, doing numbers, and nobody had been getting jacked.

"Roll through tonight, my nigga, at the Ritz. My partner just got out from doing ten on a body. He a GF nigga but me and bruh came up together since knee high," Block told Veedo, who nodded.

"I might slide through, bruh, ion know," he said.

As Block got out of the Bentley, his shooter pulled off. Right now Veedo was on high alert. He watched everything and over-thought everything. He didn't trust nothing no one said, he only went off actions. His heart was hardened because every day he had to face the fact that the girl he was in love with was a big fat lie. She was deceiving him every chance they got together. And if he would've never been told, then there was no way he would've known she was a federal agent.

Yeah, true enough, he felt something wasn't right with her. But at the same time, he didn't think she could be the police, a federal agent at that. He couldn't do nothing but play the game with her until he made up his mind what he wanted to do. Tonight, they had a movie date at his loft downtown so he would try again to fuck her, as he'd tried but failed the last time. The closest he'd came to sex with her was sucking her breast one night and her stroking his dick through his pants. His phone vibrated. He looked down and saw Monkey's number. It was a text message.

"Mandatory meet 'n greet 10pm Peach Street condos per wolf," the text said, which threw Veedo for a loop. The condo on Peach Street belonged to Kash. It was their only meeting place. But who was the wolf? Veedo sent a text back, just plain question marks, and minutes later, Monkey called him up.

"Yo?"

"What's up, brother?" Monkey asked.

"That name," replied Veedo. It was the first time he'd ever heard that name and he wondered what and who it belonged to.

"That's Kash's brother man. Shawty came back last night," Monkey informed him, which made Veedo happy because now he could put his plan in motion.

"Oh okay, cool, I'll be there," Veedo shot back. They ended the call. He had thought Kash had another three weeks before his return, but however it went, he was glad Kash was back. It was nothing else to be done today, so he decided to kill some time by surprising Lisa Pay with a visit at the rehab center.

Chapter 18

Kash had already heard everything that had been going on in the city. That was why he called a meeting. He was heated the most by the fact that Zay nor Eric complied with their payments, and even more furious to know the nigga he sent was a phony. Then the issue with Veedo and this Fed bitch took him for a loop. he didn't know what to do or what to say.

Monkey explained to him exactly what happened, he had Veedo snatched up. Everything else was cool, except the drama from Don Kill Sum, who'd made threats to get Kash when he come out of hiding. It was funny to Kash, a big fat joke that he laughed at every time he thought about the lil' pussy nigga. Kash was a king now. He refused to let some simple nigga like Don Kill Sum even think he could bring the drama to him.

It was thirty minutes before the meeting and Kash was in the woods behind Rico 'Don Kill Sum' Jones's mother's house. She stayed in a brick home right off Camp Creek. Kash crunched down in the woods and moved towards the house. This was a tactic used by Longo and Jeter that he had learned, and what better time to use it than now? He slid over the fence, still kneeling, and made his way to the brick home.

Lights were on inside and voices could be heard. Kash was up on the house. He looked up, and then around before he proceeded to climb the house with hook tip and sticky glue on his hands and feet. He smoothly made it to the upstairs window and peeked inside to find an empty room. Kash lightly tapped the window until it cracked. Then he punched the remains out with his fist. A quick lift and the window was open. He climbed into the house and removed the book bag he wore. He pulled out the bomb kit and quickly activated it, set for thirty minutes. Kash pushed it under the bed and climbed back out the window.

He made his escape and pulled off when he got to the getaway ride. It took him an hour to switch cars and make it to the condo. When Kash got there, everyone important was there, Veedo, Monkey, Poonie, Juice, a couple more niggas he had on the team, and all his shooters. It had been a month since he'd seen everyone. Kash didn't speak to anybody, he jumped straight to business.

"No longer acknowledge me as Kash. If it's personal, then it's Kash, for business, it's *the wolf.* And the wolf is to not be seen, talked about, or contacted. Cool?"

Kash didn't wait on any replies.

"Juice, I need you to step your game up. You gotta start moving at least ten a week to compete. All commands come from Monkey, per the wolf. Next in command is Veedo. Veedo, I need you on the money, meaning you do the accounting for me but continue to be on the routes over Poonie, making sure pickups are safe. Monkey, you make sure all the dope get to where it needs to get. Poonie, you still over the money, but now it's all the money instead of a few spots. You gone always ride three deep, two shooters and you. Juice, I got something lined up for you, something sweet, so continue to work the block, get yo numbers up cause position open. Every shooter in here, y'all niggas get paid to bust at all times. I want y'all niggas on Go-Go, I need everybody's number locked in my phone before y'all leave. Any message you receive, read and erase it, and handle yo end. We got plenty of drugs, plenty of guns, cops on payroll, cities on smash. We all finna be rich. Just stay down and by all means no rats allowed."

Kash finally paused, then asked, "Any questions?"

"Yeah, nigga, how was the trip?" Monkey said in a joking manner. He started laughing and everyone else did too. Kash was glad to be back. He and Veedo ducked off in the kitchen because he wanted to hear Veedo's side of the story, since he'd gotten it from Monkey and Poonie already. Veedo explained to him everything that had happened from the time he met Trish up until now. How he'd been playing her into sex with him so he could render any case built against them. Also, Veedo told him how mad he was that the niggas he rocked with flipped on him.

"You gotta understand, Veedo, where Monkey was coming from. It was the right move, my nigga, no lie. As for Poonie, I feel you on that, bruh, but let's focus on this money and see what the Fed bitch got going on," Kash said, and Veedo agreed.

"You right, bruh, you right." it was around 2am when Kash let everyone leave, except for four shooters that he hand-picked out of the sixteen that showed up.

"I'ma show y'all firsthand how I want shit done," Kash said, and they all jumped in his four-door truck, all black with heavy tents.

***

Veedo felt a lot better after leaving the condo and talking to Kash. Kash understood like he thought he would. He listened and, at the same time, asked Veedo what he wanted to do.

"I wanna crush that fuck nigga Poonie," Veedo said with visions of himself choking the life out of Poonie. Nothing was better than that sight, Veedo thought. He quickly made it to the loft in just the right time to set up his video monitor and listening devices. He also cleaned the loft of anything that could case him up.

When Trish finally arrived, he had dinner going on the stove. The lights giving the room a romantic glow. He had soft music playing on the radio. Veedo had an apron wrapped around him when he opened the door to a beautiful Trish. She stood there with that same smile she always wore when they met up.

"What's going on, beautiful?" He moved to the side allowing her in. They hugged at the door.

"Hey, handsome. Sure smells good in here," Trish said, and stepped inside. She pulled her coat off and Veedo took it while looking at her mean shape she was indeed fine as wine.

"Food's almost ready, too. I hope it's good." He hung up her coat, then proceeded to the kitchen as she took a seat on the floor at his stereo system.

"You got any slow jams in here?" she asked as she went through his CD collection. Veedo peeked his head into the living room from the kitchen.

"Don't come up in here changing my swag," he laughed.

She smiled with her reply. "This a dinner date, not a club going." Trish she found an old school slow jam and replaced the hip hop. She joined him in the kitchen where he had steak, greens, bake potatoes, and salad set out on the table. He was taking off his apron when he turned around and saw her standing there.

"Come mere." Veedo took a step, she took a step, he kissed her lips and lightly brushed the side of her face with his fingertips. Her eyes closed and stayed that way. Even after the kiss was over, she had them closed. Then she slowly opened them up, still in his embrace.

"I sure missed you."

"I feel the same," she replied.

Veedo seated her then he sat down. The food smelled so good and she looked so good, he couldn't wait to bust her. He couldn't wait to lock her in so that things could work in his favor, so he could stay out of prison and at the same time, get out the game with the perfect excuse.

Their conversation was light over dinner. Veedo just asked question after question about things like school times, first dates, and her first crush. He asked those type of questions so that she could open up more and be comfortable with him. Trish she gave him an answer to every question asked. She had a few questions of her own as well which she asked him while helping with the dishes.

156

"So what would make you go back to the streets?" It was a question out of nowhere. It made Veedo look at her, standing side by side, washing dishes together.

"To be honest, nothing," was Veedo's reply.

"That's good to know because the streets offer you nothing but death and a jail cell, and I know you don't want either," Trish told him.

"Yeah, I've done that too many times to count. It never got me anywhere but down on the ground. Since being out and not hustling, I've come up major. And then meeting someone like you sealed the deal with me and these streets."

"Why someone like me?" Trish wanted to know.

"Cause I never had someone like you, your type, your beauty and brains. I can't do nothing but count it as a blessing," replied Veedo.

"I can't help but to see that the people around you look as if their drug dealers and how you ride around with these mean looking kids."

Veedo smiled and dried his hands off before he replied. "Nawl, boo, ever since I was jacked few weeks ago, I hired a few bodyguards to have my back. Everyone thinks I'm still slanging, but I'm not, and all type of niggas coming at me sideways. All I'm tryna do is live, bae, that's it."

Trish also dried her hands. "I feel that, bae. I feel exactly where you coming from," she said and they hugged and kissed. Veedo led her to the living room. It was near midnight.

"Can I get you to watch a movie with me or must you run?" Veedo took a seat on the plushness of his sofa. Trish she did the same.

"It's late. I don't know," she inhaled and exhaled deeply.

"That's understandable, but what's also understandable is that you're grown, so late shouldn't play a role in this matter." Veedo lightly pulled her arm, pulling her over closer to him. She willingly came. "I just like to be around you," he said and kissed the side of her head.

"You sure know how to use your words, don't you?" Trish replied.

"I'm just being honest."

"And I adore that. So tell me, what movie will we be watching?" Trish looked at him. He was so sexy in her eyes.

"Ah, what movie will be watching us?" Veedo joked and got up to look at his DVD and Blu-ray collection. "I wanna watch one of them love movies, since I'm in tune with them," he said.

"Ha-ha, funny, and what you mean by in tune with them?" Trish wanted to know as she joined him. Veedo took her in his arms and kissed her deeply. She kissed him back, tongue and all.

"That's what I mean. Hey, I'm falling in love here, ion know 'bout you," Veedo said after the kiss, which made her blush.

"The feeling is mutual," she replied.

Chapter 19

Kash smoked two blunts with the four shooters while they waited outside of one of Zay and Eric's restaurants. News had already traveled in the streets that Don Kill Sum's mother's house had gotten blown up, killing nine people inside. Nobody knew what happened, though everyone speculated the cause.

Kash vowed not to spare nobody, never, not one time, for nothing. He knew not to play with no man. He wanted Don Kill Sum to go crazy before he finally whacked him. And as far as Zay and Eric, the party had just begun. The four shooters with him were Speedy, Swag, Funk, and Chop. All four of them were supposed to be the ones who were trained to go. Tonight Kash was about to see because he couldn't have pussy niggas walking around him like they was down. He just wasn't with it.

His baby's mother, Ebony, had been blowing his phone up and he wondered why, but decided not to think about it now. He said he'd deal with it later. Kash was the first one out of the ride, followed by the rest, close on his heels. Nobody knew what to do but to follow Kash's lead. He snatched the door open to the restaurant. It was closing time so no one was inside but the workers.

Kash had his gun out and aimed. Everyone with him was strapped also, and did the same. The six people inside went into panic mode once they saw how viciously Kash slapped a guy across the mouth with his gun.

"Bitch."

Whack.

He nearly knocked all the guy's teeth out of his mouth. Females screamed and males grunted as Kash and his shooters worked them all over, pistol-beating them. They trashed the restaurant completely.

"Get up, nigga," Kash snatched the store manager by his shirt. "Take me to the video." He drug the dude to the back.

"Okay, okay, don't hurt me, man, you got it. It's back here. It's right there," the guy pleaded and pointed.

"Get that shit out."

They were inside the small office room. The guy quickly punched in a code and ejected the tape. He gave it to Kash with shaky hands. Kash made everyone ball up in the freezer. He locked it and they made their getaway clean from the scene. Nobody spoke words for the first five minutes of the ride. Then Kash cleared the air.

"I go hard so that's what I expect from y'all. Nobody should hesitate on any mission 'cause y'all didn't pump fake tonight. Best believe I watched every last one of y'all out the corner of my eye, and I like what I seen. But it's what you do that I don't see that matters. I did this with y'all niggas to show that I won't ask you to do something I wouldn't do. Remember, it's the wolf and should nobody know me as Kash but y'all, ya dig?"

Everyone in the car agreed. Thirty minutes later, they all split up, going their separate ways. Kash knew it was late but he still checked in with his kids' mother, who didn't answer. So he left her a text, telling her to call him.

Home to him was an eight-bedroom brick house located in Decatur, GA off Memorial Drive. He was the only person that stayed there, but help was constantly around, cooks, drivers, cleaners, and yard details. Kash made a mental note to beef the security up on his new home.

The gate automatically opened when he pulled up to it. He pulled the Benz into his stone black driveway. His Glock sat across his lap. The video tapes with him and his shooters beating people were on the passenger seat with a book bag full of cash. Once he stored the money inside his safe, Kash stripped down to his boxers. He sat on the bed with his phone in hand and went through all his messages, scrolling past all groupie hoes and begging niggas. He read only the important ones he saw.

Asia had been texting him with updates on her training. She aced all scores and was hired by the DOC. Kash was glad to know this news. He also had seen that Meco had been texting him, saying that he was home, which was more good news. Ms. Johnson, the nurse he messed with, was able to transfer from Augusta to Jackson where Gangsta was located. Everything was working in his favor, going as plan.

Kash left his phone on the bed. He went and jumped in the shower, allowing the water to rush over his body, the heat relaxing him put his mind at ease. He was lost in deep thoughts about his next couple moves, about his next mission in life. At that moment he had everything he could ever wish for, but he wanted more. He wanted something else out of all that he was doing. Kash couldn't tell you what it was he wanted. He just felt the need to have something more.

It wasn't a female, it wasn't a nigga, it wasn't more money or more freedom, but it was something. He just hadn't figured it out yet. Once he was out of the shower and comfortable in bed, he decided to hit Meco's new number that he'd left in the text message. It was almost 2am, but Meco still picked up.

"What's mobbin'?"

"Shawty, what's up?" Kash asked.

"Shit, I been tryna get at you, my nigga, ever since I jumped yo shit been going straight to the voicemail," Meco told him.

"I been out of town on business. Text me your address so I can scoop you up tomorrow though. So what's up? What you feel like?" asked Kash as he started rolling him a blunt.

"I'm loving this freedom shit, fooly, been ten years straight," Meco replied.

"I feel that. So you ready to come into the money? Do you think you can take over yo side of Dill?" Kash asked him.

"What you mean, bruh? My lil' partna and them sling their thang ov…"

"I'm not talking about two, three spots, bruh. I'm taking bout you with yo own team type shit."

"I mean, my G, if need be, you know I'm grinding to me a check. So yeah, I can work the streets," Meco said.

Kash knew he didn't understand just yet. He knew that Meco thought it was a game. They ended the call after talking some more. Kash smoked the entire blunt and then fell asleep in the comfort of his bed.

Chapter 20

They were still balled up together on his sofa long after the movie went off. The both of them fell asleep, him holding her as they mumbled in conversation. But something awoke him and Veedo was glad it did because he didn't want to miss a chance to fuck this beautiful ass police.

She was laid nestled under him, knocked out. Veedo was on her side. He softly kissed her chin, then her neck. He looked at her and she didn't stir. He kissed her lips one time, two times, and then Trish opened her eyes. She felt his hand between her legs. His finger lightly brushed her pussy, sending chills running up and down her body. Trish kissed him back, grabbing his face with both hands. She opened her legs wider than they were. Veedo kissed her deeply with so much passion, giving her all of him.

His love, his affection, his mind, body and soul. She grinded his hand. Veedo got up, pulling her up with him as well. Once the both of them were standing face to face, Veedo kissed her. He took both her hands into his hands, walking backwards to his room. They kissed every step into his plush bedroom, where he turned Trish and laid her back on the bed. For a moment, he just looked at her beauty. Trish placed one of her bare feet on his stomach. Veedo took it. He looked down while raising her cute toes to his lips. He kissed the bottom of her feet.

"For I'll Cherish every step you take." Veedo pulled at her pants as she unbuttoned them and lifted up so he could pull them off. Trish reached out to him once her pants were off. He grabbed her hands. She sat up, then Veedo pulled his shirt over his head. She took the chance to kiss his stomach, his ripped six pack. She ran her fingers roughly across Veedo. He bent down and kissed her again while pulling off her shirt. He pulled it over her head, revealing she wore matching bra and panties.

Veedo then undid his own jeans. He let them drop to the floor. Trish was amazed at the bulge she saw in his boxer briefs. She grabbed his dick and held it while looking up to him. Still standing, Veedo placed one of his hands behind her neck. Then he pushed her back, making her lay flat on the bed.

Veedo spread her thighs, her panties still on, though damp was its center as he pulled them to the side. She had a cute, small pussy he saw and instantly kissed her there. It was warm. Her pussy and his lips both created a heat. Veedo licked around her clit as he spread her pussy lips He dove his tongue into her a couple times, making Trish moan out his name. Her insides tasted good, so good he pushed his tongue a bit deeper into her love tunnel.

"Oh, ooh, Vee, ohhh, babbby," Trish couldn't help but say as he sucked on her pussy nice and slow and deep. She found herself near a nut once Veedo pushed two fingers into her tightness. He started finger fuckin' the pussy while he played with her clit with the tip of his tongue. Trish's pussy juice painted his face and chin. He was loving the way she fed him the pussy, filling his mouth up with her sweetness.

"You like that?" he questioned.

"Ye-yes, I'm bout to, ugh. Oh, ah, mmm, shit, Veedo, baby, stop." Trish pushed his face away from her sensitive pussy.

Veedo took his hand and patted her pussy to calm her quivering body. He slid a finger into her and then kissed her clit once, twice. He slid up her body, his dick standing at attention. He rubbed his dick head up and around her wetness.

Trish pushed at his hips. "We need protect…" her words came to an end when she felt Veedo enter her walls. She moaned, "Mmm ah."

"I don't have none, baby, we safe."

Veedo stroked her deep two times and started pumping in and out of her tightness. She rubbed his back as Veedo went to work, stroking her, thrusting his hardness into her with slow, rhythmic strokes. He kissed her. He kissed her with all the passion inside him. He loved her up and down in one position, taking his precious time until he came inside her tunnel of love. Long after he came, they laid there still kissing and rubbing each other, laying side by side in a beautiful sleep.

***

The very next morning, Kash was with his daughter, Unique. He had to pick her up from school. She was sick with a cold and Ebony was at work. So before he started his day, he picked his baby up.

"Want something to eat, beautiful?" Kash asked. They were at the red light inside his Yukon truck with heavy tented windows.

"No," Unique mumbled with her eyes closed, trying to rest as her daddy drove.

"The doctor?"

"No, sir," she weakly replied.

"Okay, baby, whatever you want, just let me know," he stated.

"Okay."

Kash decided to pull up to his mother's house. She stayed in Buckhead when living in GA. His parents had the biggest home in Buckhead, being one of the richest couples in Atlanta. Kash was allowed in and parked behind one of his dad's expensive cars. He and Unique made their way up ten beautiful stone steps leading to twelve-foot double doors that were opened by the help. Help that had been around even when Kash was just a kid himself. His mom was in the kitchen helping one of the cooks when he entered and spoke.

"Ma, what's up?"

She turned to see her son and grandbaby. It was a blessing each time she saw him alive and not behind bars.

"Hey, baby. Glad you made it out here to set your old lady." She hugged him and then bent down to pick up Unique. "What's wrong wit mamma baby?"

"She sick, ma." Kash grabbed one of the cookies off the display of all kinds of freshly baked sweets. He kissed the side of his daughter's face. She had her head laid on her grandmother's shoulder. Kash took a bite of his cookie.

"What's wrong?" his mother asked him.

"She got a lil' cold. Listen, ma, I got this meeting to go to. Can you tend to her until Ebony get off? She'll come get her from you."

"Yes, that's fine. Take her and lay her down." She passed Unique to him. Kash kissed his daughter again. He took her to his mother's room where he laid her down.

"You have your phone?" he asked Unique.

"Yes."

"Okay, you got my number. Call me and daddy coming like superman. Okay?" he said.

"Okay," Unique replied. "Love you, daddy."

"Love you too, baby. I'll see you later."

Kash spoke with his mother about helping him open up a business and she happily agreed to do whatever it took. He knew she would have his back. It was just his father who would have something to say, and he really didn't wanna hear that shit so it was good he wasn't there. Not even thirty minutes later, Kash was pulling up to meet Veedo at the tire shop on Bankhead, a shop Veedo had investments in. Kash jumped out the truck and they dapped each other with a shoulder to shoulder hug.

"What's going on?"

"Man, good days 'bout to come," Kash said. They both were fresh and iced out. Veedo walked over to the Benz.

"Hop in, bruh," Veedo said. He cut the Benz on, the TV came up, and he put in a DVD and pressed play. Kash watched Veedo and Trish fucking in a bedroom. Veedo let it play for a few minutes and then cut it off. "I got three hours of us," he said.

Kash sat there quiet for a moment. He pulled out a blunt and put some fire to it.

"Just keep that shit in a safe place. We'll use that if any case come about, so keep on busting that hoe," Kash said and passed the blunt over.

"Gotta know dat," Veedo replied, hitting the blunt twice, then looking at it, and hitting it again two more times. He had his mind made up that he would continue to play dumb to Trish, lie just to see what she had going on. His team was safe for now, and Veedo planned to keep it that way. He passed the blunt back.

"Yeah, we can't be stopped no way. Look, I got a lil' partner who just got out I'm 'bout to put on the team. He one of them GF niggas, a real stand-up guy. I'm 'bout to snatch him up and take shawty shopping. What do you got going on?" Kash asked in between puffs of the blunt.

"Shid, I can roll. I need a few hats anyways. One of them lil' GF niggas' mamma house got blowed up last night, killed six motherfuckers, including his twin boys inside that bitch too." Veedo shook his head because it made no sense how far niggas took beef. Little did Veedo know, Kash was the one responsible.

"Fuck that nigga," was the only thing Kash said to that subject and Veedo quickly caught on. They got out the Benz and climbed into Kash's truck. Kash didn't give two fucks about Don Kill Sum nor his kids. Don Kill Sum was fucking with a fool and he would learn that in the end. Kash's phone rang. He saw that it was Erica's number. He let it ring over to voicemail. He didn't have the time nor day to focus on her right now.

Kash drove with his gun across his lap like always, ready for any action any nigga could even think to bring. He was ready at all times. He made Veedo leave his shooters at the shop saying, "I am the shooter, my nigga."

"Say less, bruh," Veedo laughed and knew that Kash was dead serious about bringing the drama to anybody.

Kash smoked another blunt of loud while the radio blasted. He followed the GPS to the address Meco had given him. It took them to Dill Ave, a house sat off from the streets surrounded by a small iron fence. Kash pulled up in the yard and blew the horn. Meco stepped out, looking at the black Yukon with super dark tints in his baby's mother's yard.

Kash opened the door, leaving his gun on the seat. Veedo climbed out also. He thought he recognized the GF dude with tattoos all in his face. The dude smiled at Kash as they dapped each other up.

"What's up, my dude?" Kash said. Then he introduced him. "Veedo, this my nigga, Meco. Shawty, this Veedo, my main guy."

"What's up, Bruh? Glad you made it out that bitch." Veedo gave him a solid pound.

"Same here. Lemme run in here and tell my BM I'm out," Meco said. Then he disappeared into the house. Meco came back out, followed by a dark skinned thick chick. She watched him jump down the steps and climb into the Yukon.

"Bout to hit Lenox, tear this bitch up real quick. You still smoke?" Kash pulled off asking.

"Fuckin' rite, fooly," Meco replied.

"You ready to eat in these streets?"

"Boy, what kind of question is that?"

Kash passed him weed and blunts to roll. "You still head in the mob?"

"Fasho."

"Some of these niggas wilding, bruh. I done spanked one or two of yo brothers since I been out," Kash told his partner.

"Niggas stunt mobbin' right, but I'm out here now. I'm finna show my brothers how to mob it to a bankroll," Meco boasted.

"That's what I'm talking 'bout," Kash laughed. Then he added, "Your brother Don Kill Sum, what's up with him?"

"Lil' Rico? Oh that's my lil' nigga I raised that boy. Shawty a fool wit it," Meco answered.

"Yeah, niggas paid him to run up on me wit da drama, him and a few of yo other brothers. I spared them folks on the strength of you and bigger business, but he still screaming my name on some war shit. I'm telling you 'cause I wanna know your take, cause you know how I am," Kash warned his partner. That way if Meco gave him the green light, he'd finish Don Kill Sum off, or if Meco wanted him spared, it would be a business move. It'd be like Meco owed him a favor and all Kash wanted was a nigga's loyalty.

"Yeah, dats my lil' nigga. He going through some shit right now. He don't want no drama, but I'ma introduce y'all niggas when his ordeal is over. Spare him, fooly, for me," Meco shot back, and it was a sealed deal.

All three guys hit the Gucci store up. Kash dropped ten bands on Meco three outfits and himself a belt. They hit up a couple more stores, dropping more bands on expensive gear, hats and shoes. Kash took Meco into Ice, a new jewelry store inside the mall.

"What's up? Hook my people up with the neck, wrist, and ears," Kash told one of the store owners who he was cool with. They left the mall after he'd spent over seventy-five grand on Meco, just showing him the love of a real nigga. Meco was surprised by the money, but not by Kash's actions. He knew Kash was a go-getter, but not like the shit he was on now. Walking outside, Kash saw Eric and his stripper bitch headed in. Eric had his head down, texting on his phone so didn't see Kash until they were real close.

"What's up, nigga? You got something for me?" Kash stopped in front of him and his bitch. Eric looked embarrassed and scared.

"Bruh, wh-what you talking 'bout?" Eric tried to stand firm. It was killing him.

"You get my message? Yo employee didn't tell you what I said? I must ain't speak that shit loud enough," Kash punched Eric in the mouth, sending him crashing to the ground. "Boy, stop mother-fuckin' playing wit…"

Kash went at him again but Meco stopped him. "Hold on. Whoa, whoa, bruh, we in public."

Eric's girlfriend was screaming, grabbing onlookers' attention. Kash allowed Meco to pull him away, but not before saying over his shoulder, "You know what it is, fuck nigga. I'ma show you, boy. Never send a pussy at me again, nigga," Kash yelled as he was being pulled away by both his partners.

"Da fuck that was bout?" Meco asked, once they were in the car, driving off into traffic.

"Them niggas owe Gangsta and niggas ain't paid bruh yet. That nigga the one sent yo brother to check me." Laughing, Kash said, "Bruh, he a real pussy."

"How that nigga, Gangsta, holding it down anyway?"

"Shawty good," replied Kash. "You know bruh the reason we all out here and them niggas can't cut him a check. Fuck dat," Kash was clearly heated.

"Say no mo, Fooly. I can put the pressure down on them shrimps. Don't let that sucka get you in yo feelings, my nigga, we cooling it today, ya feel me?" Meco said as he began rolling more weed to smoke.

"Really want them ducks on ice," Kash added.

"Fuck nawl, that's Gangsta's cousin, nigga," Veedo laughed at Kash, knowing he was for real.

"And that's the only reason I ain't milked his fuck ass, pussy nigga, ion know how them niggas on the west side let a pussy get all that money. Shit don't make no sense," said Kash, and he hit the highway. He was taking Meco to meet Monkey and to show and explain his job detail on what he wanted to be done.

Monkey was at the warehouse overseeing a new shipment of cocaine when Kash pulled up and parked. It was crowded with niggas moving loads from an eighteen-wheeler into vans and trucks. Monkey had the phone glued to his ear in conversation with someone.

"What's the move?" Kash wanted to know as they pounded each other.

"Tryna get this shit on the road before twelve," Monkey replied.

"Meco, this my right hand out here, Monkey. Monkey, this Meco, my nigga," Kash introduced them. Veedo was texting on his phone. He kept his convo for Monkey to a limit. If he didn't have to speak, then he wouldn't because he still felt some type of way about being snatched up.

"What's up, my nigga?" Monkey acknowledged Meco and they pounded each other.

"I'm coolin'."

"Let me show you the mojo, my nigga. Follow me." Kash took Meco to the drug room where he had hundreds of kilo's stacked in corners and in boxes. He took him through the process room and the count room where he met Poonie and a few other niggas Kash said he'd be dealing with. Kash was glad to help a nigga out he felt deserved it.

Meco was solid since day one. He had showed no flaw and when the GF members had a hat on Kash for stabbing Dank, it was Meco who made the call to fall back. And for that, Kash would forever salute him, even though he was fully prepared to war with every last GF in the prison system. Dank was a rat and snitches never get saved. Kash left with Veedo and Meco, not knowing they'd been being followed since leaving the tire shop on Bankhead. The Feds were on to them and nobody peeped the move as picture after picture was being taken.

***

"Charles McCants," she spoke his name out loud while sitting at her desk going over paperwork. She was faxed over forty photos of Veedo, Kash, and another guy. Surveillance also located a shipment spot which gave the government rights to lunch an investigation on them.

Trish was getting the final paperwork in order to be signed by the judge.

"What are you up to, Veedo?"

She asked herself the question she needed answers to. Last night was the biggest mistake of her life, when she had sex with him, and unprotected at that. Trish knew she was in love and in lust because she could not control herself. She knew that if she laid down with him, it would be hard trying to launch an investigation. But she went against all her common sense. Instead of following her thoughts, she let her emotions get the best of her and she fell into lust.

It had been nearly two years since she'd had sex with any man and last night opened up new emotions in her. Trish was in love with the man she may have to send off to prison. It was one of the hardest decisions she'd had to make in her life. She was stuck because being with this man had proven happiness for her, something she hadn't felt in a long time. She was happy at how she was treated by him. Men these days didn't do those simple things that make a woman happy. They were rare, and by Trish finally meeting the correct man, it shattered her to know that they lived two different lifestyles.

Trish stared at a picture of Veedo sitting in his Benz with Charles. She shook her head side to side, secretly hoping that all this was a mistake. And no matter how bad it seemed, she hoped that Veedo was truly done and that he was clean. Something told her if she held her breath for that, then she would die. She was startled when her captain stuck his head in her office door.

"Ms. Williams, urgent meeting in my office in seventy seconds." Then he was gone.

Trish quickly paused her session on her laptop, slipped on her heels, and made her way out of the office and down the hall, wondering what was going on that was urgent. There was a room full of federal agents when she walked into the office. The lights were dim and a video was on pause when she noticed the TV on.

"Chavez is back in the states." Her captain pressed play as everyone watched Chavez exit a G-4 private jet at the airport. He walked to a black Benz and was allowed inside. Then it pulled off.

"He's located at the Hilton for three days. This is our chance to snatch him before he gets away. I want a team on him right now. Watch his every move. If he shits, I wanna know how many turds he dropped. Don't let nothing past us, not nothing," her captain, Oliver Brown, said. Then Ms. Mathis took over, giving everyone their position, their role. The plan was to strike in two days, giving Chavez a chance to slip and show them anything that could help build a stronger case against him.

The Federal government had been running an investigation on Chavez and his entire Mexican family for the past ten years. They had never won with him, never went past go with them. This was the closest they'd ever gotten when dealing with Chavez, and the government wasn't about to let him get away. He was a wanted man. His father and son were wanted men.

Chavez was powerful, a power stemming from long runs in the drug empire, and he was connected all over the world, which made him nearly invincible to the cops. Every chance they got close to getting either guy, somehow they'd get away clean, untouched, and with more power. This time here would not be one of those times. The government was determined to put a stop to the Mexican cartel. and what better chance than now?

Trish was assigned to interrogation, which was a relief to her because she didn't have the energy to deal with anything else. She couldn't help but wonder if Veedo had any ties with Chavez. She sure hoped not because that would crush her hope. She made it back to her office to find she had two missed calls from him, a text message and voicemail. She only smiled at him for that sweetness he gives off.

"Hey handsome."

Trish sent a text back, then she made notes about Chavez that she remembered Ms. Mathis pointed out. She wanted badly to put an end to this investigation, and wanted even more badly for Veedo to get out while he could. She had to figure a way to warn him, maybe that would make him re-evaluate himself. She just wanted the man she knew him to be, nobody else mattered because he made her feel perfect. He made her feel loved. He showed her so much respect, and he had good dick. She wrapped things up in the office, feeling elated by the attention Veedo gave her.

He sent a message back. "When can I see you again?"

She sent a reply. "Whenever you want."

Trish made it down and out of the building to her car. Today made out to be a good one. She just hoped it ended on the same note. She climbed into her car, adjusted the radio, and released her hair from a bun. She was in heavy relaxation mode. New good dick made you act a certain way, and she was most definitely acting a nut case, a happy nut case at that. When would she tell Veedo the truth?

She was in love. She knew it would have to come out at some point in time. So when was the best time to tell him? how could she possibly word it? First things first, she needed to know he was not in the Game. But she knew he was dealing, every finger pointed to him, even some facts. But Trish didn't want to believe them.

She found herself making excuses up for him, just hoping he was a changed man. All she could do was hope. Deep down she saw them faced off in the federal courtroom, but something had to be done to change that. Trish wasn't a drinker, but today she needed a few shots. Veedo would have to know the truth as well because she would hate to see the day she put him behind bars.

Jerry Jackson

Chapter 21

Terry and Zay were having dinner when Eric pulled up with his girlfriend. Terry knew something was wrong by the way Eric came into their home unlike himself. Eric was the cool, calm type, but right now, he was moving fast paced and looking crazy. Zay slowly stood up with the help of his crutches. Eric's mouth was bloody.

"What happened, bruh?" Zay started walking towards his sports room. It was a spot in the house you could almost always catch him at, especially when his friend came over. Terry, being the nosey one, got up and followed them.

"Man that nigga Ka…"

"Hole up," Zay stopped him from talking when he saw his girl enter behind them. "Baby, lemme holla at Eric."

"No, I need to know what's going on." Terry stood firm, unmoved. She wasn't hearing Zay right now.

"Terry, go head on now," Zay fully turned around, facing his pregnant girlfriend.

"Boy, stop." She rolled her eyes, stepped around Zay, and looked at Eric. "What happened to you?"

Eric walked away when she asked. Zay stepped back up in her face and leaned down on the crutch. "Terry, don't never disrespect me, shawty. Get up out of here. This street business, you know what we talked about," he said.

Terry rolled her eyes at him again and walked around him.

"Eric, don't do me. What's going on? What is Kash doing?" Terry didn't care how Zay felt because she felt that she could put a stop to whatever it was that Kash was doing, or trying to do. Eric flopped down on the sofa chair and looked at Terry.

"This nigga Kash stole on me at Lenox this morning. Nigga pulled out a gun and all out there," Eric said defeated.

"Man, that nigga is nuts," Zay added, "I never fucked wit him when he used to come to the hood back in our teen years. He was always kicking that bully shit."

"What he wanted?" Terry already knew the answer. She just wanted to make sure her man wasn't lying to her.

"This fuck nigga want us to pay him for Gangsta, thirty-five percent of our worth every month. That nigga crazy as fuck," Eric stated.

"Get that nigga knocked off," Zay said as he eased down on the sofa supported by the crutches.

"Lemme talk to Kash 'cause he not finna break my family. All the money he got, he don't need to be acting like that."

"Ain't no talking," Zay said. He was fed up with Kash acting like he couldn't be touched. He knew money talked and bullshit ran a thousand miles.

"Just let me holla at him." Terry had her mind made up whether Zay liked it or not. She left them both in the cool room. She was determined to put an end to the bullshit that was going on.

Terry went to get her daughter. She was already late for her doctor's appointment and now mad and in her feelings. Kash had to stop whatever it was that he was doing to Zay and Eric. Gangsta wouldn't want him to be doing that.

Keshana was in her room playing with toys.

"Come on," Terry demanded, walking away to her own room. She was grabbing her phone and house keys when Keshana followed. That morning she woke up feeling joyful, hoping that Zay healed and that thing with Kash had calmed, and now this? Eric ruined a perfect day with news of his run in with Kash. And Kash's ass was doing entirely too much. She wasn't feeling him acting like this. He wasn't acting like family.

Terry buckled her daughter into the back seat and climbed into her Infinity truck, Terry saw the living room door come open as she backed out of their driveway. Zay was stepping out, waving

178

his hands for her to stop. But Terry put her truck in drive and pulled off. Kash was tripping.

Jerry Jackson

Chapter 22

"Stand by for regional inspection. Stand by for inspection. Make sure all beds are made, all lockers and walls correct, shave, boots shined. Have a nice day gentlemen."

Gangsta heard the intercom say. Then he looked at the time and saw that it was 1:15pm on Wednesday. And they calling for inspection? He wasn't feeling getting out of his comfort zone, but knew it was best to comply rather than buck. So he got up from his laying position and started to make up his bed. Gangsta couldn't afford any type or trouble right now. He was about to receive his first visit and a chance to see and hold his son, so Gangsta complied with all officers at all times, giving them no reason to book him.

He was more than ready to see his son, see him woke, see his eyes, see his smile. He was ready to touch his little man. He needed to touch him. It'd been a month since Jr woke up and he was doing excellent. He was still growing, still learning. Gangsta took off his tennis shoes and put on his black boots with the shining tips. He was already state dressed coming from a morning inspection. He quickly presented himself and his room the way the prison required.

Once he got straight, Gangsta stood at the door. He looked out at Ms. Pitts in the control booth with a trainee. Flip was standing in his door messing with her on some lovey dovey shit. The trainee couldn't figure out what was going on since she was fairly new.

"You ready for inspection over there, old man?" Gangsta asked Flip through the doors.

"Yeah, I'm afraid so," Flip replied. The dorm officer on the floor had everything under control, everything was running smoothly. Gangsta double checked his own cell and saw that he was straight. If you looked at Gangsta, had a conversation with him, or watched him from afar, you couldn't tell he had the death penalty. He still carried himself in a normal manner. He still smiled, laughed, and at all times he sought to learn something he didn't know about life.

He did not let the judge break him. He did not tremble under the pressure. Gangsta just accepted his fate like a champ and, strange thing, but he wasn't mad at how things ended up. After about ten minutes of standing around in the cell, the inspection team came around. The warden's name was Mr. Jones. He was a hard nose black man in his early forties. He was real strict, very mean, and too direct. Today Mr. Jones had visitors and on days when the commissioner showed up, Mr. Jones made sure his entire prison was spotless and that everybody was on point. When and if you weren't, then he punished you with time in the hole and all sorts of restrictions.

Mr. Jones was the type of man most people hated, other than his family. He was sharp about everything and never thought he was wrong, he was always right in his book. He and Gangsta had never had a run in. It had always been about respect with him and Gangsta. Gangsta seemed to always be on point with his shit and that was something Mr. Jones liked.

The sergeant of the cert team and the prison captain led the inspection team through death row. They went first to make sure people were up and ready before the warden made his stop at the door. It was a big inspection because the whole cert team was there, along with three visitors and some trainees.

Gangsta had to do a double take when he saw Mr. Jones' new secretary. She wasn't your average secretary for wardens, old, white, bad body. No this lady had the youth, the face, and the body. She had every nigga in the pod looking hard at her. Once she got close, Gangsta's eyes got bigger. She wouldn't look at him as she stood next to the warden when he stopped at Gangsta's door.

"Jackson, how you doing?" Mr. Jones asked.

"Good, sir, and yourself?" Gangsta replied with his own question. With his heart pounding away in his chest, he was confused.

But it was good seeing someone he knew. She still refused to look. Even when they walked off to the next cell, she didn't cut her eyes and acknowledge him in any form. Gangsta kept watching her as they made it around the whole dorm. She was still super bad, even in a business skirt and pumps.

Gangsta remembered sex with her, how beautiful her body was. "Asia," he said to himself in a mumble as she walked out the door behind the warden. *What is Asia doing? This is strange*, Gangsta thought as he took off his boots. *Damn, Shawty tough*, he thought while sitting on his bunk. It was time to smoke. He needed to blow a stick of weed, but didn't have any. Gangsta hit the wall to get Flip's attention.

"Yo."

"What's going on, neph?" Flip yelled

"I need me one, unc, a one and one." Gangsta had started smoking cigarettes since being on death row.

"I can hook that for you, neph."

"Cool," Gangsta shot back. He picked up his writing pad and a pen to start a letter to Kash. He wanted to know if Kash had anything to do with Asia being down at Jackson State Prison, which just happened be the same prison he was in. He made the letter brief and ended it with his love and a favor asked. Gangsta sent the mail to his mother. She would get it to Kash.

His mind couldn't stay away from seeing Asia with the inspection team. This shit was like a movie or something. He had to laugh at it. The shit was confusing but funny. After Gangsta seal up the letter to Kash, he went to the door so that he could get his stick of weed and cigarettes. Flip would send it over on a line and he would send the food back to pay for it. That was what they did.

Even though Flip looked out and always gave Gangsta weed and cigarettes, Gangsta still spent money with him. He would smoke, and then eat his lunch. So Gangsta began making some fire with two batteries and two razors. He had the bottom of his door stuffed so the smell wouldn't escape. Gangsta smoked both to the head, not saving anything, not even a pinch. He laid back in his bunk, waiting on the trays to be delivered so he could put something other than junk food on his stomach.

***

Nene and Erica listened to Terry explain what was going on with Kash, Zay, and Eric. She told them from front to back what had taken place up until now. Nene was totally shocked at how badly Kash was acting up. He wasn't being the man Gangsta wanted him to be.

"I thought Kash was pose to protect us." Nene made the statement, speaking her thoughts out loud.

"I know right," Terry said. She had tears in her eyes, scared, hurt, and frustrated about the situation. Nene put her arm around Terry's shoulder.

"It's gonna be okay. Erica call Kash. Tell him to get over here. It's urgent," Nene told her sister. Keshana and Junior were playing on the floor together. They had a brother and sister bond unlike anything else.

"Ok," Erica said, pulling out her phone. She wanted to see Kash anyway. She missed him, wanted to hear his voice, feel his touch, and more.

Nene walked Terry over to her sofa, where they both took seats. Terry was big, almost ready to have that baby. She didn't need to stress right now, and Nene knew it.

"We're about to get this fixed. I promise."

"He on the way," Erica said. She now had a glow on her face, a slick smirk as well. Her sister noticed but said nothing about it as she continued to pat Terry's back as she cried silent tears.

"Ok," said Nene. She couldn't believe how Kash was acting. She knew him better than that. He shouldn't come home fresh from prison acting all stupid and shit. Look at his friend and where he was at. Look at Junior Look at where he just came from. Nene couldn't figure who would be stupid enough to wanna risk going back to prison or worst, be killed in the streets. Kash needed to slow down or one or two would soon happen. Either way, it was a sad day, a sad evening.

Terry finally dried her tears and was able to talk normally. She held Junior while talking about how she just wanted everyone to get out the game. She talked about her kids and her future. Terry showed a side she rarely showed people. Nene and Erica both felt her pains and understood her vision.

It took Kash two hours to get there. He pulled up with two more dudes in his truck, but neither got out. Nene was standing on the porch when he walked up the walkway and the few stairs to the porch.

"What's up, sis?" Kash hugged her.

"Mm huh, I'm mad at you," Nene hugged him back and walked away, into the house. He followed and saw the kids, Erica, and Terry.

"What's up y'all? What's going on? Let me guess, y'all mad at me too?" Kash asked through a smile. Him and his nephew gave each other dap, and then he bent down to kiss Keshana.

"I am," Terry pouted.

Then Nene asked, "Kash, why is you messing with Zay and Eric? Why you stab that boy?"

"And why did you trash that restaurant?" Terry added.

Then Nene cut back in, "You supposed to be protecting us, the kids. You know we family, Kash. Eric is Gary's first cousin. Don't do them boys like that.

"Look, check this out. That nigga Zay, he not right, Eric either…"

"Kash," Terry cut in, "what have they done to Gary? Nothing. What have they done…"

"For Gangsta," Kash cut her off. "Nothing. Nan one of them niggas sent bruh a dime in four months."

"How you know?" Terry raised her voice and rolled her eyes.

"I asked them niggas."

"Well, Kash, for the sake of us, just let it go," Nene stated.

"Please," added Terry as tears started to fall from her eyes again.

"Man…"

"Please, Kash, do this for me," Nene begged.

Kash looked away from all three girls. He shook his head side to side. He didn't expect to come over for this. It was bad enough Zay and Eric had pussy niggas and lames asking for them to be spared. Now they got the family involved.

"Nene, them niggas owe," said Kash.

"What do Zay owe you?" Terry asked.

"He owe Gang…"

"How much?"

"Terry, I fucks with you, shawty, and I know Zay your baby…"

"Kash, listen, she don't need to keep stressing. It can hurt the baby. Okay, Zay and Eric, they not real as you and Gangsta are. So fuck it, just let us give you whatever it is they owe and that's that," Nene said.

Kash shook his head again. *Damn*, he was thinking. "Nene, y'all putting me in a fucked up position." He wanted badly to just walk out, but Nene was right, they were family.

"Just do this one favor for me, remember you the one who said that whatever I want, I can have. Well I'm asking right now, face to face, leave them alone, Kash, please," Nene spoke, looking directly at Kash, who looked at a pregnant Terry.

He looked at the kids. He had so much love for these people. He just did not have love for a fuck nigga. Terry and Nene wanted him to do the unthinkable, and only for the love of Gangsta did he agree to leave them alone.

"Under one condition," Kash said.

"What?" the girls both asked at the same time.

"They both give bruh half a million, and I know they got it. If not, then I can't leave them alone."

"Kash, don't nobody have that type of money," Terry shook her head at him.

"Okay, okay, two hundred fifty, no exception."

"Fine," Nene concluded the conversation. "I just want our family to be a family again, Kash, that's all."

"And it is," Kash replied. He hugged Nene, and then Terry, before walking out of the house with Erica, who had a big smile on her face. So much weight was lifted off Terry's shoulders. When Kash left, she was feeling so much better. She hugged and thanked Nene.

"Girl, thank you. That boy let us double team him," Nene said, giving Terry a high five.

They both smiled at each other, happy with the outcome. Nene decided to go out with the family since it'd been forever and a day since she'd been out to enjoy anything. It would be Junior's first time leaving the house, too, since he'd been home. They ended up at Ryan's, the all-you-can eat place. Things were smooth as can be, but NeNe nor Terry knew they were being followed. Erica was so busy playing with Keshana that she didn't pay attention either.

Jerry Jackson

Chapter 23

Kash jumped in the smoked out truck and pulled off from the corner store. Meco passed him a blunt. The music was pumping Monsta Swole's new mix tape *Da Run Down*. Kash had just noticed a text message in red, blinking across his phone screen. He opened the message, which was from Chavez. Kash read it fast because it automatically erased. He had an urgent flight out to Miami and the plane would leave at six.

"Damn, I gotta dip out, fooly," Kash said, putting the phone down. "I'm gone make one more stop then I'ma drop y'all niggas off."

"Say no mo."

"Everything Gucci, bruh?" Veedo asked.

"Hell yeah, bruh, everything good," Kash shot back. "I'm headed to Miami for a lil' minute, that's all."

"Okay, cool."

Kash pulled up to the house Veedo met him at before. Veedo noticed and then remembered the girl who worked at Augusta State Prison. Kash got out. He knocked on the heavy wooden door twice before someone opened it, and it was her, Mrs. Johnson, standing before him. Kash pulled her towards him. She melted in his embrace as they shared one of those *I miss you* kisses.

"What's up, baby?" she spoke. Her name was Tiffany Johnson and she was thirty-six and divorced, due to Kash, and so in love with him.

"What's going on?" Kash entered the crib.

"Nothing much, just some spring cleaning on my off day. Here, I got that blood for you," Tiffany said as she disappeared in the room and came back out with a table of blood. It had a strip with Gangsta's name and GDC number on it. Kash laughed and took it.

"How you pull this off? You good?" He quickly stuck the tube in his pocket and he kissed her again.

"I guess he had a birthday or something because the lab had just taken his blood the night before they was waiting on them to be picked up. When I got to work yesterday, I saw it and stole it and erased the data out of the computer."

"So he never got to see you?" asked Kash.

"No."

"You never got the phone to him?"

"No, I told you, I'm not giving no one nothing if it's not him. I got it. I will just try again Monday when I go back in," Tiffany shot back to the man she had come to love.

Kash had stayed on her since the day they met and with time, she finally fell for him. She destroyed her marriage to be with Kash, and so far so good. Even though she only got eight percent of his attention because ninety-two percent was elsewhere.

He kissed her once more and left the crib. He climbed back into the whip and pulled off, blasting the radio. He reread the text just to make sure he was right about the time and date. Kash took Veedo back to the tire shop and took Meco back to Dill Ave. They both got out in the yard and dapped each other up.

"Here," Kash went to the back of the Yukon. As the back raised up where Meco's clothes were, Kash said, "Grab that book bag too. That's your loyalty fare."

Meco also took the bag Kash pointed out. It was a bit heavy. He said nothing, just took it and threw it over his shoulder.

"Say no mo, foo. Hit me when you get back in town." They dapped once again, and then Kash got the hell on. He only had a few hours before he had to be at the airport.

Ebony and the kids were in the kitchen when Kash entered through the side door. Unique got excited when she saw her daddy.

"Daddy," she yelled and got Sheen from her chair. Charles Jr. wanted to act like his sister also and jumped over, hugging Kash's leg as he held Unique in the air, kissing her lips.

"Hey daddy's pretty girl." He put her down and then picked Charles Jr. up with one hand under his arms. "What's up, big guy?"

Then he put him down. He walked over to where Ebony was over the stove. She was frying chicken. "What's up, woman?"

"Hey, Charles, what's going on?"

"Hungry. Glad I showed up."

"Well I gotta drop some more chicken 'cause we didn't expect you. This is a surprise to see you two times back to back," Ebony said in a joking manner, but was so serious.

"You'll start seeing me more often," Kash added.

"Yeah."

"I'm dead ass, I'ma be around so much you gon' think I stay here."

"The kids will sure love to see that," said Ebony. She would too, but she refused to tell him so.

"For real, though. I'm coming around more. I just gotta tie up some loose ends. Then I can be more into my family," Kash took a seat at the table. His daughter ran over and stood between his legs.

Ebony turned to look at him. "You need to get out them streets. That's a start."

"I'm not in the streets, the streets in me," he replied, and that got him a mean eye roll from her, which made him smile. He kissed the top of his daughter's head. He knew Ebony wanted nothing but the best for him, and that was cool. But at the same time, Ebony knew what she was dealing with when they first met. He understood she'd chosen her path for herself but he couldn't let her create his journey because if so he'd end up being the police and that's not good.

Ebony only shook her head. Then she walked off, back to the stove, leaving him to play with his kids. Kash knew she was mad but he never cared about how nobody felt. He always did what pleased him and people had to deal with it, or not. He stayed over and ate dinner with them. He helped bathe the kids and put them in the bed.

Kash read them a bedtime story while Ebony watched from the corner of the room, adoring the sight of him being a father to his kids. This was the side of him she loved. She always wanted to see him like this. Kash left around 8:30 because the airport was closer to her house. The Feds kept a tail on him the entire time and were able to get pictures of him and Chavez getting on a G4 flight.

Chapter 24

Old National Highway was crowded out tonight. The whole strip was packed with a slew of different flavored people. Every club on Old National was popping. Every open parking lot was packed and crunk. Music blasted from hooked up cars on big rims and females killed the scene from all angles, sizes, and shapes.

Poonie rode shotgun in a white Range Rover with heavy tint. Two shooters rode up front, both strapped and ready to bust if need be. They were some young niggas out the Bluff, Simpson Road. Poonie had grown to like them both in the months' time they'd been appointed by Monkey to ride with him everywhere he went. They had yet to prove themselves, but they were some cool young niggas who be wilding the fuck out.

"Pull up at the plaza over there," Poonie told Red Nose, who was driving. The plaza had a host of cars posted as the Range pulled in and cruised down through the crowd. Poonie, sitting up in his seat, saw who he expected to be right there. "Slow down too."

Poonie rolled down the window. He had his eyes locked on this honey colored female with jeans on that fit her near perfect body. She stared at him a moment. The girl was amazingly beautiful with a body to kill for. Her long hair flowed down her back, it was reddish brown.

"Hey, didn't think you would show up," she said leaning into the window, smelling like fresh fruit and looking like something he could eat.

"What's up, bae? You know I'ma pull up on you. Get in. I got something for you." Poonie opened the door and slid over. The girl looked back over her shoulder to her three friends.

"I'm not going nowhere," she said and got in with Poonie.

"You looking good, bae." Poonie he gave her a small box. The girl smiled and took it. He'd always surprised her with gifts since they started talking. He did it to stunt on her peers. Plus, she was bad so she deserved it. Her name was Tootie. She was nineteen. Poonie was a lot older than her, but he didn't care because she was his side chick. She was his lil' baby, that's what he called her. She opened the box to find a Michel Kors watch with diamonds in its front.

"Happy b-day, baby girl."

"Thanks, daddy," Tootie leaned over and they shared a kiss. Poonie also passed her a few grand for her pockets.

"Go enjoy yourself. I got some business to handle, but it's me and you tonight after you done turning up. You know I'm tryna bust this." Poonie reached between her legs and touched her pussy print.

"Around three, bae, I'll be ready. Are you picking me up or you gonna come to my spot?" Tootie asked

"I'ma come scoop you up." he kissed her again and she gave him the okay. He watched her get out of the truck, showing off her birthday gift from him.

The Range pulled off. Poonie peeped how her friends jocked the whip and those in it. He smiled and sat back, loving life and how this position fell in his lap. He'd never dreamed of the kind of money he was getting now, and his job was easy all around the table. The only thing he did was pick up the money from everyone all throughout the day and take it to one place to be counted.

Poonie had everything he wanted, cars, clothes, and a banging crib. He also had a spot he cooled it at, where he took his side hoes to fuck when he was not in somebody's hotel room. Overall, he stayed under his baby's mother, Nikki, because if she found out he was creeping, she'd end up in somebody's jail cell and he knew it. Plus, family was more important than any fling.

He was happy to be able to care for his kids because all their short lives, he'd hardly been able to take care of them due to him being in and out of jail, plus being on powder was bad too. He was glad he gave that high up cause it was sho taking him down under.

They rode down Old National. Poonie had to make two pickups. He met Juice at her shop where she gave him 150k in one book bag. He went down the street to meet Man-Man for another pickup that went smooth.

As bad as Poonie wanted to play, as bad as he wanted to hang out tonight, he knew one of Kash's main rules was to get his money safe and then do whatever else you want to do. He felt like if a nigga couldn't do that, then it was like saying fuck him, and that he would not tolerate at all. Poonie wasn't trying to mess up his money train, so he told his driver to take him to Hollywood Road, a count spot they had on gun club. Poonie's phone started ringing crazy. He looked and saw that it was Nikki calling.

"Hello?"

"Poonie, you need to get over here and calm Zay down. Him and this girl is going at it. They done damn near trashed the house. You know she pregnant and shit. Then Zay ass can barely move. His ass so mad though that he walking 'round without his crutches," Nikki rambled off.

"Wait, did Zay hit her?" Poonie asked.

"Nawl, but he done hit everything else," Nikki shot back.

"I'll be there in a few."

"You need to come now. This can't be put off, baby," she wouldn't give in.

"Okay, give me fifteen minutes." Poonie wouldn't stop his mission just to run to Terry's rescue. He didn't want her stressed, but he wasn't thinking about no relationship shit right now. Poonie wished Nikki would've left him out of it, but that was his girl and that was what she did. He knew that he could talk some sense into Zay, being that they all grew up together.

He made it to Hollywood Road safely, and put the money up. The set up was well put together with six niggas on post twenty-four seven, all of them strapped with choppers. Once Poonie was free from that mission, he had to complete this situation with terry and Zay. Then it was back to Old National he'd go because the night was just beginning and he was ready to get in his groove of things, and most definitely was ready to fuck Tootie tonight.

When he made it to Terry's house, the police were there. Things had gotten out of hand. Zay was in the back of the police car. Police had Terry sitting on the porch. Poonie smoothly got out of the Range Rover. He was strapped but left his gun inside the vehicle. He motioned with his head for his shooters to get out as well.

"What's going on?" Poonie asked his pregnant baby's mother. Nikki was two months pregnant, with three kids already, all by Poonie. they shared a quick kiss and hug.

"Oh, they started picking up weapons," Nikki said, and saw Roxanne had showed up also.

Poonie acknowledge her and kept it pushing towards Zay, where he was cuffed from behind, looking at Poonie through the glass. He had a hateful look upon his face, shaking his head side to side.

"Say officer, can I holla at my brother?" Poonie asked the policeman that stood guard. The officer cracked open the door.

"Man, Terry tripping, bruh," Zay said. His mouth was busted.

"What's up with y'all two?" Poonie laughed, leaning down to get another look at Zay, which made him smile hard and laugh longer.

"She doing too much, bruh, she just doing the most." Zay shook his head. he couldn't really talk and Poonie caught on so he turned back to the police.

"Y'all bout to lock him up?"

"I don't think so. They both just need to calm down," the officer said, looking from Zay to Terry.

Poonie agreed. "You right," replied Poonie. He then walked over to Terry, who was surrounded by police officers. One female officer talked to Terry, also attempting to get Terry to calm down.

Poonie walked over. He hugged Terry and kissed the side of her face.

"What's up, fat girl?" Poonie couldn't help but to be nervous. It was too many police around for him. Terry saw that he wanted to talk. He gave her that look and walked away. She decided to calm her nerves because neither Zay nor Terry wanted to go to jail tonight.

Police said if the both of them calmed down, then they would not lock him up, but he had to leave. Terry told them he was on bed rest and that he couldn't really leave the house, and it was clear she was having a baby soon so she most definitely couldn't be out and about. The debate only lasted five minutes top, with the police on their side. They agreed to leave the family with threats that if they were called again, the both of them are going to jail.

"What's going on, bruh?" Poonie asked Zay once the police left. Terry was in her room packing her and Keshana's bags.

"Man, shawty tripping. She stepping to Kash. You know me and bruh slick beefin' so she went and made a deal with this Nigga, bruh, when I told her to stay…"

"He was gone kill yo ass. You see the boy ain't playing."

Terry walked into the room they were in and walked back out, rolling her eyes.

"Bitch, that nigga ain't talking 'bout nan," Zay shouted to her back, then turned back to Poonie. "This bitch think I'm 'bout to pay this nigga Kash. She crazy as fuck."

"What da hell y'all beefin' bout, bro?" Poonie couldn't help but ask.

"Long story short, he stressing a nigga disloyal to Gangsta. But Kash don't even know what's going on, bruh. He just wanna do all the talking. Really and truly, the nigga getting beside himself," Zay said back.

Terry walked back into the room. She looked at Poonie.

"This nigga just want two hundred fifty grand for Gangsta. Shit, that's the least you can do nigga…"

"I'ma send bruh money on my time. I know how I wanna do my shit," Zay raised his voice, cutting her off.

"What's two hundred fifty grand to all the millions you got? Two fifty to kill a problem that you know you don't want," Terry shot back.

"Bitch, fuck you."

"You a fuck nigga, Zay. Bitch, bye," Terry stated. Her words had to hit a nerve because Zay lunged towards her, but Poonie stopped him.

"Let him go Poonie. Let him put his fuckin' hands on me. I bet his ass die."

Tears threatened to fall from her eyes. Poonie wouldn't let him go so Terry walked off. She was leaving Zay. If he wanted to be stupid, then that was on him. She wouldn't sit around and be killed by him and his choices. Zay was rich and that little money wouldn't even faze him. He had plenty money so Terry didn't understand why he couldn't just kill the problem.

Poonie and Zay ended up riding to Old National. It was Zay's first time out in a long time and it would be a night to remember.

Chapter 25

"Com'ere Tootie," Dontay said from his crowd of homeboys and girls. They were walking through the parking lot. He was a member of GF. He was one of their main hit men. He was wild and everyone knew it. Tootie was his girlfriend, and everybody knew that also. She was one person he didn't play about. He was crazy over her and didn't give a fuck who liked it. None of her friends liked Dontay because he had control over Tootie and she stayed in denial. Tootie excused herself from her friends.

"Hey, boo, what's up?" she asked Dontay as he looked her up and down, checking out her expensive outfit Poonie had gotten for her that he knew nothing of.

"What's up with you? Happy b-day." Dontay hugged her, kissing her jaw.

"Nothing, about to go in the club in a few," Tootie said. She kinda was uncomfortable for two reasons. One was that her brother didn't like Dontay and her brother was somewhere on Old National, and two, Dontay didn't know nothing about Poonie. She would surely regret the day he found out about him and tonight wasn't the night she wanted it to happen on, not on her birthday, hell no.

"How long you plan on staying out tonight? I hope you don't think you finna pull an all-night flight."

"No, I'm not. For your info, I'm only going to this club, then to the waffle house." Tootie's friends loved when she lied to Dontay. They were the ones who encouraged her to start talking to Poonie.

"Girl, he a made man," they would say. But little did they know.

"You need someone like Poonie. He's your security," they added all the time.

"You got one when you got Poonie," all three of her friends told her on different occasions, and eventually Tootie fell for it and started talking to Poonie, only on the friend level. Then Poonie started spoiling her with attention and gifts while Dontay gave her drama and rough sex. She still hadn't had sex with Poonie in the three months they'd been sneaking around. He knew about Dontay, but Dontay didn't know 'bout him. Dontay hugged her again and passed her a birthday present.

"You betta call me when you leave this club. Hell, I might be in the parking lot when you done anyway, just make sure you call," Dontay demanded like he always did. Then he walked off with a group of lil' niggas willing to do whatever to prove their Gangsta.

"I will," replied Tootie, walking away. Tootie knew she had to go inside the club fast and get lost because Poonie was sure to show up on the strip.

"I don't see how you still under his command," one of her friends said as they all walked towards the club and a long line of people. VIP wasn't a problem as long as she had Poonie with her. But tonight she would have to stand in this long ass line if she wanted to save the money she got. Tootie paid for five VIP passes to go directly in the club. It was her b-day so fuck it, she thought as the music vibrated her body.

***

Zay and Poonie pulled into the Ritz parking lot. The crowd had become aggressive and didn't want to clear the way for the Rover to ease through. The horn blew as the truck inched up more. A dude just stood there like he had some issues. He was mean-mugging and then stepped out the way as the Range pulled fully into the parking lot.

"Fuck wrong with that nigga?" Poonie said.

"Ion know, but he can get it though," one of the shooters said while looking for a place to park.

"I'll bust dat lil' baby up," the other shooter finally spoke. He mug the dude who wore tatts between his eyes and around his lips.

"Fuck them niggas," Poonie spoke. He had his mind on Tootie and how he was gonna eat her out from sun down to up and down again. He was so ready to get the pussy, some pussy he'd never had the privilege to touch the few months that they had been together.

The line was long, Poonie noticed. He pulled out his phone and sent Tootie a text. "Which club you in?"

He got a reply back moments later. "Ritz."

Poonie walked in behind a limping Zay and paid for VIP seating, and also purchased the bar, just to stunt for Tootie, who watched him put on, throwing away money like it grew on trees. Only for a minute did Poonie stay away, he was up on her first chance he got, all in her ear talking numbers, a future, and spoiling her until he could no more.

True enough, Poonie loved his baby's mother, Nikki, and loved his kids, but Nikki had lost the flavor he sought. She wasn't young anymore. She wasn't stacked like she used to be. Tootie she was well put together. She was fine as fuck, Fat booty and pretty face. She didn't have kids. She was smart and striving to be something, where Nikki had three kids and counting and didn't have a job at all. Whereas, Tootie worked a twelve hour shift. Poonie didn't have plans on leaving Nikki because that would end up ugly, but he most definitely was trying to lock Tootie in as his side piece.

***

Dontay linked up with Meco and Don Kill Sum outside the club. Tonight was the night the mob celebrated one of their brothers been released from prison. GF was out deep tonight, crunk and drunk at the same time. Meco was feeling all the love he got, and most definitely appreciated Kash for stunting for him today.

Kash being the plug was the last thing Meco thought, but it was real because money talked and bullshit walked a thousand miles.

Kash gave him two guns and a hundred grand to get started with. That was a blessing unlike any he'd had. Plus, Kash was the plug, telling Meco to lock his hood down because he'd provide the product. It was simple and easy to do such things, he just needed his brothers to be on the same page as he was because lately they had been wilding out in the streets, not getting no real money but causing all kind of beef.

Meco also made Don Kill Sum his right hand because Don had almost lost his mind when his sons got killed in a house bombing. Meco knew this was one of the ways to calm Don down because he was killing niggas left and right for nothing. He'd just snap out of nowhere and Meco wasn't with that because most times he was with him when he got to showing out.

They all stepped into the club twenty deep. Everyone wore black shirts with GF written across the front. VIP was already paid so the mob took over their section. Hoes flocked from all over the club when the DJ announced that Meco was out after doing ten years and was back in town. The statement made a group of blood members from Etheridge walk over. Some of the GF members grilled them as they approached, but Meco, on the other hand, smiled at one blood in particular.

"I am my brother's keeper." Both Meco and Block hugged each other tight.

"What's up, nigga?" Meco said, elated to see his childhood friend.

"Had to come out and rep with my nigga," Block passed him a tall bottle of Hen. It was Meco's favorite drink as far as Block could remember.

"Man, we just mobbin' easy."

"Well I'm over in the cut, bruh, go head and enjoy yourself, my nigga. We'll link up later," Block gave him pound.

"Say less, Foo," Meco replied and turned the bottle up, taking a big swig of the drink. The strong burn in his chest made Meco's eyes shut tight. He shook his head side to side and held the bottle up, looking at it. A group of girls were passing through. Meco noticed as his mob brother grab one of the baddest.

"Com'ere." Dontay pulled the girl away from her friends.

Meco could see him checking her about some issues. He couldn't understand what was being said but knew it wasn't pleasant because the girl tried to walk off and Dontay snatched at her arm. She snatched back wildly. then Meco and Don Kill Sum moved in to stop whatever it was that was about to pop off. Meco took Dontay around the neck.

"Come on, bruh, don't mess a Don's day up 'bout no pussy."

"Dat hoe trying me, bruh." Dontay was heated looking back at her over his shoulder while Meco pulled him away.

"Get out your feelings, Don. Let a Hoe be a hoe, my nigga. We can never change that, ya feel me?" Meco stated.

"I feel you, Don. You right, bruh, fuck that hoe." Dontay allowed his brother to pull him away.

"Yeah, lil' nigga, we finna be straight. Don, I'm out here now and shit already moving in the mob favor. What I need for you to do is be my eyes, be my ears while I stamp the city Good Fellas," Meco said, giving Dontay the bottle of Hen. It was the worst mistake he could've made, giving Dontay some liquor while he was already geeked on pills and in an emotional state. Meco didn't know how possessive his lil' partner was over that girl. He didn't know Dontay was as insecure as he was, and on GoGo because it was how he was. All Meco knew was that Dontay was on GoGo because it was how he was raised. All that other shit Meco was blind to, but soon he would find out.

Jerry Jackson

Chapter 26

Poonie saw, from a distance, his girl and a group of niggas in an altercation. He wanted to but didn't move because he wanted to see how Tootie would handle it and, to his surprise, she handled it right, just walking away from the dudes. Poonie waited a minute before he sent his shooter to go get her. Tootie walked over, minutes later, with a disturbed look on her face. He could tell she was aggravated, her whole mood had changed. Her three friends followed.

"Hey," she spoke once she stopped in front of him sitting on the sofa.

Poonie moved to the side and patted the seat. "Sit down. Let me holla at you." he pulled her arm. "Y'all come on over too, it's all love. Her friends, our friends, ain't that right y'all?" Poonie told the other girls, but asked his two shooters who replied in unison.

"We all friends."

"What's up?" Tootie sat next to him. She carefully looked out at the crowd of people. She was praying Dontay didn't catch her over there. She knew she was playing with fire so she had to be quick.

"What's wrong with you?"

"Nothing."

"Who was that nigga?" Poonie asked

"Nobody."

"Don't lie to me, Tootie. Why he snatched on you like that?" Poonie was asking her low in her ear because he didn't want anyone around them to hear what he was saying to her. Tootie was uncomfortable and he knew it.

"That's Dontay. Okay?" She rolled her eyes. "I used to talk to him."

"Use to, or still do?" Poonie questioned.

"I told you that I had a lil' friend anyway, when we first met. You acted like it was alright but now…"

"I'm saying, you just said use to talk to or still fucking with, 'cause from what it look like to me, you still talking to that nigga." Poonie wasn't liking this at all.

"I talk to you more. I mean, he know things are different with us so ion know. Poonie, I gotta go. I'm leaving this club. It's too much drama in her tonight. It's my birthday, I don't got no business stressing," Tootie said and was about to get up, but his hand on her thigh stopped her.

"So it's me and you strong, right? He dead, right?"

Tootie stood up. She had to get away from both these niggas. "Yes, it's us. We need to talk, though. I'll hit you once I get to where I'm going."

"We got a date still, right? I got the suite and all at the Double Tree."

"Yup, I'll call you," Tootie replied and quickly got out of the VIP section with Poonie all in her ear. Her three best friends made an exit.

"Bitch," Tootie heard. But she didn't see him, just felt a sharp pain to the side of her face as Dontay back-handed her outside the club. He was waiting on her when he saw how she let some nigga drool all in her ear. Tootie would've hit the ground if one of Dontay's brothers wouldn't have caught her fall.

"Whoa, whoa, lil' homie." somebody grabbed Dontay but by then it was on and popping. All three of Tootie's friends went at Dontay. Tootie got her feet right and with a busted nose, she also pounded and pounced on Dontay. The bouncer ran in to break up the fight ass the girls fought four mob members.

All the commotion made people peek out the club. Some decided to leave the spot and to witness the madness in the parking lot. Poonie and Zay were amongst those that came out, and what they witnessed instantly made Poonie mad. He saw Tootie and her friends being held back by the bouncers of the club and other people, and a group of niggas being held by other niggas. One of them was the guy from earlier in the club. Poonie and lock eyes with him and the dude spit at him.

"What the fuck mobbin' nigga, fuck you stalking?" Dontay said towards Poonie.

"Come on, young nigga, let's dip," Meco pulled his brother who was doing too much.

"Shawty, you don't want none," Poonie quickly looked Dontay up and down. Then he turned his attention to Tootie. "Bae, what's up? You straight..."

"Bae? Bae? Nigga..." Dontay tried to break loose from Meco but Don Kill Sum held him also. Poonie turned around back towards Dontay. He saw that he'd struck a nerve.

"What's up, nigga?" Poonie said, getting aggressive.

"Fuck nigga, what's up? What you wanna do? Let's bust some," Dontay yelled while he struggled to break free of being held back by his brothers.

"Let that nigga go," Poonie shouted. More security rushed up to stop what was about to start.

"Guns up, pussy nigga," Dontay yelled. His face turned hard. He was too mad.

Poonie he walked away from the bouncers. He, Zay, and his two shooters walked to the ride. He saw the GF nigga go in the opposite direction. Then he looked around for Tootie, but he didn't see her. So he climbed in and called her phone it rang a few times before she answered up in a frustrated tone.

"Hello."

"Baby where you at? "

"Why did you do that, Poonie? Why? Was that called for?" she questioned. He could hear the tears in her voice. He could feel the vibes in her voice.

"It slipped. I just seen yo motherfucking mouth busted and I couldn't help it. Baby, fuck that nigga. I can protect you. He ain't talking 'bout shit. He just a lil' boy that don't know nothing," Poonie told her.

The ride pulled into traffic as Poonie sat in the back seat talking. He wasn't worried 'bout no lil' kid. He was more worried about her wellbeing rather than that fake ass gangsta shit her lil' boyfriend was kicking. Poonie knew he could be better, do better, and perform better than lil' dude.

"You don't pose to do that, Poonie, for real, for real," she said.

"Where you at? I'm 'bout to pull up."

"No, you not. I don't want to see you right now, I swear," she cried hard.

"Man, ba…"

Poonie's words came to an end when the car was riddled with bullets from a semi-automatic weapon. Lil' Dontay hung out the sunroof while Don Kill Sum hung out the window.

Tat. Tat. Tat. Tat. Tat. Tat. Tat. Tat. Tat. Tat. Boom. Boom. Boom. Boom. Boom.

Instantly, the passenger got hit. Then Zay was chopped up and Poonie, but he managed to open the door and fall out. The driver also climbed out, unhit by the bullets. He aimed his Gloc and let off in the van the mob nigga was driving. They pulled off, but the shooter emptied his clip.

"Oh sit, boy, call the cops." Poonie looked and saw that he was hit in the stomach, his guts hung out. He got dizzy, just lying on the ground, losing too much blood. People screamed, cars stopped, and people ran. Poonie started to panic when he looked inside the car and saw Zay crunched over with blood leaking out his head, dead. It seemed like forever for the cops to arrive and when they did, Poonie had done passed out from the loss of too much blood.

Veedo was in the bed sleep when he kept constantly hearing his phone vibrate. His eyes quickly shot open because nobody called his line at this time of the morning if it was not an emergency.

"Yeah." Veedo picked up. He looked at the clock. It was 3:50am.

"Dem boys Poonie and Zay just got murked on the Nat." the Nat meant Old National. "Them GF niggas. Meco in the clear though. Bruh tried to stop them niggas," Block said.

"Huh? What? What happened?" Veedo sat up in bed. Trish was sound asleep.

"Zay and Poonie just got whacked at the red light. They got into it with some GF niggas 'bout a bitch. Shit led outside. Everyone went their separate ways. Then the next thing you know, it's gunshots up the street. The GF niggas got caught red handed though. They killed three of your people. One Nigga got away before the police got there," Block said.

By now Veedo had gotten fully up out the bed. He looked back at Trish to see if she was still was asleep, and she was.

"Whea you?"

"Shid, I'm back in the Ridge, what's up?"

"I might need cha. Lemme make a few calls. I'ma hit you back in a second," Veedo said and disconnected the phone call.

He hit Monkey, who wouldn't pick up. He knew Kash was with the plug so he didn't bother to hit his line. Veedo quickly got dressed because this shit didn't even seem right.

Trish was still asleep, or so Veedo thought as he snuck to his walk-in closet to retrieve his only gun in the house. He put it on his hip and smoothly left his room and Trish sleeping in bed.

Last night they made love for the second night in a row and it was even better that time, and longer. Last night Veedo took his time and pleased her. She returned every favor as well. They made love until they both passed out. Now that call all of a sudden got him out of his bed and in his Benz headed to meet Block. What did Poonie and Zay have going on? Veedo's mind clicked. He pulled the phone out and scrolled his contacts until he found Juice's number, who picked up on the second ring.

"What's up, V?"

"What da fuck happened out there?" he jumped on the highway headed to the west side of Atlanta.

"Man, apparently Poonie got into with Rico and Dontay 'bout some lil' chicken-head and one thing led to another. Zay was just caught up in the midst of shit. Police all on the Nat. But they got Rico and Dontay in custody," Juice said.

"Damn, that's what's up. And they both slumped?"

"Hell yeah, V. its three bodies been laying under sheets the past two hours."

"Okay, cool. I'll fuck with you later." Veedo shook his head at the notion of what was going on. He wondered what the fuck happened. Monkey needed to wake the fuck up. Veedo called him two more times and then decided to go over to Monkey's crib instead of meeting Block.

"Fuck this," Veedo thought, and changed lanes to get off the highway and head back the other way.

Chapter 27

Trish opened her eyes when she was sure he had left. This was her only chance to snoop around his crib in hopes she didn't find nothing that could land him in jail. She slid out the bed naked, in only his long t-shirt. The first place she went was to his closet to search for a safe, but found nothing but fashion of all sorts.

She checked his bed and under it, and then started searching the walls for a hidden safe, like any drug dealer would do. Trish rubbed her hand smoothly across the wall, tracing picture frames and all. That's when she saw the wire, a painted wire camouflaged to the wall. She followed it to his walk-in closet, where it disappeared behind a shoe shelf. Trish pulled at it and it gave a little. She pulled harder and it gave more. She pulled the entire section out to find a video monitor that was actually going as she looked. It had to been running nine hours. Trish counted back in her head.

"Fuck," she shouted because she'd been there nine hours on the head. She quickly came back out the closet. She followed the wire until she found the eye that watched her. She eventually found six in his room. Tears crept into her eyes at the thought of what had happened. Trish pressed stop on the monitor. She ejected the disc and then pushed it back in.

Her heart beat rapidly in her chest, hoping she wouldn't see what she knew she would see. The video started and it crushed her from the moment she saw herself walking into his home. Trish fast forward to the scene of them having sex and her whole world was crushed. She wondered why. She thought all his love and affection for her was real. Tears fell from her eyes at thoughts of the first time they had sex.

She thought about how he played her for a sucker. She instantly started looking for the other disc that had to be around. She looked top to bottom in his house, but found nothing. Trish went back to the monitor and erased the entire disc, then put everything back how she had found it. She couldn't help feeling crushed as she sat on the bed in his room. It was 5:30 by the time she decided to leave, heartbroken because her hope was that he was pure in intentions, but she was fooled again.

She finally was able to make it to her car without destroying his home and expensive furniture. She had gained a hate for him now, and decided that everything he said out his mouth was a lie. He was going down, and she would make sure of it. But first things first, she had to clean up her tracks. She would have to get around anything personal that could be said. Trish let more tears fall from her eyes, the more she thought of Veedo not being the man she wished him to be.

Chapter 28

Kash, Loco, and Chavez all entered the abandoned warehouse to find both the strippers who set him and Jeter up. There were two more niggas. All four of them were tied and duct taped to the chairs. a few Mexicans stood round holding weapons.

"My friend, so these are the guys who had nuts enough to come at the cartel and, better yet, shoot my son down like a dirty dog in the streets," Chavez said as he pointed. "And these two females, they were stupid enough to let these guys trick them into playing a part in this ordeal."

Chavez pulled up his sleeves up on his gloved hands. He calmly walked over to the four of them, the two dudes and two girls. As Kash and Loco watched, Chavez grabbed one of the girls around her throat. He started choking her with one hand. The girl kicked out but couldn't move because duct tape held her bound. With his free hand, Chavez stuck his thumb into the socket of the girl's eye, pushing her eye ball completely in and smashing it at the same time he choked her. She shook violently a moment or two and then life left her. Chavez pulled his finger out of her eye socket and looked at it drenched in blood.

"I am the reason you should work hard and earn your money instead of taking from the one who grinds."

Chavez went to one of the dudes. With both hands, he grabbed the dude's head, and with one hard twist, he broke the guy's neck. He kept turning the head until it was backwards. Kash and Loco just watched as Chavez went into maniac mode. Before Chavez could get to his next victim, they all heard a loud bang. Then the smoke bombs were thrown.

"FBI, freeze, don't move."

Gunfire erupted from the Mexicans as federal agents poured into the warehouse, ducking behind whatever to dodge the bullets. The first couple agents got hit as Loco, Chavez, and Kash also pulled out their guns and started busting their shots and moving to the back, away from the agents. But they didn't know that more agents and swat was in the back also.

The first shot hit Kash in the back of his thigh as he backed up, shooting at any cop he saw. He winced in pain and turned around to aim but got struck again, two times in the stomach. Chavez snatched Kash, pulling him to cover and shooting his gun towards the Feds. The cartel of Mexicans had the first load of Federal agents at bay, hiding behind things not to get hit by the spray of bullets. Kash was losing breath as he reloaded his clip.

"Hold on, wait, hold on," Loco said, looking down at Kash. He looked around and then pointed to the exit door to their left.

"The door." Chavez was the first to make it to the side door. With one massive kick, it flew open and he went out of it, fully prepared to gun down any police in his way. Loco helped Kash to his feet. They both shot at the Feds together, going out the side door.

"Come on," Kash heard Loco say as they made it out the door. Then a spray of bullets tackled Kash to the ground, knocking him out the door. Lying flat on his back, all he remembered was Chavez telling Loco to pick him up. But as soon as Loco went to grab him, more Feds came around the corner in the alley and some poured out the door. As Chavez and Loco disappeared from the scene, Kash passed out.

Chapter 29

"God no. God no. God no." Terry cried her eyes out once Mr. Jackson called and told her the news of Poonie and Zay being killed. She was over Nene's house. It was all over the news. That morning when they all woke up they received the call. Nene and Eric both sat on either side of Terry as she rocked and cried, cried so hard that snot was coming out of her nose. Her entire face was beet red, her hair was a mess.

"It's gonna be okay. It's gonna be alright." Eric tried to convince her that things weren't as bad as they really were. In Terry's mind, it was Kash who had who had Zay killed. It had to be. Zay didn't have no issues with nobody but him. She was hateful towards Kash. The way she was feeling right now, she could get on the stand on his ass.

"God no," was all Terry said as kept rocking back and forth. She was devastated of her loss. She couldn't believe it. Zay probably went to confront Kash and had gotten himself killed.

"Terry, come on, girl. We gotta stay strong. You gotta go meet Zay's mom, don't you? "

"Yes, but girl I can't deal with them right now," Terry cried, shaking her head.

Nene hugged her again, but this time harder than before. She was feeling the pain of Terry's loss. She understood exactly how Terry must feel. Why did so much violence come to them? Nene wondered time and time again. She wasn't understanding Kash and what he'd created of himself. Nene didn't know what happened or why, but she felt Kash was behind all of this drama.

"Come on, let's get these kids up." Erica turned the TV off when the news went to the weather of the day. The girls all got the kids up and dressed to leave and meet up with Zay's mother at the police station. When they arrived, Nikki was there. She took Poonie death very hard. The police had to get her medical attention because she passed out and was pregnant. Roxanne was there as support. She was the one who told Terry what really went down last night on Old National.

"Girl, it was some GF niggas. They was trying to rob Poonie and Zay." Roxanne only told them what she had heard.

Zay's mother was being held by one of the detectives in the case as she cried, rocking back and forth.

"GF?" Terry asked, confused. She looked at Roxanne for understanding. What did someone wanna rob Zay for? He didn't floss his wealth. It had to be Kash behind this, and now he was trying to make it out like it was someone else doing this shit. She hated Kash.

"Yeah, Dontay and some other dude. They both on Rice Street," Roxanne said while reading a text message in her phone.

All kinds of people were calling and texting about Zay and Poonie being killed. Terry still couldn't believe it. She shook her head side to side, still in denial of what she was hearing. More people started walking into the police station. Poonie's folks and more of Zay's people. Terry was questioned about Zay and his friends, then she was allowed to leave with Nene and Erica.

Mrs. Jackson was outside waiting on them. She hugged Terry. "Baby, call me if you need anything, and stop all that crying. You know you have that baby inside you," Gangsta's mother said. She then hugged her grandkids.

"Yes, ma'am," replied Terry, tears still in her eyes.

"Nene and Erica, y'all care for her, okay?"

"We will," Erica said while moving a strand of hair out of Terry's face that got caught by her tears.

"Okay, that's good, and y'all call me, okay?"

***

Kash was in ICU at a Miami hospital, being helped by the machine. His room was guarded by two federal agents. He had survived eleven shots. He was blessed. His body was banged up and he was weak. He was woke but couldn't move. He was strapped down to the bed. His body was really weak from being cut open for surgery. All Kash could do was think.

He was thinking about how he would get out this mess. How could he beat this case? The Feds must have been following Chavez and Loco to know they were at the warehouse, and it had to be a bust because it was too many of them to count. Kash remembered hearing the loud bang. Then he heard the Feds. He heard gunshots, and when he saw that Loco and Chavez started dumping at the cop's, he followed their lead.

It wasn't something he wanted to do, but it was something that had to be done. Kash knew that it was over when he got hit in the stomach by two slugs. he felt his defeat but he was willing to shoot to his death. Now he was stuck. Now he was down bad, cuffed to a hospital bed with tubes running out of him. What could he possibly do? Who could he possibly call? Kash wasn't ready to see another jail cell. It had only been some months and already he was on the way back. But this time, he was going to the big boys' playground.

Kash's heart dropped when he thought about how he failed Gangsta. He felt bad because he knew his brother would be disappointed at him. Gangsta sacrificed too much for Kash to take it all down the drains. He thought about his kids and how sad they would be. He thought about Ebony and the talk they had before he left her at the kitchen table. Kash thought about his mother, his father, and how happy his mother was to know he was doing okay and that he was trying to start a business. Kash felt defeated. He wanted so badly to sneak out of the hospital, but he was too weak to move.

Jerry Jackson

Chapter 30

Trish landed in Miami at 5:30 pm the day after the warehouse shooting. She was still torn up by the fact of Veedo videotaping her, but her job called for her to be there. She was shocked to hear that Chavez and the agents had a gun battle that left four Mexicans dead, six shot, and eight federal agents wounded from bullets. She could not believe Chavez and his son were able to get away when they raided, but they did. And now here she was leaving the airport, headed down to the hospital to interview the Mexican and Charles McCants aka Kash, a man she'd seen with Veedo a few different times. She knew he was a piece to the puzzle. She saw it in his face.

She thought about Veedo and wished they had never met. She still wasn't able to confront him about the disc but she was sure he knew something was up. She knew that it was very likely Veedo was still a drug dealer, she just held hope that her gut feeling told her wrong this one time.

She was just shocked to know he'd been recording her, and worse, while doing the nasty. She felt so disrespected and dirty because she trusted him to be that man he portrayed himself to be and it hurt deeply to see that mask come off his face. But what was done was done as her best friend, Brit, said. Trish just wanted to run home to Augusta GA and hide in her mother's embrace. She wanted to hide her and her heart deep in the confines of her mother's love because she was for certain that woman would never hurt her, never trick her.

As Trish was riding to the hospital with a few agents, she heard over the radio that all federal agents, local police, and state troopers were to report to the hospital. There was a gun war going down.

"Oh my God," Trish said as the Tahoe roared a little faster down the highway. She wondered what was going on. She wasn't even dressed for war. She had in tactical clothes, no vest, no nothing. All she had was her gun and ID because she was only on an interrogation assignment. Nervous wasn't the word, she was scared shitless. She could only imagine what was going on at the hospital. The government was dealing with the Mexican cartel so there was no telling what was going on. All Trish knew was to be prepared for the outcome.

***

Kash saw the red beams bouncing off his wall, coming through the window. He wanted to duck for cover. He couldn't take another slug right now if he wanted to. After he saw the beams, all the power shut down making the hospital floor pitch black dark for ten seconds until the generator came on. But then there was a scream and Kash heard gunshots. Kash watched as both the federal agents were gunned down by some Mexicans posing as ninjas, wearing all black, black masks covering their entire face. Two of them entered the room, then two more entered pushing a wheel chair and holding a doctor with a gun to his head.

"Make sure he lives for the next twenty minutes, my friend."

Kash and Longo made eye contact as the other ones rushed to uncuff and unstrap him. Kash was helped up. He was drugged up as well so he couldn't find his balance as he tried to fully stand. The staples in his stomach caused him to be hunched over in pain, but the pain had him numb.

He was placed in the chair, rushed out of the room, and down the hall. It was commotion all over the hospital floor. A whole lot of Mexicans were standing guard, ready to die or to kill something. They took the elevator to the ground floor and quickly made it to the ambulance. It was the perfect getaway. Once Kash was placed in the back, the ambulance pulled off into traffic with the sirens blaring. The Feds and police was just pulling up, jumping out and running into the hospital, not knowing Kash was gone. No matter how many gunshots he heard or how many people screamed and shouted, the morphine was taking control of his body. Minutes into the ride, Kash fell into a deep sleep.

Jerry Jackson

Chapter 31

Veedo was still in the streets trying to figure out what was up. Meco was at Walmart with his kids when Veedo and Monkey wanted to meet. Meco wasted no time telling them to come on with it because he knew that they felt some type of way. Meco met them in the food section of Walmart. He had both his lil' girls with him.

"Man, what da fuck happened out there, bruh?" Veedo was the first to speak after they all took seats.

"Bruh, real shit, both then niggas was on some tender dick shit. All this shit is about a hoe, my nigga, a hoe that was playing both them niggas. Bruh, I tried and tried to stop that young nigga, get that nigga to fall back, but he wild and insecure, my nigga. So after the fight outside, I left everybody. I had to get home. A nigga just got out, I'm not with that bullshit," Meco explained the best he could.

"Damn, bruh, that's some fuck shit. All 'bout some pussy? And how did Zay get caught up?" asked Monkey.

"Who? The Nigga with the limp?" Meco didn't know Zay nor Poonie.

"Yeah."

"Man, he was coolin' he didn't even jump in it when the fight broke out. Ion know how he end up gettin' whacked."

"Word, he got hit two times in the head," added Veedo.

"Yeah, them young niggas pulled up on shawty nem at the red light with them sticks, which you already know what that toy do," he replied.

"Say less, bruh. You good, right? We just waiting on the wolf to get back so we can continue business 'cause right now shit is real," Monkey told Meco. Then he and Veedo left.

They'd already gotten the 411 from the only dude who didn't get touched, one of the shooters, and he'd told them exactly what Meco was saying. Veedo shook his head. Pussy made niggas go crazy. Three niggas dead behind one nigga's pussy. Veedo didn't understand niggas, he never would either.

He checked his phone and there was still no call from Trish. He guessed she was at work and too busy to talk or text. He hated the fact of leaving her in his bed like he did. Veedo had plans to get the pussy again early that morning and send her off. But this situation called for his attention. He was tired now and needed to shower and get in a power nap. He sent her a text.

"Baby I'm missing you. Hope all is well."

He pocketed the phone and headed to his house. The streets were off the chain and he really didn't have a reason to be in them. It was time to retire. Veedo constantly said it in his head, but he was loyal to Gangsta and he knew what Gangsta's plan was, so Veedo wanted to help who helped him.

He wanted out of that lifestyle though because Kash and them were younger than him. He'd played the street enough. It was time to be smart with the money. Veedo's kids needed more of him. His grandmother was getting old and he was getting no younger, so the time was now, rather than later, to get out the game. Veedo made it out to the crib and went inside. He walked to his bedroom, hoping he could see Trish laying there still waiting on him. But he knew that was only a fairy tale.

He knew because her car was gone. It wasn't in his driveway anymore and her purse wasn't on his sofa like when he left her. Veedo retired to his bedroom. He was about to lay back when he thought about the video tape that was still playing. He got back up, wondering if he would see Trish snooping around the house. He was pretty sure he would find her doing something she had no business doing.

Veedo entered his closet and went to his shoe rack. he pulled at it and removed the shelf. The monitor was off. Veedo powered it up and ejected the disc. He looked at it and pressed play, but nothing came up. Veedo pressed rewind and then play again to get the same thing.

"What da fuck," Veedo was baffled.

"I know I started this shit," he said to himself. Then he looked around his closet. He walked around his entire house to see if anything was out of place, but found nothing. He made it back to the monitor and tried it again. He pressed record and it started recording. He pressed play and it showed what he'd just recorded, which was just a few seconds. He put everything back in place and returned to his bed. He was confused and was thinking crazy.

Could it be that Trish found the monitor? Why did he up and just leave her in his shit when he knew she was the Feds? Veedo picked up his cell phone, still no call from her. He called her four times, back to back. Then he text her twice. Now he knew why she wasn't replying to his calls and text message. She had to have found out that he was recording her. Veedo looked around again. He looked at the wire on the wall, it was hidden good. He knew she didn't find that, she couldn't have, or could she? Veedo was baffled big time as he kept calling her phone.

***

Trish was down town Miami at the federal headquarters, piled with paperwork and more coming in. the Mexican cartel pulled off yet another one of their stunts when they entered the hospital, killing two agents and wounding three. Then they removed every one of their own men including Charles McCants.

The government did not give badges and pictures to the media because they did not want to show defeat to the world. They did not want to show people that the cartel was nearly impossible to nab. They worked hard to keep it under the rug because once the media got it, then it was on.

Trish's phone constantly rang and vibrated, text after text, all from Veedo. And as bad as she wanted to answer, she couldn't. If she could, she would. But she refused to do so around her coworkers and the loud chattering going on around the office.

"Call me ASAP!"

She read one of his many messages and replied, "At work in Miami. Will call you when I can." she sent the text, then put her phone back in her purse. She was still shocked and hurt by the video, and still wanted to know his reason. But she also missed him, and that was crazy. That was insane, she thought. She could not keep him off her mind, no matter how hard she tried. He'd just invade he thoughts.

"Ms. Williams, we have a witness."

Trish she looked up from the pile of paperwork to one of the agents standing in the doorway.

"He? She? Where are they?" Trish stood to her feet. She was ready to get away from all that damn paperwork. She was ready to do some talking and learning of what was going on and who was involved. So she followed Steve down the hall to an empty room where an old white woman sat at a table smoking cigarettes. Trish looked in at her and then back to Steve.

"Where did y'all find her?"

"She was one of the warehouse workers. She works for the cartel," Steve smiled.

"Oh my." Trish straighten her shirt. "Has anyone spoken to her? Got statements? Anything?" she asked, prepared to go inside and question the woman.

"Yeah, we have a verbal statement made at the scene. Called her in and she came, to our surprise," Steve shot back. He opened the door to allow Trish inside. This was the start of a big case. She planned to finish with victory under the government's belt. This was a case Trish wouldn't lose. She would convict everyone involved with the Mexican cartel, even if it was the one she loved and wanted to be with. Trish walked into the room with the lady. The room was stale of old cigarette smoke, which made Trish ball her face up as she pulled a chair out to take a seat.

"Hello, I'm federal agent Williams and your name is, ma'am?" she politely asked the woman.

"My name is Sandy and listen, lady, I need protection if I talk to you," the woman pulled another cigarette out, ready to put some fire to it, but Trish stopped her.

"Please don't. It's smoky enough in here. And it depends on what you tell me if I can get you witness protection."

"This is the fucking cartel, lady." The lady tossed the pack of cigarettes on the table.

"So what do you know about the cartel other than they're Mexican drug dealers?" Trish wanted to know.

"I know all about the cartel, honey. I been working for them for twenty years," the woman spoke confidently.

"So why are you willing to sell them out?"

"Cause they sold me out. I was loyal to those bastards but they drew first blood. I was too loyal, honey." The white woman picked the pack of cigarettes up off the table. She pulled one out and lit it up.

"I see. Well okay, tell me something. Have you ever met Chavez? Tell me something about him that you think I should know." Trish looked over at the woman.

"I know he owns the limo shop downtown. It's how he traffics his money and product."

Trish wrote down what the woman said and at the same time asked, "How do you know he's the owner?"

"I've been working for them twenty years, ma'am, believe me, I know all about Chavez and his family," the white lady replied as Trish kept notes. Then she finally looked up.

"How long have you been working in the warehouse?"

"Six years now," replied the woman. She put some fire to her cigarette, inhaled, and exhaled a cloud of smoke.

"Where else have you worked?" Trish kept writing on her note pad.

"His home in Riverdale and limo service, trust and believe if I say it, I mean it. I know what I'm talking 'bout."

"Okay, so tell me everything there is to know." Trish looked up from her pad.

"I need protection first."

"You got it. I can have that arranged for you," Trish replied and was all ears.

The white woman made a thirty-five minute verbal statement against Chavez, telling everything she knew from her first day until her last day. In between, she had smoked four more New Ports, almost killing Trish in the process.

Trish made sure to record everything the woman said and also write down main subjects. Things were looking even better for the government now that some of Chavez's secret had been exposed. The old white woman was given federal protection, being the government's first and only witness against the notorious Mexican drug lord.

Trish's phone kept ringing and vibrating text messages. She kept ignoring it because what Veedo wanted wasn't as important as the conviction of the Mexican cartel. So he would have to wait. Plus, Trish was still heartbroken by fact that he video recorded them. She couldn't trust him anymore, but she still loved him and what he could be. Trish returned back to the office to get her bag. She had a plane to catch back to Atlanta, and some drug dealers to put behind bars.

The Streets Bleed Murder 3

Chapter 32

His vision was blurred. The pain killer had his mind in a daze. It was like he was in a constant dream. It was like anything he thought of somehow turned into this dream so vivid that it felt like he was woke.

Chavez. Did he see his face? Loco was standing there too, both at a distant, watching as doctors worked over him. Kash couldn't move. He couldn't feel, but he saw and heard.

Then Chavez, Loco, and the doctors were gone and the room wasn't cold anymore. The room was warm and comfortable. It was a bedroom. He saw a TV mounted on the wall.

Ebony. He saw Ebony walk past him. She didn't look his way. She walked into another room. She was gone. Kash wanted to scream, but he couldn't say any words. He couldn't move. He couldn't get up. He could only watch, look, and see.

Sleep took over again. His eyes gave way and he was out.

***

Ebony walked into the bathroom to get towels and rags to clean the blood drops in her kitchen from when those Mexicans first got to her house bringing Kash inside on a hospital bed, hooked to all types of machines, shot up. Ebony knew what was going on already because he was on worldwide news on CNN, wanted dead or alive, when they got there with Kash glued down to a hospital bed, she didn't question them.

"I have doctors that's gone attend to him every day until he's well. When he wakes, give him my best regards," one Mexican told her. He spoke clear English to Ebony. None of her instincts kicked in. she forgot she was a homicide detective. All Ebony saw was that Kash was hurt and he was hurt bad.

"Okay, and your name?" Ebony asked.

"I'm Chavez ma'am." And he was gone.

Ebony she was glad the kids weren't home this morning, glad they didn't see their father so messed up.

"What have you done, Charles?" she asked herself, walking back into the room with him. She did not know what to do, who to call. All she could do was stare at her kids' father. Kash needed help. He needed help badly. But who could she call? What could she do to make things better for him? Should she call family? Should she call her own doctor? But didn't Chavez say doctors would tend to him?

Ebony constantly prayed that Kash made it out of this ordeal. He looked so bad, so many holes in his body. His entire body was smaller. If it wasn't for the machine and him breathing hard, you would think he was dead.

Ebony noticed a note pad on the nightstand inside her guest room, the place she told them to put Kash. She saw that it was a to-do list when it came to tending to his wounds. It was instructions on how to bathe and feed him. Ebony read two pages of instructions with two phone numbers at the bottom for doctors. When Kash finally did make it out, she promised not to let him go back into them streets, no matter what he said. She remembered the talk they had before he had left. She heard his words. She heard them loud and clear.

He spoke his own situation into existence. Kash just needed to sit down. He needed to just chill, be a father to his kids, just let the streets go. But it seemed he just couldn't. Ebony vowed to put a stop to him, no matter what it took because shit like this wasn't called for.

***

The next day, Veedo heard a knock at his door. He was tired, still asleep, and didn't really wanna be bothered. With his eyes open, he just laid there looking at the ceiling. Then the knock came again. His clock read 7:35am. He wondered who it could be.

Veedo threw the covers off of him and sat up in bed. the first thing he looked at was his phone, and saw that he had nine missed calls and a few text messages, all from Trish. The knocking at his front door continued, so Veedo stood to his feet, making his way to the living room. He snatched the door open with a man scowl on his face. Trish walked in, right past him, without speaking. And as always, she looked amazing. Veedo closed the front door behind her.

"And hello to you, too," he said, taking her jacket as Trish took a seat on the sofa.

"You must haven't received my calls," was the only thing she said while looking at the screen of her phone.

"You must haven't got mines," Veedo shot back, hanging her jacket up and then facing her.

"I been out of town working. I couldn't take no calls, but as soon as I got free, I blew your phone up."

"Been sleep, baby." Veedo sat down next to her. "I'll never not answer your call," he stated.

Trish she just looked straight ahead for a moment, in thought or something, and Veedo watched. He said nothing either because right now he didn't know what to think, what to say. He knew what he wanted to say, but not how to say it. Should he expose her now orc wait? Should he put everything on the plate now or wait?

"Damn. Why me?" was his thought. He was in love with a lie, and it did something to him as they both just sat there in silence, deep in their own worlds, not knowing how to open up the conversation. Veedo got up from the sofa. He walked into his room and came back out holding his phone.

"Latrisha, do you trust me?" Veedo asked, and she instantly looked up at him strangely. She was stuck for words. She never remembered telling him her real name. He thought that her name was Trish.

She finally spoke. "Yes, I guess. Why do you ask?" she answered nervously.

"Cause I wanna know."

"Well do you trust me?" she quickly shot back.

"Kinda sorta, I'm not gone lie." When he said what he said, her facial expression changed up. She wasn't expecting to hear that from him.

"Oh," she said, nodding her head up and down.

"I'm just saying, I have good reasons behind that," Veedo added.

"You do?"

"Yeah. Where do you work Latrisha Williams?" Veedo asked. He sat down beside her again, but she got up this time, got up shocked.

"I told you that already..."

"You do not work for no law firm, shawty. You work for the government. You lied off top." Veedo also stood up he reached in his pocket and pulled out a photo of her and all her info on it. He gave it to her.

"You lied too." Trish read the paper. "And the only reason I never told you was because I wanted to see how serious we were," she said, balling the paper up.

"Don't make no sense."

"But you lied about being a fucking drug dealer. Plus, you recording us and shit." Trish pointed to the eye in the corner of the living room. Veedo turned and looked at it.

"I only did that when I found out you was the FBI. What the fuck you expect me to do? I had to have my own back just in case this here was a set up?"

"A set up?" Trish was mad. "Boy, you the one who stopped me the day we met."

"So what's up? You tryna put me in jail or what? Am I under investigation?" Veedo he wanted to know.

"Putting you in jail is the last thing on my mind," Trish lied, it was the first thing.

"I'm in love with you, Trish, but I'm in love with a lie," Veedo admitted.

"Same fits, you lied and tricked me too, Veedo."

"So do you love me?" he asked.

"I do," she replied.

"So what's up? What are we gonna do?" he took a step closer.

"Honestly, I don't know because stuff don't seem the same. So how many discs do you have of us? "

"None, you erased the only one I had, I promise, but you gotta understand why I did this."

"That day you was at the warehouse, did you really get robbed?" Trish to a step back.

Veedo paused to think carefully. Should he tell the truth?

"Yeah, I really had got robbed that day," he lied. At the end of the day, she was still the police, and police he didn't trust at all. He wasn't stupid at all.

"I just…"

"Look, listen, so my question to you is what are we gonna do now that everything is in the open?"

"I don't know, Veedo. I'm fairly confused," she shot back.

"You must be building a case on me?" he questioned.

"I'm not, but your friends are in deep trouble. Your best bet is to leave them alone, Veedo."

"My friends?" he asked confused.

"Yes, Charles McCants. I'm surprise you haven't heard," Trish said.

"Charles McCants? How you know I know him? I never mentioned his name to you."

"I been watching you for some time now 'cause I just couldn't believe you wasn't in the drug game. I mean, I've fallen in love with you as a man and I'm a federal agent so I had to watch you in hopes that all you have told me 'bout you was true."

"And it is," Veedo said.

"It's not, Veedo. You're in the game deep and that crushes me. But most of all, you recording us," Trish was clearly hurt.

"All sins are the same, Trish. You lied too. You played games too. But I'm serious when I say that I'm not selling drugs. Do I be around the niggas who do? Yes, 'cause it's all I know. It's where I'm from, but not where I'm going. I wake up every day to try and figure an out a route, but it's not easy as it seems. So don't fault me for that. But in the end, I'll be everything I told you I will be. I'm sorry that you feel like I've played you by the video, but over stand my position when I learned you was the feds."

"I don't know, Veedo. I just don't, 'cause you're telling me one thing but you showing me something else. Don't get me wrong, you're a good man and I'm in love with who you can become too. I dislike who you are. You're right, I am the federal government and I have been snooping, sting watching you, but it was only to see if I should open up to you or not. I'm not building a case against you. No, but I still needed to know," replied Trish. She sounded hurt. She looked hurt. Veedo could almost read her honesty and it was something inside him that made him walk up closer. This time she didn't step back. Veedo pulled her by the waist. She didn't pull away.

"I love you," he said.

"I love you, too," she replied.

"So listen, can something good come out if this? I mean, I know shit rocky right now and your trust isn't the greatest with me, but I'm being honest when I say I'm really trying to find another way in life. It's like you are the kind of woman I need. And I know that I'm a good nigga, I just got these mishaps that I must workout.

Let's start over since we know what's what." Veedo felt her tense up at his words. She lightly removed herself from his embrace.

Trish walked away saying, "I can't see it working. I'm scared, first of all. Second, we live too different, no matter if we love each other or not," Trish said with her back to him. Veedo walked up behind her. She tensed again, and then said, "I'm scared, Veedo. I can lose my job."

"Trish, I'm not in the game and the thing is if me and you continue to work, then it helps me stand clear of the streets. I'm just saying, I would adore the chance to keep what me and you got going."

"Where is the first disc, Veedo?" Trish turned in his arms and asked. Veedo looked directly into her eyes. For a moment, he didn't say anything, he just looked, battling with his own thoughts. He let her go and then took her hand and pulled her into his bedroom. They walked inside and Veedo let her hand go. He walked to his bed and flipped the mattress. Then he flipped a thin mat also, revealing a safe molded into the box spring of the bed. Trish looked and was amazed that he had a safe made into his bed. Veedo punched in the codes and the safe cleared. He pulled it open and turned and looked at her.

"Com'ere," he said. Trish walked closer and saw loads of cash money, more money than he was supposed to have. Veedo reached under a few stacks of bills and retrieved the disc. Then he gave it to her.

"Is this the only copy?" Trish looked at the disc and then up to his face.

"I promise it is." Once the words left his mouth, Trish broke the disc.

"One day at a time, Veedo, is all I can say," Trish said as Veedo kissed her lips. She quickly kissed him back and then walked away again because right now she was still confused, still heartbroken, and still distrustful to words he spoke. Veedo followed her into the living room. She went straight to her coat that was hanging up.

"You leaving?"

"Yes. I must go," Trish said.

"Will I hear from you again?" Veedo walked with her to the door. She opened it and then turned around to face him. Trish had so much hurt and confusion in her eyes as she looked at him solidly.

"I'll call you, Veedo," and with that, she was gone out the door.

He watched her go. Veedo knew that it was time to get right because now he was playing with fire. He couldn't trust her right now. She couldn't trust him. But things were out in the open and neither knew what to do from here. Veedo knew what he wanted but what he wanted wasn't good for him, or was it? If he and Trish could figure out a route to this relationship, it could help him stay clear of the streets.

Veedo was a street nigga, so being with a federal agent wasn't a good look. What would his partners say once they found out Veedo was serious about her? If they found out he was in love with that woman, then what would happen? Was it possible for Veedo to live on both sides? Could he figure something out that would work for them all? Only time would tell the truth of this matter? He gave her the disc because he wanted her to trust him, but Veedo wasn't stupid enough to give her every copy, just in case she wanted to try a stunt and build something against them.

He had to play it safe. He had to be careful and stay one step ahead of the game. First things first, he was about to move his stash of money just in case she flipped.

***

Nene was as nervous as she'd ever been. Her palms were sweating, her stomach in knots, and her body shook. It'd been so long since she'd last saw him, touched him, smelled him, kissed him. Today was like a dream come true, a dream she'd waited to be revealed, a dream she went to sleep every night chasing.

He was the only man that gave her these feelings, gave her this glow, and made her heart pump. He had the only key to her heart, the only key she'd ever give away. If it wasn't Gangsta, then no other man could move her like he could. Junior was standing between his grandmother's legs while Keshana sat on Nene's lap eating candy. Both of them were kid fresh from head to toe. Mrs. Jackson looked across to Nene and smiled. She saw that Nene was nervous.

"Baby, you look like you 'bout to fall out," Mrs. Jackson spoke in a joking manner, which made Nene crack a smile.

"I am," she replied.

This prison was different from the ones she used to visit him at. This prison seemed like death. The walls were cold, the floor was colder. Every officer walked around like a zombie. There were four officers escorting Gangsta into the room where his family waited. Nene saw him. He saw her. But then his eyes went to his kids, especially Junior, who had his neck turned. Gangsta just stood there. Keshana climbed down off Nene's lap.

"Daddiiiee."

For a moment, not knowing what to do or what to say, he just stared at Junior as Keshana rushed his legs. Gangsta picked his daughter up with a big hug and kiss. He kissed her a few good times and Keshana was loving it. Gangsta was amazed to see his son living.

"There go your daddy," Gangsta's mom turned Jr around to face the man who helped make it possible for him to have the life he had. Junior looked up to Gangsta and took a few steps towards him to make sure it was his father. Nene and Mrs. Jackson also stood to their feet. Gangsta bent down and opened his arms, and Junior ran into them.

On first contact, so much weight was lifted off his shoulder. Junior felt so good to him. This day was the day he'd prayed for. This day was the day he'd waited for day and night to see, and it was finally here. Gangsta kissed the side of his son's face. God was good was all Gangsta thought. He scooped Junior up and then embraced his mom and Nene.

"I love y'all," he said.

"We love you, son," replied his mother. Gangsta kissed his son again and then looked at Nene.

"Com'ere," he said. Nene stepped closer. Gangsta kissed her lips one time, two times, and pulled away. "Thank you, Nya, thank you so much."

"For what, Gary?" she wanted to know because if anything she should be thanking him for being one of the greatest men she knew to walk the face of the earth.

"For being as beautiful as ever, for raising my son, taking care of him, and for believing in me. Thank you for coming down here, for staying down through all I've put on your plate. You are amazing to me and not never will I hurt you nor my son anymore," Gangsta spoke the words from his heart.

"No, thank you," Nene replied back. Then they kissed deeply and hugged some more. She was happy, but most of all, he was amazingly happy with how life played out for him. Mrs. Jackson walked off to get him some food to eat, giving the both of them the chance to talk more. Junior was sitting across his lap as Gangsta sat across, looking at the woman he needed to marry. She was just right, perfect to him. She was the right one for him and she knew it.

"So what's up, baby? How he been doing?" Gangsta asked.

"More worried 'bout you than anything."

"I'm good. I'm holding my end down, you just continue to hold your end down as well for us."

"Poonie and Zay was killed last week. Have you heard?" Nene asked. The shocked look Gangsta gave her confirmed that he didn't know.

"Fuck no. What the hell happen?"

"Poonie got into it with some dude about a girl and Zay got caught up in the crossfire. At first, everyone thought Kash had something to do with it, but Kash got shot as well, in Miami."

"Kash?" Gangsta looked dumbfounded now. "What?" he asked again, confused.

"Nobody knows where he's at. The Feds have a manhunt out for him and some Mexicans. Say he was in critical condition. He escaped from the hospital in Miami and killed some FBI agents."

Nene told him. Then she finished telling him about everything, including how Kash was doing Eric and Zay. Gangsta didn't know what to say. All he did was hold his son in deep thought.

"How did you get caught up, my G?" Gangsta asked silently because this wasn't in the plan at all, not his partner getting shot down out of his king seat. Gangsta couldn't believe what he was hearing, but he listened to every word spoken from his baby's mother's mouth. Nene was looking amazing to him. She was still as beautiful as ever. His son had fallen asleep in his arms as Nene and his mother updated him about what was going on.

Then Nene hit him with, "Gary, we are moving out the state next month. I'm going to Texas for a while to get away from the madness in Atlanta."

"When did you decide this?" Gangsta wanted to know.

"As soon as Junior woke up out his coma. She's planned this and I'm helping her. Baby, it's entirely too much going on in Atlanta for Nene to stay. This girl is trying to position herself and her career and protect your son, so leaving is the greatest idea she could have come up with," his mother said.

"You mad?" asked Nene. The last thing she wanted was for him to be mad at her for making the decision to leave because leaving was for the better.

"No, I'm not mad, baby girl, but why Texas?" he asked her.

"Cause I have family there and two job offers," Nene replied.

"Okay. Well yeah, that's cool. You have money, right?" Gangsta had left strict instructions to Kash, telling him to give Nene his cut of profits every month.

"Yes, every month Kash had been out he's forced money on us."

"Is he okay, ma?" Gangsta asked his mother

"I don't know, baby. News said if he didn't show up to a hospital soon, then he would die from loss of blood and no medical attention. He was taken from the hospital and went missing. It's been four days now and when I tell you he's on every channel, I mean it."

Jerry Jackson

Chapter 33
Dank

"Two thirty-one top, pack up, you leaving out tonight," Ms. Green, an old white correction officer told Dank when she opened his cell door. Dank, who was on his phone in the dark under the covers talking to his girl, raised up, phone hidden.

"Whea I'm going, Ms. Green?" he asked.

"It don't say but pack all your stuff 'cause you're not coming back." She pushed his door up and walked off. Dank threw the covers off him and put the phone to his ear.

"Bae, they just told me to pack it up, I'm gone," he said excited. He climbed out the bed and opened his locker box.

"For real, baby?" his girlfriend, Nina, said. She had been his girlfriend the last three years, riding strong by his side day for day, holding him down. Dank had been locked up nine years for killing Danny and Tonya in '99. It was 2008 and he was on his way to the halfway house. He was approved to go last week when his security got dropped down.

Dank was so tired of being locked up and was so ready to be free again. He was a changed man now. He had a business mindset now. He wasn't on the stupid shit no more. He wasn't going back to the streets and Nina was gonna make sure of it. He just wanted to take care of his kids. He just wanted to live the life he'd missed. Dank knew that what he had to do was stay focused and not panic when life got hard. He'd been in all kind of prisons and boy was he tired.

"Call my sister. Let her know. I gotta go sell this phone real quick. Let me get this shit packed right quick. I love you," Dank told his girl.

"I love you, too."

Dank wasn't scared but he was fearful because he didn't want to fail when he finally did hit the streets. He knew he'd end up staying at the halfway house nine months, stacking his money. Plus, the money he had from hustling in prison, so he should be set once he was free. After he packed and pulled his stuff outside his door, he went to one of his partners' room and knocked hard on the door.

"I'm gone, shawty." Dank looked in through the dark.

"Fareal, bruh?" Dude came to the door. "Whea? Halfway?"

"Halfway."

"That's good, bruh, hold it down, boy. Write my number down," the dude said and Dank went to get a pen to do so.

"I need you to sell this phone for me, bruh," he said after returning with the pen. Then he wrote the info down.

"Say no mo, just erase everything. You know I got you, big bruh," the guy said.

"Bet." Dank walked around to a few more niggas' rooms to say his goodbyes. It was finally over. His day had finally come. His chance to do it all over again was not waiting around. He could finally get it done. Ms. Green took inventory of his property and sent him to ID to have him processed out.

"Whea I'm heading, sergeant?" Dank asked the sergeant, a guy he'd been was cool with since being at Dodge State Prison. He had worked for him a few times on different occasions. The sergeant looked at some paper, and then up at Dank, smiling.

"Halfway house, son," he said.

"Bout time." Yes, now it was time to live the life meant for him. Dank was one happy man now. He knew his sick mother was gonna be happy about this news. He quickly went through the process and got back to the dorm. Ms. Green was in the control booth with the other officer. Dank walked to his partner's room who was supposed to sell his phone for him.

"Say, bruh, lemme see dat bitch so I can let shawty know I'm going to the halfway house," Dank said, tapping on the door and looking into the dark room.

He saw movement and then heard, "It's over wit, bruh, fuck from my door, rat ass nigga."

Dank couldn't believe his ears but he knew he heard correctly. He looked in, both hands covering either side of his face. "What you say, my nigga?" Dank was far from a pushover. He always was ready to rumble for his respect, and niggas knew this. But it wouldn't be no fight tonight. It wouldn't be no drama and Dank knew this as well.

"It's over with on this phone, pimp, I'ma holla at cha," the dude said on the other side of the door.

Dank couldn't do anything about it because now Ms. Green was coming into the dorm about to put him in his room. He only shook his head and walked off to his room mad as fuck. He could kill that nigga who was hiding in the room like a bitch. Dank vowed to send a hit at this nigga.

"Pussy ass nigga."

"Yeah, yeah, yeah," the dude said.

***

Asia

"Shit, baby," her husband, Gerald, moaned while holding her head and gyrating his hips into her mouth. She sucked slowly but with pressure, and stroked him intensely. Every so often, Asia would place his dick at the back of her throat and take it out, kissing up and down, still stroking him.

This was a man she didn't love, didn't like, and couldn't wait for the day he met his maker. She was disgusted by him and his nasty ass ways. She didn't respect him at all and it had been like that since day one. Asia married Gerald Johnson only for a position of mind control and closeness. She married him because that's what it took to help Gangsta in the plan Kash set out. She just played her part, that's it, all for the love she had for Gangsta.

Asia started sucking and stroking the tip of his dick, which was pretty big, and to her surprise, he could fuck.

"You like that?" she asked, still sucking, still stroking.

"Yes, lawd yes, baby, right there." he rotated his hips faster. Feeling his cum about to shoot out, he grabbed her head to hold her in place. He pushed harder into her mouth. "Keep going, keep going."

Asia hated this part, but it was all a game, a scam that had to work. She had invested too many years to not see this plan work. She was never going to be the one to mess up the plan. She felt his dick swell up in her mouth. Then she tasted the nasty, salty liquid as it entered her mouth, disgusting her even more. Plus, he wouldn't let her head go.

It had been years seven years since her whole life changed. Seven years of fake kicking it, of playing a role. She was ready to get this over with and done. Asia had been married the last four years. It was something she had to do because she needed say so with him. And what better way to get it than being his wife? So now today was the day she begged him to make happen. Today Mr. Johnson was installing TVs and radios in every room on death row because his wife begged him to. She felt like if these guys were gonna die, then at least let them be comfortable.

It took three years of begging before he finally gave in and let her put it together. Asia instantly put her act into motion. She made the call to Kash and Kash put the plan in motion to make everything work right.

"I love you, girl," Gerald said.

"Love you, too, bae," Asia spoke with a mouth full of cum. she got up and went into the bathroom to rinse out her mouth. It was 5:30 am and boy was she ready to get it over with. She couldn't wait until she got the call that he was dead and she reaped all the benefits, even though she didn't care about none of that. She just wanted out and wanted Gangsta out.

They both got up to get dressed. Today was the first day things would get started. She was to supervise the detail today while her husband ran his prison. Mr. Johnson was the head warden over Jackson State Prison and Asia was still his secretary and had been for the past seven years. He was a hard man to crack, but Asia somehow got under him and now she knew him like the back of her hand. She was smooth how she swindled her way into his heart.

She had him wrapped around her finger. He'd been so in love with her since the first day they started dating and since the first day they met. Making him fall for her was all in the plan. Asia had only seen Gangsta twice in the seven years she'd worked at Jackson, and each time she acted like she didn't know him. Even when he made every gesture to get her to notice him, she played it off cool because it was all in the plan and nobody could mess it up, not even Gangsta.

It had been plenty of times when she wanted to break. It had been times she'd wanted to send him mail, put him on point about what was going on. Many nights she'd wanted to hug him, kiss him, and feel him. But all that she wanted didn't matter because it was about what Gangsta needed. Asia jumped into her ride as Gerald climbed into his own after their morning kiss. He followed her to get coffee and something quick to eat. Everyone knew them in the little town they stayed in, so when Asia walked through the door she was greeted.

"Morning Ms. Johnson, what can I get for you?"

Asia smiled at the woman, a fake smile that she hated to paint on her face, but it was something she had to do because it was all an act, point blank.

***

Veedo, Monkey, Loco, and Longo, along with another dude, walked into the prison after they were cleared through the front gate. A correctional officer escorted them down to the warden's main office where Monkey and Asia made eye contact. It had been years since he'd seen her and boy was she looking like a star. She was still bad, still fine as fuck, he noticed.

"Officer McCord, take these guys to death row so that they can get started. Go the opposite direction of the inspection team," Asia told the officer, who was new here at Jackson.

"Yes, ma'am," the correction officer replied and led the way through the prison to high max and death row. Veedo and Monkey paid attention to everything as they followed. Nobody was nervous and the plan was working just as Kash expected it to work.

They made it to the dorm where death row inmates were housed. The guard in the control booth let them in and waved to the officer escorting the workers. Veedo, Monkey, and Loco instantly started pulling out measuring tape and tools, while Longo counted the cells to be worked on.

Longo and Gangsta made eye contact. Longo kept going, acting as if he didn't know him. He kept working but he saw in Gangsta's face that he was lost. Veedo walked over to the control booth where Mrs. Pitts nervously slid him a cell key. He cuffed it and walked away to the dude who was with them. he gave the dude the key and whispered something in his ear.

Loco pressed the button, sending the signal, and moments later, all the power shut off in the jail. It was day time so you could still see, but that's all they needed to kill the video monitor for a second. The dude rushed over to Gangsta door. When Gangsta looked at him, it was like he was looking at a mirror. He didn't know what to think as the dude stuck the key in his cell door and smudged it open. He slid in stripping out of his clothes.

"Switch with me," he said to Gangsta, who was baffled and looking around. But time was running out and he still hadn't moved yet until Loco peeped in.

"Let's go," he said, which brought Gangsta to the reality of things and he quickly got with the program and traded clothes with the dude who looked just like him. Gangsta didn't know what was going on, but seeing Loco and Longo and Veedo and Monkey, he knew it was for him and he knew it was illegal.

"Take this." dude gave Gangsta the key and pushed him out of the cell door as soon as the generator cut on running the power again. All five men stood to the side after Veedo gave Ms. Pitts the key back. Moments later, three guards came up to do emergency count time to make sure no inmate had escaped.

Veedo and his crew had to wait outside the prison while this was done. Gangsta had knots in his stomach as he walked with them down the hall. He made sure to keep his head low because all the officers knew him and the last thing he wanted was to alert someone.

They made it down to the gates and were let out by the captain, who was coming into the prison. Gangsta was scared for the first time in his life because he really didn't know what was going on. It felt like a dream he was stuck in and couldn't move. It had him confused, excited, and fearful. Outside, they all piled into the van Longo was driving.

"Welcome home," Veedo was the first one to speak and hug Gangsta tightly. He really missed a real nigga.

"Welcome home," Loco said next, smiling.

"What the fuck?" Gangsta was still shocked at what was going on.

"Surprised, I know," Loco said. "Kash surprised us all."

"Shawty hell," replied Gangsta, also smiling because he was happy to be free. But was he really free or was he locked in a cage of life? Being out was a dream. Gangsta knew that he'd never see the streets again, no matter what. So being out now was something unimaginable to him. It was something he would never think of but facts are facts and he was free. He was with his friends in a van, riding somewhere off in the wind, or was he dreaming? Would he wake up in his cell at breakfast call? Would he hear the radio traffic and the clinging of the cell keys? Would he wake up and smell death because right now all he smelled was freedom.

***

Dank had knots in his stomach as the van pulled up to the half-way house in Atlanta around 1pm. He hadn't had this much freedom in such a long time. Everyone on the van with him was extremely happy to finally have their shot at going home. They were happy to finally see the day that being locked up was almost over. It was eight of them that stepped off the van into the fresh air of freedom, into the city lights and the morning dew.

Dank was more excited than anyone because he was supposed to have a life sentence. He was blessed and vowed to do something good this time around. He knew it was some niggas that were mad at him, that hated his guts, but he wasn't stressing that. Dank had to think about his kids and his family. That was why he told on Kash and Gangsta.

Did he regret it? Yes, he regretted every day he woke up that he took them down with him. But what was done was done and he couldn't change that.

"Everyone grab your bag off the back and stand in a line. Hurry up, hurry up," one of the employees said to the group of inmates. Dank was amongst the first to grab his bag and stand at attention, waiting to be instructed again.

Everyone lined up side by side with their heads held in the air as the head person of the center came out to speak. Nobody saw the two dudes across the street running in their direction, holding choppers down by their sides until they were too close. Then they aimed and let off a burst of shots aimed all at Dank.

Boom. Boom. Boom. Boom. Boom. Boom. Boom. Boom. Boom. Boom. Boom. Boom. Boom.

The chopper bullets hit his chest, his face, and legs. His body twisted and turned under the impact of the bullets. two more people also got hit with the spray of bullets.

"Oh my God. Oh my God. Call the police," someone yelled as the two dudes tucked their guns and ran back across the street, ducking low.

***

Kash rolled the window up on his Bentley as he witnessed Dank's body and face being ripped to shreds. The driver pulled off into traffic. Kash leaned back with a smirk on his face. He and his crew had made it through the trenches and come out on top.

The main reason everyone was safe was because Veedo pulled off a major stunt with the FBI when he married an agent, meaning he got out the game in exchange for all evidence on the cartel and Kash. Trish was six weeks pregnant at the time when Veedo proposed the deal to her.

It was something he had to do or everyone was going down in a major way, no questions asked. It took so much begging and so many promises to get Trish to even consider jeopardizing her job and all she'd worked for just for the sake of love. She loved Veedo, she had been captivated by him so deeply that she couldn't help but to step out on a leap of faith and hope he wasn't playing her for a second time. Veedo got her to erase all evidence against the cartel and Kash and place loop holes all through any documents that the government had that she couldn't destroy.

In the long haul and with great attorneys, Chavez and his father beat the Fed case. Loco also got away clean with the rest. The Feds really didn't have much on Kash so it was easy to sweep him under the rug and his faults. After Kash had been shot eleven times, he laid up in Ebony's house for a year, healing and running the city with an iron fist.

He put Meco over Atlanta and let Monkey have Miami and Texas. They both held their end down like champs. Juice was also major league and handled all the money. He had bloods, crips, and Good fellas all united slanging and getting money together. GDs also were on his team, but they were on some growth and development with the youth, which was Veedo's out route.

He had come up with a non-profit organization called Support-Team which aimed at the kids. Veedo also opened up two youth centers with his wife that he allowed one of the head GDs to run. Kash was rarely seen in the streets, and when one did see him, it was in passing because he really didn't kick it. He was the owner of nine gas stations, six clubs and four apartment complexes. Everyone around him was straight.

Kash still kept an eye on Nene and Junior, who were doing great. Junior was smart and driven, just like his father. Kash made sure he had anything he could ever ask for. Keshana and Terry were living great and her and Kash were back on talking terms, but at first she wouldn't speak to him until she found out the truth and saw the two GF dudes get convicted for the murders.

She had a Lil' boy by Zay who looked just like his daddy. Roxanne and Nikki were still around and also, living good on the strength of Terry. Kash made sure they didn't hurt for nothing. Kash was the wolf, it was what the city called him, and everyone knew the wolf didn't play at all. Kash didn't mind having niggas killed or hurt badly. He was with the bullshit at all times, but this time he just sent in orders and shit happened fast. Everything was laid out for Gangsta, just like it was supposed to go, so now he could take over. Kash patted his own back for the stunt he pulled, for the plan he put together to free his bother.

It took years to get everyone in position, and a lot of patience, a lot of motivation to Asia, who wanted to quit so many times until he reminded her that all this was for Gangsta. Asia was the biggest help of all. She was the main reason everything worked and that was why she didn't have to ever lift a finger again if she didn't want to.

Kash was loving everything about today. He got to see Dank get murdered in cold blood, and he was loving it. Plus, his brother was finally out. He could finally take the king seat he deserved because Kash was tired.

The Bentley pulled up into a parking lot where his entire squad was waiting on him. Kash couldn't help himself. When he laid eyes on his brother from another mother, he jumped out the Bentley before it could even stop.

"Fuck going on, my nigga?" Kash opened his arms wide.

"Hell going on, fooly?" Gangsta's smile was big as the both of them hugged tight, rocking side to side in an embrace. This was a moment to remember, to keep close, and to learn from. Gangsta had risked so much to make sure everyone of his niggas was right, and them same niggas made sure he seen the streets again. And for that, it would forever be some love. Gangsta trusted Kash would handle his business, and he did. Gangsta trusted that Kash would do exactly what he asked, and he did.

"Come on, bruh, let's get you fly. You gotta surprise everyone while we can, 'cause nobody but the squad know you out, Nene, yo mom, nobody, bruh," Kash said, walking over to the ride.

"How did y'all niggas pull this one off?" Gangsta still was trying to figure what was what because shit had happened so fast, he didn't have time to think nor ask questions.

"No jail can hold you, my nigga. That's all you need to know. Come on, let's dip and get to this city," replied Kash, pulling his brother to the Bentley. Gangsta couldn't do nothing but laugh and follow his lead. They ended up at Kash's mansion, where everyone was there who was on the team and who had rank in the organization. Gangsta dapped and hugged all type of people. Kash stood up in the middle of everyone and raised his arms up wildly.

"Yo, listen up, our bother back and from my own mouth, I crown him king. Shawty the reason behind everything. Without him and my motherfucking migo squad, none of us would be here. So salute to the big homie. I can finally say, 'call him don't call me!'" Kash said and they all fell out in laughter.

THE END

Stay Connected with Us!

Text **LOCKDOWN** to 22828 to stay
up-to-date with new releases, sneak peaks,
contests and more…

Thank you!

Submission Guideline.

Submit the first three chapters of your completed manuscript to ldpsubmissions@gmail.com, subject line: Your book's title. The manuscript must be in a .doc file and sent as an attachment. Document should be in Times New Roman, double spaced and in size 12 font. Also, provide your synopsis and full contact information. If sending multiple submissions, they must each be in a separate email.

Have a story but no way to send it electronically? You can still submit to LDP/Ca$h Presents. Send in the first three chapters, written or typed, of your completed manuscript to:

LDP: Submissions Dept
Po Box 870494
Mesquite, Tx 75187

DO NOT send original manuscript. Must be a duplicate.

Provide your synopsis and a cover letter containing your full contact information.

Thanks for considering LDP and Ca$h Presents.

Coming Soon from Lock Down Publications/Ca$h Presents

BOW DOWN TO MY GANGSTA

By **Ca$h**

TORN BETWEEN TWO

By **Coffee**

BLOOD STAINS OF A SHOTTA **II**

By **Jamaica**

WHEN THE STREETS CLAP BACK **II**

By **Jibril Williams**

STEADY MOBBIN

By **Marcellus Allen**

BLOOD OF A BOSS **V**

By **Askari**

BRIDE OF A HUSTLA **III**

By **Destiny Skai**

WHEN A GOOD GIRL GOES BAD **II**

By **Adrienne**

LOVE & CHASIN' PAPER **II**

By **Qay Crockett**

THE HEART OF A GANGSTA **III**

By **Jerry Jackson**

LOYAL TO THE GAME **IV**

By **T.J. & Jelissa**

A DOPEBOY'S PRAYER **II**

Jerry Jackson

By **Eddie "Wolf" Lee**

IF LOVING YOU IS WRONG... **III**

By **Jelissa**

BLOODY COMMAS **III**

SKI MASK CARTEL II

By **T.J. Edwards**

BLAST FOR ME **II**

RAISED AS A GOON V

BRED BY THE SLUMS

By **Ghost**

A DISTINGUISHED THUG STOLE MY HEART **III**

By **Meesha**

ADDICTIED TO THE DRAMA **II**

By **Jamila Mathis**

LIPSTICK KILLAH II

By **Mimi**

THE BOSSMAN'S DAUGHTERS 4

By **Aryanna**

Available Now

RESTRAINING ORDER **I & II**

By **CA$H & Coffee**

LOVE KNOWS NO BOUNDARIES **I II & III**

By **Coffee**

RAISED AS A GOON I, II, III & IV

By **Ghost**

LAY IT DOWN **I & II**

LAST OF A DYING BREED

BLOOD STAINS OF A SHOTTA

By **Jamaica**

LOYAL TO THE GAME

LOYAL TO THE GAME II

LOYAL TO THE GAME III

By **TJ & Jelissa**

BLOODY COMMAS I & II

SKI MASK CARTEL

By **T.J. Edwards**

IF LOVING HIM IS WRONG...I & II

By **Jelissa**

WHEN THE STREETS CLAP BACK

By **Jibril Williams**

A DISTINGUISHED THUG STOLE MY HEART I & II

By **Meesha**

PUSH IT TO THE LIMIT

By **Bre' Hayes**

BLOOD OF A BOSS **I, II, III & IV**

By **Askari**

THE STREETS BLEED MURDER **I, II & III**

THE HEART OF A GANGSTA I & II

By **Jerry Jackson**

Jerry Jackson

CUM FOR ME

CUM FOR ME 2

CUM FOR ME 3

An **LDP Erotica Collaboration**

BRIDE OF A HUSTLA **I & II**

THE FETTI GIRLS **I, II& III**

By **Destiny Skai**

WHEN A GOOD GIRL GOES BAD

By **Adrienne**

A GANGSTER'S REVENGE **I II III & IV**

THE BOSS MAN'S DAUGHTERS

THE BOSS MAN'S DAUGHTERS II

THE BOSSMAN'S DAUGHTERS III

A SAVAGE LOVE **I & II**

BAE BELONGS TO ME

A HUSTLER'S DECEIT I, II

By **Aryanna**

A KINGPIN'S AMBITON

A KINGPIN'S AMBITION **II**

I MURDER FOR THE DOUGH

By **Ambitious**

TRUE SAVAGE

TRUE SAVAGE II

TRUE SAVAGE **III**

By **Chris Green**

A DOPEBOY'S PRAYER

By **Eddie "Wolf" Lee**

THE KING CARTEL **I, II & III**

By **Frank Gresham**

THESE NIGGAS AIN'T LOYAL **I, II & III**

By **Nikki Tee**

GANGSTA SHYT **I II &III**

By **CATO**

THE ULTIMATE BETRAYAL

By **Phoenix**

BOSS'N UP **I , II & III**

By **Royal Nicole**

I LOVE YOU TO DEATH

By Destiny J

I RIDE FOR MY HITTA

I STILL RIDE FOR MY HITTA

By **Misty Holt**

LOVE & CHASIN' PAPER

By **Qay Crockett**

TO DIE IN VAIN

By **ASAD**

BROOKLYN HUSTLAZ

By **Boogsy Morina**

BROOKLYN ON LOCK I & II

By **Sonovia**

GANGSTA CITY

By **Teddy Duke**

A DRUG KING AND HIS DIAMOND

A DOPEMAN'S RICHES

By Nicole Goosby

<u>BOOKS BY LDP'S CEO, CA$H</u>

<u>TRUST IN NO MAN</u>

<u>TRUST IN NO MAN 2</u>

<u>TRUST IN NO MAN 3</u>

<u>BONDED BY BLOOD</u>

<u>SHORTY GOT A THUG</u>

<u>THUGS CRY</u>

<u>THUGS CRY 2</u>

<u>THUGS CRY 3</u>

<u>TRUST NO BITCH</u>

<u>TRUST NO BITCH 2</u>

<u>TRUST NO BITCH 3</u>

<u>TIL MY CASKET DROPS</u>

<u>RESTRAINING ORDER</u>

<u>RESTRAINING ORDER 2</u>

<u>IN LOVE WITH A CONVICT</u>

<u>Coming Soon</u>

BONDED BY BLOOD 2

BOW DOWN TO MY GANGSTA

Jerry Jackson